# KEEPING SCORE

JO COX

Copyright © 2023 by Jo Cox

All rights reserved.

No part of this book may be reproduced in any form or by any electronic or mechanical means, including information storage and retrieval systems, without written permission from the author, except for the use of brief quotations in a book review.

This is a work of fiction. Names, characters, places, and incidents are either the products of the author's imagination or are used fictitiously. Any resemblance to actual persons, living or dead, businesses, companies, events, or locales is entirely coincidental.

# 1
## JAX

"Five, four, three, two..."

BANG!

"Son of a!" Jax cried out as the clubhouse was plunged into darkness and her leg hit a heavy wooden stool. It had come to something when you needed to wear shin guards off the pitch as well as on.

She fumbled a hand over the bar, trying to find her phone so that she could use the torch function, but was beaten by the strobe ceiling lights as they flickered and eventually glowed steadily again.

"Are you okay?" Jenna asked, completely unmoved from her position atop the offending bar stool. "That sounded painful."

Jax's face screwed as she squinted though blobs of tears. The fridges had been tripping the electrics like a teenager on acid for weeks, but she'd ignored the emails asking for money to repair them in favour of an extended Christmas break. Now it was coming back to bite her in the ass.

"This wasn't how I planned to see in the new year," she answered, finally grabbing her phone and watching the slew of generic Happy New Year messages battle for supremacy on her notification screen. Why did people do this? If she wanted to exchange pleasantries with vague acquaintances who only contacted her once a year, she could just as easily chat to her dentist. At least then she got something out of it. "Is it a bad sign that I got a smack rather than a kiss on the stroke of midnight?"

"If it helps, I didn't get a kiss either."

"Yeah, I know buddy, but you didn't get a kiss because Abi is still in Spain visiting family for the holidays. I didn't get a kiss because—"

"You've worked your way through every available woman in a fifteen-mile radius and none of them are speaking to you anymore?"

Jax tucked her phone into her pocket with the messages unread. "Why did I bother busting my ass to get here from the airport?" After three weeks in Nebraska catching up with her family for the first time since Covid, she thought it would be fun to make it back for the big football team party. She was wrong. So far, she'd succeeded only in fielding endless questions from Greg, the chair of the men's club, about approving repair invoices. Then she'd injured herself. Now she was also faced with the riot-laugh of being teased by Jenna. "More to the point, where in the hell did I get this reputation?"

"From sleeping around?" Jenna took a sip of her half-empty pint but then spat it back into the glass. After a second or two, she held out the cocktail of lager and saliva. "Sorry, I just remembered it's past midnight and we're doing Dry January. Do you want this?"

"Do I want a pint of lager you just spat in? Um, no. And please don't say *sleep around* like that. Last time I checked, having sex wasn't a crime, and it's not like I set out to have flings. I'm just unprepared to start a relationship for the sake of having someone around when I know I don't really give a shit about them. I can't stand people who do that."

"Don't you want a relationship that lasts more than three dates, though?"

"Sure I do, but with whom?" Making a point of looking around the clubhouse, Jax put her hands on her hips. "Honestly, buddy. This village isn't exactly overrun with mature, single women. Yeah, I've found a few I'd spend a couple of nights with, but it's been a long time since a woman's come along who I can imagine having an actual relationship with."

Jenna sucked her teeth and drummed her fingertips on the bar. "Almost five years, isn't it? I'm starting to wonder if that's the real problem. You're still hung up on *her*. The woman."

"Don't start again." Added to her long list of regrets was telling Jenna anything about that and choosing tonight to give up her occasional cigarette habit. Even ordering a consolatory drink backfired when Jax tried to flag down the barmaid but only attracted the attention of Greg. She pivoted so that her back was to him, then glanced over her shoulder to make sure he wasn't coming towards them.

"It's completely natural." Jenna smiled at Jax's discomfort but chose to supply no help whatsoever. "You met someone who blew your mind enough that you asked her to leave her husband, for goodness' sake. She must have been pretty special to you. All I'm saying is I hope you're not putting her on a pedestal and stopping yourself from finding someone else."

"She *was* special to me, but I promise I'm not holding onto a fantasy, okay? She made the decision to stay with her husband and even if she'd chosen differently, I know that it may not have worked out."

"How did you meet her? Maybe you can replicate some of the factors."

Jax laughed because she knew what Jenna was angling for. She'd made intermittent attempts to pump for details ever since hearing the vague gist of the story a few months ago. "Nice try, but I'm not giving you any more information. She was just a friend who I developed feelings for. The rest is all ancient history."

"I wonder if being friends first is the key, because I was friends with Abi before we fell in love and that's the best relationship I've ever had."

It was never long before the conversation returned to how loved up Jenna was, but Jax didn't mind. She'd rather listen to her gush than tease, probe, or start yet another argument about how Arsenal would win the league this season. "Oh, are you in love? I don't remember you telling me about that."

"I know, I've hidden it so well."

"I'm happy for both of you but not everyone needs a relationship and as I've told you over and over again, I'd rather be single than with the wrong person."

"I know you don't *need* a relationship, but I also know you want one. That's why you've still got Becky in your spare bedroom. I thought it was only meant to be temporary?"

"It *was* temporary two months ago, but it's ended up working out, so I've asked her to stay." What was the point in having two empty bedrooms when a friend was struggling to find somewhere to live? Besides, they got on well, and Jax had to admit that she enjoyed the company of a lodger. Even if Becky contaminated the bathroom with a dizzying array of luminous hair dyes. "It works for both of us. I finally have someone to watch Match of the Day with on a Saturday night, Becky has somewhere affordable to live, and she's also close to the football club which is convenient for her coaching the under eighteens and—"

"Let me guess... convenient for you now that you've roped her onto the committee?"

"Exactly." The committee had fallen apart spectacularly since Jenna stepped down as treasurer at the start of the season. The secretary had followed soon after. Now the chairperson had also decided to retire due to ill-health and it meant Jax was doing everything. Including fielding all those annoying enquiries from Greg. "Becky's taking over the secretary role but we're still down a treasurer and a chairwoman. Any ideas?"

"I guess I could come back as treasurer if you're desperate, now work is a bit less crazy. As for the chair, that's harder. I'll give it some thought."

"That's the best news I've had so far this year."

"Pretty sure it's the only news you'd had so far this year, but whatever."

With a treasurer back in place, Jax started to wonder if she should quit whilst she was finally ahead and go home. She realised that she wasn't quite as ahead as she thought, though, when she scanned the clubhouse for Becky and found she'd just started a game of pool with Greg.

"How bad would it be to leave her here?" Jax asked as she peered over the bar towards the snug at the back of the room.

Jenna laughed. "Very bad. You might have to brave it."

"I knew you were going to say that." Letting out a huff, Jax weaved through the groups of people still chattering and enjoying the party, until she reached Becky's side. "You okay there?" she asked, folding her arms. "If he's bothering you, just ram a pool cue up his ass."

"I don't need to," Becky replied before lining up her shot and cracking a ball into the far pocket.

Despite knowing Becky could handle herself, it was hard not to feel protective of her. She'd been in such a state when she'd arrived in the village over the summer, fresh out of a shitty breakup and dealing with her mum's announcement that she was moving to Scotland to run a bed and breakfast. Being hit on by Greg wouldn't improve her life in any way.

"You know, Greg, eventually you might consider finding a woman your own age."

He pointed the tip of his pool cue at Jax. "Bit rich with your reputation."

"I prefer them older rather than younger."

"Yeah? Well, I'm still young at heart. And as handsome as ever."

That part was annoyingly true. He was a good-looking guy if you were into that sort of thing. Greg was pushing fifty but kept himself fit, always dressed well, and had a passable personality when he wasn't either going on about invoices or leering over women who were young enough to be his daughter.

"How are the kids?"

"They're in Spain with my ex-wife and her new husband, so they're having a brilliant time. I had them for Christmas and she got them for New Year." He took his shot and then stood with a hand on his erect cue, the other rubbing his hair as if to make the point that he still had all of it. "For the record, despite younger women often enjoying the maturity of a slightly older man, there is absolutely nothing like that going on with Becky. We were just having a game whilst I tried to find out if anyone on your committee has a clue what they're doing."

Jax clutched her chest. "Ouch." She let her hands drop and forced a laugh, so he knew she wasn't taking it seriously. "Don't worry. Our treasurer is back now so if you send over the invoice, we'll chip in with our share for getting the fridges fixed. We'll also pay anything else that's outstanding."

"You're still without a chair, though, I hear." At that, Becky winced and mouthed an apology for dropping Jax in it. "The offer to merge still stands. Maybe we should revisit the idea. If the ladies and girls came under the umbrella of the boys' club, you wouldn't need to worry about your own committee anymore."

After a long flight, two trains, and a taxi ride, Jax's left eye twitched uncontrollably. Then again, it might be rage. She hated the idea of merging the clubs and Greg knew it. The ladies and girls needed autonomy to ensure their interests. Greg only wanted them under one committee so he could secure more grants for the boys, not because he really cared about women's football. "No, thanks. We're all set."

"Won't that be the decision of the whole committee...?"

It would be, Jax had no doubt about that, and when they found a new chair, she'd make sure it was someone who shared the same ethos. "I'll raise it with them at our next meeting. Thanks for your concern. Do you fancy heading back?" she asked Becky, who'd just potted her final three balls in quick succession. "I've already offered Jenna the spare bed. We could finish the party at home."

"Perfect," Becky replied as she sunk the black and rested her cue against the table. "I'm finished here anyway. Thanks, Greg. Enjoyed the game, although it's a shame you couldn't last a little longer." She glanced down at an imaginary watch. "What was that, ninety seconds?"

Jax hung Becky a high five as Greg waved them goodbye. Then she zipped herself into the big black North Face Arctic edition parka she'd gifted herself for her fortieth a few months back and flipped out the handle of her suitcase. Whilst everyone else was ringing around trying to find a taxi firm who weren't booked up on New Year's Eve, Jax only had to roll her luggage five minutes down the road.

With Becky and Jenna trailing behind her, gossiping about something or other she didn't care about, Jax powered on in front. The trip back to Nebraska was always one she enjoyed, and it had been great to catch up with her sister after the pandemic had put a halt to her annual visits, but it no longer felt like home.

"It's so good to be back," she said to herself as she pushed open the front door and the warm air hit her. The lingering smoky scent from the wood burner was better than a two-hundred-dollar perfume right now. You couldn't beat it.

"Are you okay?" Becky asked as she squeezed past Jax's body in the doorway. "You look like you're having a moment but you're letting all the heat out."

"I *am* having a moment. It's a good one." Jax tilted back her head and closed her eyes, but she had to move when Jenna pushed her out of the way less gracefully and then turned to close the door.

It prompted Jax to wheel the case into the kitchen, where she found another comforting aroma. In the centre of the room was a rustic wooden table with four matching chairs. Jax took off her coat and hooked it over the back of one, then peeped under a checkered tea towel in the middle of the table, revealing a freshly baked focaccia.

"Help yourself to that," Becky said as she wandered in behind and pulled open the fridge.

"Will you stay forever?"

"Not like I have anywhere else to go. Do you want a drink? I stocked up with those Belgian lagers you like, to make up for staining the bathroom grout. Again."

"What colour have we got this time?" Jax asked, trying to discern by inspecting the hair protruding from under Becky's beanie. When she pulled it off, the nondescript brown Jax had left her with was streaked with pink. It fell out of a shoddy bun and cascaded over her shoulders. "Looks good."

"I wanted to do my whole head, but I haven't used this shade before, so I thought I'd test it out first."

"So wise," Jax agreed as she took one of the bottles Becky had just handed her and twisted off the cap. She held it up and clinked the air. "Cheers and Happy New Year. I hope it's a better one for you. No cheating boyfriends or homelessness. Can't be too difficult, right?"

"It'll be really easy if I stay away from men."

"I always stay away from men," Jenna replied distractedly as she came in tapping at her phone. "Abi says Happy New Year, by the way. Also, I've been thinking."

"That's dangerous," Becky and Jax said in unison. Perhaps they had been living together for too long.

Jenna would usually have a retort, but she was still preoccupied. "Now I'm back on the committee, I want to help find a new chair. Someone brilliant." She finally looked up, but the phone remained poised in her hand. "We had a new girl come along whilst I was covering training for you before Christmas. Only sixteen but good. I think she wants to dual sign for the ladies and under-eighteens, which she totally could."

"The blonde?" Becky asked rhetorically before swigging her lager. "You're right. She left the rest of my under-eighteens for dust."

That was all very well and good, but it didn't explain how Jenna had solved the committee problem. "We're desperate," Jax agreed. "But we're not having a sixteen-year-old chair."

Becky sniggered whilst Jenna only glared. "Of course not. But I got chatting to her and she mentioned that she played for the club ages ago, back at like under ten and eleven level, and guess what?"

"She knows Sarina Wiegman and has convinced her to get involved on the board of a little grassroots team on the side of managing the England squad? That's handy."

This time, Becky snorted and had to spit lager back into her bottle to keep from choking, but Jenna still didn't find it funny. She pretended to throw her phone at Jax. "Would you stop making stupid comments and listen to me? I'm trying to be helpful here."

"I'm sorry. How can she help us?"

"*She* can't, but I think her mum might. Turns out that she

even has experience."

"Of running a football club?" Jax clutched the top of Becky's arm. "Her mum's not Karren Brady, is she?"

Jenna rolled her eyes and they both laughed again. "No. She was on our committee back in the day, though, so you might know her."

"Yeah? What's the kid's name? I'll see if I can remember."

"Isla. Her mum's name is—"

"Carolyn." Jax released Becky's arm and swallowed hard, the laughter stopping dead. She knew exactly who Jenna was talking about and it was no longer funny.

## 2

# CAROLYN

Fumbling for the hallway light switch, buried behind a stack of boxes and winter coats, Carolyn ripped off a shoe with her spare hand. At least the cold had numbed the pain of a new pair of heels. She didn't know why she did this to herself when she had dozens of far more comfortable options. Surely at fifty-two she'd earned the right to wear whatever she wanted with a cocktail dress. Even a pair of cushion soled trainers.

The thought made her chuckle, and she gave up on the switch in favour of winging it using only the light trickling down from the landing. One last push over the next few days and she'd finally rid the house of moving paraphernalia, but for now, perhaps it was best that she couldn't see the chaos.

She inched forward but stopped when she reached the kitchen doorway, sniffing the air. What was that smell? There were traces of burnt popcorn, but she couldn't work out what on earth accompanied it, besides the orange and cinnamon Christmas diffusers she'd dotted around to get them in the festive spirit.

After a moment, she pulled off her other shoe and dropped it to the ground. Then she stepped over the threshold, but as she spotted the outline of a box on the central island and walked towards it, she tripped on the shoe and stumbled, a hand shooting out and saving her from face planting the granite worktop. That central island was going to take some getting used to, even if the kitchen had swung her decision to place a higher offer and secure the house. It had a large dining area with room for a formal table, too, and Carolyn couldn't wait to start entertaining again.

"Mum, is that you?" rang out from upstairs.

Resisting the urge to yell back, Carolyn straightened up and trod more cautiously out of the kitchen, almost tripped on another moving box at the foot of the stairs, and then ascended them.

"What were you going to do if it wasn't me?" she asked as she reached the landing, half-joking but also genuinely interested to know. Her daughter had led, by most teen's standards, a sheltered life. How she'd cope with university next year was a growing cause for concern. "I could have been an intruder."

"Don't worry. If it was a burglar, I'd just have given them all your jewellery."

Laughing again, Carolyn leant against the inside of Isla's bedroom door frame, but it stopped when she found the source of the smell. Isla and her friends had created a chocolate concoction that had fused itself to her new crockery, and it had also dribbled dangerously close to the antique writing desk Carolyn's dad had gifted Isla before he passed away.

"Have you had a good time?" she asked, reminding herself to relax and unclench her tightening fists. It was nothing that couldn't be fixed and tonight, she was just going to be grateful that Isla had made new friends so soon after the move.

All four girls confirmed, offered thanks for letting them stay, and complimented Carolyn on her figure-hugging outfit. They certainly weren't going to struggle to get themselves free drinks during Fresher's week, even if they'd starve.

"Did you have fun with Gran?" Isla didn't look up from the careful work of painting her friend's toes a lurid pink.

"The food was good," Carolyn replied, not strictly answering the question but somewhat distracted at the thought of nail polish on her new cream carpets. Her fingers began to curl again because she'd had the house fully redecorated before they moved in six weeks ago and she had hoped her fresh start might last a little longer into the New Year. "You will be careful, won't you?"

Isla didn't quite roll her eyes but the same sentiment came across in her tone. "Yes, mother. And don't worry, I'll clean the kitchen in the morning."

"Why, how bad is it? I couldn't see in the dark."

Finally looking up, Isla glanced at each of her friends in turn. "Maybe don't go down until I've tidied."

"Hmm," Carolyn grumbled, too tired to mount any real complaint. "Just make sure you do. And don't stay up too late. I want to finish unpacking the boxes before you go back to school on Monday."

"You're the boss."

Carolyn smiled. "And don't you forget it."

She wished them all good night and clicked the door shut, trying to dampen the noise. There was no way they would be sleeping any time soon. Then she ventured back downstairs because she was equally sure that Isla wouldn't be in any fit state to clean the kitchen tomorrow and she hated the idea of finding a mess when she wanted to enjoy her morning coffee in peace and comfort.

"Oh, Isla," Carolyn sighed when she hit the kitchen light and revealed the extent of the damage to her lovely clean house. Then her shoulders rolled forward and she looked down at her best black dress. Maybe she should've changed it before tackling this, but she didn't have the energy, and it wasn't like she'd be wearing it again for a while. She might as well get the most out of the outfit before dry cleaning and tucking it into the back of her wardrobe until next year.

Ten minutes later she'd cleared the worktops of bowls, plates, and cutlery. The majority of it could be stacked in the dishwasher. What she was meant to do with her new saucepan, though, which was coated in what looked to be burnt Mars Bars mixed with Rice Krispies, was anyone's guess.

"I thought I promised to clean up," Isla said, swinging off the door frame with a water glass in hand. She bit down on her bottom lip and winced as if predicting the bollocking that would've come if Carolyn could be bothered to dish it out.

"I know you did but I wanted to be able to make breakfast."

"Sorry, Mum."

"It was my choice to do it, don't panic, but you can still empty the dishwasher in the morning." Carolyn flung a damp blue cloth at Isla's middle. "And you can wipe down the worktops before you go back upstairs." She squirted antibacterial cleaner over them all and then set the bottle down by the sink. "Deal?"

Isla agreed, leaving her glass on the central island and then wiping some Rice Krispies into her hand with the cloth.

Whilst she did that, Carolyn ran hot water in the sink and left her saucepan to soak. Then she retrieved her shoes, which were still discarded by the door, and tidied them away. She could hardly complain at Isla when she'd left a trip hazard.

"I'm glad you went out tonight," Isla said as she scrubbed at a stubborn patch by the sink.

"Is that right? I bet you're hoping I go out again at the end of the month, too. That'd be mightily convenient around your birthday."

The cloth was discarded with the job pretty much done.

Then Isla wiped her hands on her T-shirt and sidled up for a hug, letting Carolyn press a kiss to her temple. She stayed quiet, before finally replying, "No." Then she stepped away and let out a little laugh. "Well, yes. But I also think it's good for you to get out, you know. Be with people your own age."

A louder burst of laughter shot out of Carolyn. "People my own age? I was with your gran and she's eighty!"

"It was a step in the right direction. Maybe eventually you could go on a date. Get a life instead of just hanging out with me and Gran all the time."

A life? Wow. Trust a teenager to believe that you didn't have one just because you weren't dating. "The ink has only just dried on the divorce. Give me a moment to breathe."

"Dad's dating."

Carolyn bristled, because he was dating long before the ink had dried. That was something they'd chosen not to share with Isla, though, so she shook it off. "Well, we're all different. There's a lot more to life than romantic relationships, and it'll happen when it happens."

Not that there was any point trying to convince Isla of that. Carolyn had become increasingly suspicious that she had a boyfriend lurking somewhere or, at the very least, a crush. Carolyn had definitely interrupted a related discussion in the living room earlier, before heading out to dinner, but she wouldn't ask outright. They spoke about most things, and it would come up eventually.

"I know there's more to life," Isla agreed, grabbing the tea towel and holding it for show. "I'm just saying that I don't mind. You know?"

"That's very good of you. Thanks."

"You're welcome. Old people deserve love, too."

If she hadn't already got it in hand, Carolyn would have

thwacked her with that tea towel. "Careful young lady, or the party's off."

"Does that mean I can have it?"

It was tough to deny her after all the upheaval of the past year, and Carolyn found herself close to agreeing. She would just need to work out how to keep their new home from burning to the ground. "I'm considering it."

"And can I invite the girls from football?" Isla asked suspiciously cautiously.

"Why wouldn't you be able to invite the girls from football?"

She shrugged and set down the tea towel, then hoisted herself onto the work surface she'd just cleaned. "I don't know. Just because they're older."

"A year older." When Isla remained silent, swinging her legs and looking around the kitchen, Carolyn pressed. "A year older, yes?"

"Sure. Well, I mean some of them are like, in their twenties I guess."

Now the penny dropped. She hadn't meant girls from the under eighteen team, she'd meant the senior squad. "I get the picture. No. I don't think that's appropriate."

"But Mum!"

"Don't *but mum* me. They're adults and you're only just turning seventeen. It's one thing playing football with them but I'm not sure about grown women in their twenties and thirties coming to a teenager's birthday party." Besides which, Isla had so far only been to one training session with them, in the run up to Christmas. She hardly knew anyone yet.

Isla folded her arms, which wasn't exactly strengthening her argument. It only made her look more of a child. "Not even one or two? Or, like, one?"

One? Carolyn could read her daughter far better than she thought. Did she have a crush on someone from the football team? If so, the answer was a firmer no. Not because it was a woman, but because they must be way too old for her. "Don't push me on this or the whole thing is off."

"Fine, but can I watch their first game of the season next Sunday instead of going to lunch with Gran, since I'm missing training this week to have dinner with Dad?"

Carolyn nodded. They'd already discussed how it would be hurtful to turn down dinner when he was only in town for one night, and she wasn't going to get into another argument. "Yes, but I want you to make sure you at least send your gran a text or, better still, give her a call."

"Great. I really want to meet the coach."

"The coach? Didn't you meet her before Christmas? Jenna, was it?"

"No, she only covered the session because the normal coach was away. She's brilliant, though. She plays striker and she's the captain. She also runs her own businesses, and used to be on the committee, and is just totally capable."

Isla continued to ramble about Jenna whilst Carolyn's heart lodged itself in her throat. When Isla had asked to go back to her old club, she'd felt similarly, and the only thing that had stopped it was learning there had been a change of personnel in the intervening five years. Now, Carolyn had the awful sense that she may have relaxed too soon.

"So, who is the usual coach if it's not this Jenna?" she barely dared ask.

"Jazz? Jules? I don't know, I don't remember her, but you probably will when you see her. She was around when I played before." There was a pause before Isla began rattling off more incorrect names.

Carolyn rubbed the ache growing in the middle of her chest. "It's Jax, sweetheart. Her name is Jax."

# 3
# JAX

Jenna followed Jax's line of sight towards the leisure centre car park. "Why are you so twitchy?"

"I'm not twitchy," she grumbled quietly, shuffling from one foot to the other. "I just didn't sleep well."

Usually being kept awake all night by a woman would be a good thing, but not in this instance. Jax wasn't prone to worrying or overthinking but hadn't been able to control the urge to go over every possible scenario. Would Isla remember her? Would Carolyn want to see her? Would they have the husband with them if and when they turned up to another training session?

Hoping she might be more successful at pushing it from her mind if she focused on coaching, Jax grabbed a stack of cones and began laying them. Training was important, especially with a tough game at the weekend, right after Christmas when everyone was still sloshing with beer and carrying five pounds of extra sausage meat.

"Do you want me to take the warmup?" Jenna asked, already counting the players trickling through the gate and changing into their boots. She was power-hungry as ever and seemed to have really enjoyed her stint as head coach in December, which was no surprise given it allowed her to boss people around even more than usual.

"Are the team safe?"

"Probably not, but you seem preoccupied, so I was trying to be helpful."

Jax dropped the last cone and then looked over at the car park again. This time, it made Jenna frown. She'd been too caught up with Abi's return from Spain to connect the dots and realise that the woman she'd teased Jax for being hung up on and the woman she wanted to bring on board as their new chair were one and the same. It wouldn't last forever, though, and Jax needed a cover.

"I *am* preoccupied," she admitted, just about managing a more casual tone. "You said that Isla wanted to train with us again and given we're so desperate for a chair, I was going to try to chat with Carolyn. I figured it was best coming from me, since I already know her."

"I had the same idea but Becky just told me Isla's not coming tonight. She was at under eighteens training yesterday but apparently had something else on this evening. She'll be back next week, though, so we'll try then. Or *you'll* try then, since you're our secret weapon."

The thought of waiting another week made Jax's stomach flutter a little. Was it relief or disappointment? She honestly had no idea how she was going to feel when she saw Carolyn again. The only thing she knew for sure was that, far from being their secret weapon, she could be the reason the plan bombed.

"I guess there's no reason for me to keep looking at the car park, then," she said, trying for a smile as she patted Jenna on the shoulder. There was definitely disappointment in the mix because she knew it hadn't come off. "Or for you to take the warmup. Sorry, buddy. You'll have to delay your bid to take my job."

"Damn."

Damn was about right. Damned either way. Carolyn would be a great chair, in fact she was everything they'd been looking for, but there were numerous scenarios that could make it hell for Jax. If they got on well or if they didn't, it was all a potential minefield.

"Are you coming to take this warmup then?" Jenna asked, snapping Jax from another spiral of what ifs and supposition whilst staring blankly into space.

"Yes. You know what, I may even join in."

On the rare occasion that she felt emotionally off balance, football always helped, and Jax definitely felt off balance tonight. Even the prospect of going over on her dodgy ankle wasn't going to stop her. She'd happily play through the pain of another cold night aggravating the metalwork holding it together if it took her mind off Carolyn.

The plan worked for the majority of the session, and trying to save face whilst Jenna and Becky did everything possible to show up her rusty skills even provided everyone with a laugh. That stomach flutter returned with a flock of friends, though, when a young woman ran across the astroturf, her dirty blonde hair flying in all directions. Jax recognised her as Carolyn's daughter in an instant.

"Sorry I'm late," Isla shouted as she reached the pile of bags and trainers the team had discarded earlier. "Is it okay if I join in with the end of training?"

They'd stopped for a throw in and Jax instructed them to continue as she stepped over the sideline, jogging around the perimeter of the pitch until she reached Isla's side. "Of course you can."

"I don't have my boots because I've just come from a family dinner, but I can play in trainers. I don't care."

Jax finally managed a genuine smile at the confidence Isla

had radiated in thirty short seconds. There could be no doubt whose daughter she was, even if they hadn't looked so alike, and it was good to see her thriving. "I'm Jax, the manager. Do you remember me from before?"

Isla scrunched her face. "Not really. You know my mum, though, right?"

"Yeah, I know your mum." Jax couldn't resist glancing at the car park again, a little excitement edging back into her voice. "Is she here?"

"No, but she's bringing me to watch the game on Sunday if you want to say hi."

"I'll make sure I do that. For now, we're just playing a five-a-side match to end the session. You can take my place."

"Are you sure?" Isla unzipped her coat and dropped it on the floor, then her jumper followed. There was nothing she could do about her jeans, though, or the bright white trainers she would inevitably destroy.

"Yes, I'm sure. Do you want my spare hair band?" There was always one on Jax's wrist and she pinged the elastic so that it snapped back against her skin.

"Um, maybe." Isla took the band when Jax held it out. "Thanks. I wasn't planning to come so I'm a bit disorganised tonight, but I needed to let off some steam."

"Yeah? Everything okay?"

Isla shook her head slightly. "Yes. Totally. Just one of those days, though, you know?"

"Oh boy. I sure do. It's why I've been playing when I really shouldn't. There's more metal in my ankle than bone but sometimes you just need a game, right?"

"Right. What happened to your ankle? If you don't mind me asking."

Jax stuck out her left leg. "Broke it. Badly. That's the age-old story of how I ended up coaching rather than playing. It's not just because I'm old."

Isla laughed as she tied her hair into a ponytail. "You don't look *that* old. You're also not as scary as I expected. A few of the other girls said they don't mess with you. Even Mum looked a bit terrified when she found out you were still the coach the other day rather than Jenna."

That was true, Jax definitely had a reputation for taking no shit, but Carolyn had no reason to fear anything. They'd never had so much as a cross word, and Jax suspected it may have been shock rather than terror if Carolyn had assumed Jenna was now in charge. "I'd be more scared of Jenna. Some of the team threatened to quit if I didn't come back from The States after Christmas. I'm guessing your mum doesn't mind you playing with us, though, despite the disappointment of finding out I'm still here?"

Isla's confidence faltered for the first time. Her eyes darted around, before she finally replied with, "No. She doesn't mind me playing with you guys, but she doesn't *technically* know I'm here tonight. We agreed I'd have dinner with my dad whilst he was passing through on his way to London for work and she might not be too happy when she finds out I cut it short."

Jax's heart thumped at the implication. "Passing through? Is he not living here?"

"He's still in Manchester but Mum wanted to move back when they split. You two should totally catch up so she can fill you in properly. I keep telling her she needs to hook up with her old friends rather than just hanging out with me."

It was hard to imagine Carolyn sat in. She'd always been outgoing and a big part of the community, volunteering with the football club and Isla's school, and compassion superseded whatever else Jax had been feeling. "Is your mum doing okay?

Break ups are tough, especially when you've been together a long time."

"Yeah, and she's been happier for sure since we moved into the new place. Even if she has become obsessed with keeping it super tidy."

"I expect she just wants you guys to have a nice home."

Isla didn't seem to have considered that, and her brow creased before she replied, "Yeah. I guess that's what it is." She shook her head again. "Anyway, is it okay for me to play now?"

Jax had completely forgotten that she was holding up the real reason Isla was here, and she stood aside. "Of course. Sorry. Show me what you've got."

Jax bent down to pick up Isla's clothes from the ground, hooking them over her arm to keep them dry. Then she pulled out her phone and opened the list of contacts. Carolyn was still in there. Should she call to say Isla was here? No, probably not. They'd decided not to stay in touch and Jax didn't want to stick her nose into whatever dynamic Isla was escaping. She would just make sure Isla had a way to get home safely and see what happened on Sunday.

At the reminder that she had a team to pick for the weekend, Jax returned her attention to watching the rest of the training session. It was quickly drawn to Isla again, though, who had settled into the vacant place in defence. Was it her usual position? Jax had been too preoccupied to ask, but Isla was holding her own. She'd even just dispossessed Jenna, which was impressive.

She carried the ball up the pitch and slotted it through to Abi, who banged it into the net. The move was brilliant and she clearly had vision because she'd read the run perfectly. Not that it was a surprise to find Isla was good. She'd always been the star of her youth team, however much Carolyn had tried to play it down to keep her from becoming big-headed or complacent, and Jax could remember various other clubs sniffing around before she left for Manchester.

Twenty minutes later a light drizzle meant that Jax had tucked Isla's clothes inside her jacket as best she could. They'd overrun the session and the caretaker wanted to shut off the floodlights, so she finally called an end to the game and gave her usual speech about putting the team sheet out on Friday. Then she handed Isla her things and began packing away the cones and balls that Becky was collecting and dropping at her feet.

"How are you getting home?" Jax asked as Isla tugged on her jumper.

"I hadn't thought that far ahead."

"Given it's dark, raining, and your mum doesn't know you're here, I'm going to get one of the girls to give you a lift home. Where's your house?" There was no response until Isla had zipped herself back into her coat, and even then, she only *ummed* and *ahhed*. "Okay?"

"I don't want to cause a hassle. I can just walk."

"I know you *can* walk but your mum would kill me if she knew I'd left you here. Don't be responsible for that."

Isla laughed. "My mum can be pretty scary too when you get on the wrong side of her, so sure. We're on the new estate."

"That's where Jenna lives, hang on." Jax craned to yell over her shoulder in the direction of where Abi and Jenna were ambling towards the car park. "Can you take Isla home? She's near you!"

"I'm going to Abi's!" Jenna shouted back. "But I can detour if you need me to."

It was well out of her way, so Jax let her off the hook. "Don't worry. See you Sunday."

"I'm in the team then?"

"You're the captain!" Jax laughed and tied the top of the ball bag. Then she handed it to Isla. "Looks like you're coming with us, so you can make yourself useful and help carry."

"Maybe you can speak to her mum," Becky whispered as she bundled the last of the cones onto the stack.

She was a long way from inconspicuous and, unsurprisingly, Isla heard. "Why do you want to speak to my mum?"

Whilst they walked to the car park, Becky reeled off the plan she'd concocted with Jenna to get Carolyn onboard as chair of the club. She'd just finished when they reached the back door of Jax's battered old 4x4, and Isla dumped a bag of balls on top of the excess equipment already lining the floor of her boot.

"Do you think she'd be up for it?" Jax asked, enjoying a simultaneous game of Tetris with the rest of the kit.

"I keep telling her she needs to get out more, so yeah."

"I'm not sure rejoining the committee counts as getting out. Wasn't your mum always into dancing?"

"Really?"

"Yep," Jax grunted as she squeezed the door shut. Then she chuckled and bashed the mud from her hands, enjoying Isla's continuing judgement of Carolyn's lack of social life. "You might be surprised by what she used to get up to. She even did a charity dance event one year. It was like a local version of Strictly Come Dancing where they paired up community figures with dancers and had them compete."

"I don't remember that!"

"Ask her to show you her winners medal."

Isla's mouth was agape. "She won?"

"Of course. This is your mum we're talking about." Jax remembered more about that competition than she was prepared to let on to Isla or even Becky. She'd helped Carolyn learn her dance moves in between sessions with the professional dancer and been in the audience for the big finale. "I think she clinched it with a salsa. You should also ask her about clubbing in the early nineties. I've heard that was a completely different style of dance, but she'd know best."

They all climbed into the car and buckled their belts, Isla behind Becky on the back seat. She leant forward and grabbed the headrest, her interest still piqued. "I can't imagine my mum clubbing. What else do you know?"

"I said to ask her about it, not that I was going to tell you all her secrets." Although Jax would admit to knowing a fair few. It had hurt to lose such a good friend, as much as anything else, and remembering quite how close they were made her smile falter.

"I *am* going to ask her, and I'm going to make sure you catch up properly because she needs someone to take her out dancing. Also, if you become friends again, it will totally help my chances of getting into the squad."

Jax laughed as she clunked the car into reverse and swung out of the bay, her wipers squealing across the windshield. "You know, you're a lot like your mum, except in one area."

"What's that?"

"Subtlety."

## 4

## CAROLYN

"Why are you going so slowly?" Isla asked without looking up from her phone.

The speed with which her thumbs moved across the screen distracted Carolyn for a moment, and she glanced over with a frown before shaking her head. It dislodged a wave of hair from behind her ear and she tucked it back there. "Gravel," she replied. "I don't want to chip my paintwork."

"Mmm."

"Don't *mmm*. Just come out with it if you don't believe me."

"You're being weird."

Knowing she was being weird and wondering how to cover, Carolyn frowned. Should she just tell the truth? No. That wouldn't go down well. No one liked to think about their parents having sex. Isla wouldn't want to know that her mum had almost slept with her football coach. Or that, for a not-so-fleeting minute, she'd almost ended her marriage over it. What a mess that would've been. At least an amicable divorce had spared Isla two warring parents.

"Are you sure you want to keep training with the ladies?"

Carolyn asked, trying to pass off her frown as concern. "It's a big step up to playing with fully grown, adult women."

"Are you saying I'm not good enough?" Isla finally looked up from her phone, the slight tilt of her head implying she saw it as a challenge rather than a cause for offence. "Because I'm totally capable of competing at this level. The training match I played on Wednesday went really well."

The comment precipitated another frown, because Carolyn was unamused that Isla had ended dinner with her dad early and had him take her to football. They'd already hashed that out on Wednesday night, though, and she didn't want to keep going over it. "Of course I think you're good enough." They stopped on the end of a row of cars, in front of a large thorny bush. "But it's also a lot of extra time dedicated to sports when I thought you were going to get a part time job."

"I *will* get a part time job. I just need to write a CV."

"In what time, exactly?"

"I'll find some. Trust me. If it works out with the senior team, I'll drop under-eighteen games and get a Saturday job. I just need a bit of breathing room to figure it all out."

"It's your choice, sweetheart. I still think you'd be better off sticking with the under-eighteens and gradually joining in a few senior training sessions, but you need to start making your own decisions. I'm only here for support and guidance."

"Thank you. Your concerns are all duly noted but I've got this."

Carolyn didn't doubt that for a moment and now regretted talking Isla out of playing when it was partly for her own selfish reasons. "I have complete faith in you and I'm sorry if it sounded otherwise. Jax is tough and has high standards, but I'm sure you can cope with whatever she throws at you."

"So you keep saying, but she seems lovely."

No sooner had her name been mentioned but Jax came into

view through a break in the dew-stained leaves of the bush. It was providing Carolyn with useful cover. They hadn't seen each other or spoken in four-and-a-half years but Jax's last words, the admission of her feelings and the resignation in her face when they were denied, still made Carolyn's heart hurt a little. Sometimes she wondered what would have happened if she'd responded differently but it never lasted long. She had no doubt that she'd done the right thing for Isla and that was enough to quash any regrets.

"Are you sure you don't want to stay and watch the game with me?" Isla asked, snapping Carolyn from her thoughts.

"Hm?" she responded absently.

"The game. You. Watching. With me. You and Jax could catch up."

Carolyn shook her head again. "No, don't worry." Just because Jax had been having a walk down memory lane when she'd kindly dropped Isla home on Wednesday night, didn't mean she'd want one for real. Especially not on a match day, which she always took seriously. "Just give me a call when you're ready and I'll come to collect you."

Isla shrugged and flung open the car door, swivelling in her seat and catching it as it rebounded back. "I'll be done at four. You can just get me then."

With a little salute that made Isla roll her eyes, Carolyn said goodbye and then watched her daughter practically skip across the gravel car park towards two friends from the under-eighteen team.

Carolyn reversed back the way she'd arrived, taking care not to also damage her paintwork on the bush, and then swung the car around. In the rearview mirror she caught another glimpse of Isla, only this time, she was chatting to a much older blonde. Was this Jenna?

Before she could get lost in wondering again, Carolyn sped

off down the drive and pulled out of the T-junction onto the main road leading out of the village. It was beautiful here on crisp winter days, the sun bright in a clear blue sky. She'd missed it. Missed this routine. Missed home.

Ten minutes later, she was pulling up on her mother-in-law's driveway. Her ex-mother-in-law, to get technical, but after almost three decades, you didn't divorce what little family you had. Not that Sylvia would have let her, in any case.

"What a treat!" Sylvia called down the drive as she threw open the front door. There was no way that woman had just turned eighty. Carolyn refused to believe it.

"You knew I was coming, and you only saw me on New Year's Eve."

"Yes, but it's still a treat." Sylvia wandered across the block paving, despite being entirely bare foot, and peered into the passenger window of Carolyn's Lexus. "Where is my granddaughter?"

"I'm afraid you've lost her to a football match. Didn't she text you?"

Sylvia smiled, a hand coming to rest on her hip. She had the usual glint in her eye, and an air suggesting that an effortlessly witty retort was about to slide over her lips. "In my day we worried about losing them to sex or drugs."

Carolyn couldn't help but laugh because she had a feeling that in this instance, they *had* lost Isla to sex. In a manner of speaking. She didn't want to get into the inappropriate crush front of Sylvia, though. She'd only encourage it. "You're looking far too well."

"I used to imagine you said things like that because you were hoping to get your hands on my money sooner rather than later, but since you no longer have any entitlement to it, I suppose the compliment must be genuine."

"It's always been genuine." Carolyn rounded the car, her

hands tucked into the pockets of her coat, and gave Sylvia a peck on each cheek.

"So, Isla's playing football with the ladies team now? She even cut dinner short on Wednesday evening, I hear."

"Yes, that's where she is today. Marcus wasn't overly upset, was he?" Carolyn followed Sylvia into the house and slipped off her shoes, then her coat. It was always like a sauna and today that was welcome, although the sudden change in temperature made her shiver.

"No, he wasn't worried. He knows what Isla's like with her football." Sylvia led them into the large, shaker style kitchen on the back of the house, and flicked on the kettle.

"Even so, I thought she wanted to spend time with him. Do you know what they talked about? She won't say a word to me, but I know something's up. And then yesterday he asked if she could visit in a few weeks, which was odd because the last couple of times he's arranged it with Isla directly."

Sylvia turned, her face creasing. "That is perplexing, but no. He seldom calls me these days. Always too wrapped up in work."

That rung true. Carolyn could phone him, of course, but she'd wait to see if Isla said anything first. "I'm probably worrying about nothing."

"I expect so. There are so many things for teenagers to disagree with their parents over. Mostly trivial. They probably just had a spat about their dessert order, you know how they both get when it comes to cheesecake."

Her concerns somewhat allayed, Carolyn pulled out a chair at the kitchen table. She was still navigating solo parenting. Marcus was around, of course, but on a day-to-day basis she was solely responsible for Isla's upbringing, and she'd found Sylvia a useful sounding board. Even if they did have markedly different parenting styles. "I think I'm going to buy her some driving lessons for her birthday. Marcus always said he'd teach her, but that's not really practical now."

"That's convenient, because I was thinking of giving her my car."

The BMW? It was very generous, but Carolyn struggled to stop her frown from returning. "Would she even get insurance on it?"

"Oh." There was a pause, Sylvia hovering next to the kitchen table holding a pair of her best Wedgewood tea cups with matching saucers. "You're probably right. I don't use it anymore, though. My eyesight just isn't up to snuff. Maybe I'll sell it and buy her something more fitting for a seventeen year old."

"I did actually think that when she gets a job she can save up for her own car. Something to give her a sense of achievement and responsibility."

Sylvia set the cups down. "Oh tosh. She'll have enough responsibility at some point. Let her enjoy being a child a while longer."

This was exactly where they differed because, although Carolyn agreed with letting her be a child, Isla would soon be an adult. An adult who'd been around a degree of comfortable wealth for her entire life and would suddenly find that maintaining that on your own was a difficult prospect. The job and housing markets were not the same as when Sylvia and her husband had started out sixty years ago. They weren't even the same as when Carolyn and Marcus met in the nineties.

"I'm not sure working a few hours a week at seventeen is taking away her childhood," Carolyn countered. "A lot of her friends have been working for a year by now. I just want to set her up for the real world."

"Well, it's your choice my dear. If you'd prefer that I don't give her a car then of course I shan't."

"Thank you. I appreciate that."

Sylvia turned to pour from the kettle to her tea pot, set it on the table, then began hacking at a carrot. "Food will be ready soon. Anything else to share whilst I peel the vegetables?" She turned to look over her shoulder, her brow creasing again. "You still look troubled. You're not worried about Isla and Marcus, are you? They'll work out whatever problems they're having."

Carolyn paused. "There is something else on my mind. Some*one*."

The vegetables were long forgotten at the hint of any intrigue, and Sylvia wrestled to pull out a chair. "A chap?"

"An old friend who I'm going to have to see again."

"You've lost me already, I'm afraid. I thought you were keen to reconnect with your old friends down here?"

"I am. Mostly. But there's one in particular who I didn't leave on the best terms with, and I didn't think we'd see each other again, but it turns out we will. Imminently. I'm a little nervous."

"That's not like you. Usually, if someone slights you it's stiff upper lip and best of British about it."

Carolyn poured tea into her cup. Then she peered over the top as she raised it to her lips and blew across the steam. "They didn't slight me. Far from it." She wondered how much to say. Sylvia had known her for twenty-seven years and was a good friend, but she was still Marcus's mother. Would it be odd to admit there had been someone else for Carolyn, too? Despite his affairs. "I don't know whether I should say too much."

When Carolyn set down her cup, Sylvia gripped her hand on the table. "You're worrying me now."

Carolyn shook her head. "Oh, no. It's nothing to worry about. But this person had feelings for me whilst I was still married to Marcus, and I've never told anyone before. I wasn't sure how you'd react."

"Was it reciprocated?"

After pausing for a beat, Carolyn confirmed with a nod. "I

didn't go looking for it, we were just friends and nothing more, but eventually it spilled into romantic feelings. On both sides. We never acted on it, until Marcus was offered the job in Manchester, and even then we only kissed. Once."

Far from being shocked, Sylvia seemed enthralled by the drama. She took Carolyn's hand again, this time urging her on. "So, what happened?"

"I was a little naïve, I think. I hadn't even realised my feelings. Then, when Manchester was floated, the idea of leaving them put me in a tailspin. I kept crying for no reason and I thought it was just menopause or the thought of being so far from Dad."

"But it wasn't."

"No. It wasn't, and eventually it all came out. They told me that they hadn't wanted to say anything because I was married, but they were falling in love with me and desperately wanted me to stay so we could make a go of it. That's when I realised I felt the same way."

The oven timer pinged in the background and Sylvia shooed it away. "Why on earth did you go to Manchester then?"

Was she really asking that? Carolyn sat in stunned silence for a second, and then tried to answer. "How could I not? Marcus was desperate to take the job and excited for us all to have a fresh start. He thought it was going to fix all of our marital problems and help us reconnect. Then of course there was Isla to consider. It would've meant her parents being in two different cities, and introducing a new person into her life who it may not have even worked out with."

"Isn't that what's happened now, though?"

"It's different now. She's almost seventeen. We've also given the marriage another shot and proven it really doesn't work."

Sylvia released Carolyn's hand and sat back. "Gosh. And have you seen this person or spoken to them since you moved?"

"No. We decided not to have any contact. This will be the first time I've seen them since I said I was going, and that I wasn't leaving Marcus. They were very gracious about it, in all fairness, and I think understood. But all the same, you can see why I'm a little apprehensive about the reunion."

After pouring herself a cup of tea, Sylvia nodded. "Well, several years have passed. They may have found someone else now. I expect it'll all be water under the bridge." She pushed out the chair and stood up. "Just bite the bullet."

That was a lot of metaphors, even for Sylvia, but Carolyn desperately hoped they were true. Jax had never been short of female attention and even if she was still single, she'd probably have put it well behind her. "You're right. I shouldn't assume there will be any awkwardness."

"You should never assume anything, my dear. Just go in with an open mind and remember that whatever happens, you're a strong and confident woman who is more than capable of handling the situation."

That was right. Carolyn *was* a strong and confident woman, and she was more than capable of handling whatever reaction she got from Jax. It was more her own reaction that she was suddenly worried about, but she wasn't quite prepared to admit that yet. "Thanks."

"You're welcome. I hope you know you can come to me for advice any time, and it never gets back to Marcus. For now, though, let me feed you."

Carolyn did let Sylvia feed her. In fact, she let Sylvia stuff her past the point of comfort, partly out of guilt that Isla had let her cook enough for three people. Then she said her goodbyes and drove back to the football club. It was almost ten past four by the time she pulled into the drive, and the pitch was empty. Everyone had probably headed into the clubhouse, so she hit Isla's number on her in car phone system.

When it rang through to voicemail, she tried again. Then again. And one more time just to be absolutely sure that she was going to need to get out of the car. It was either that or sit in the car park for an indefinite amount of time, and that was not a proper course of action for a strong and confident woman, it was the course of action for a coward.

Chip fat. Beer. Sweat. It was an unholy trinity and it hit Carolyn square between the eyes when she pulled open the side door to the clubhouse. It made her smile to think that she'd been so desperate to spend an evening with Jax, once upon a time, that she'd chosen cheap bottles of generic white wine in here over a meal in a nice restaurant or drinks with friends in an upmarket bar. That woman really had done a number on her sense of taste.

Credit where it was due, though, someone had decorated and installed a new blue carpet with only one or two stains, while the original colour of the old one had no longer been discernible. They'd also invested in three huge televisions, so you were bombarded by the Sky Sports commentary from almost every angle. It was a useful distraction from the sudden thundering of blood through her ears when Jax entered via the kitchen door behind the bar and their eyes locked. What was the correct protocol in this scenario? Before Carolyn could think, she'd smiled again and raised a hand to signal that she came in peace.

"Hi," Jax mouthed, stock still in the door frame. Unlike the clubhouse, she'd barely changed in five years. She still wore head to toe black. Still looked perpetually like she was in her late twenties despite the fact that she must be at least forty by now. Still had a pair of sunglasses on top of her head even in the depths of winter.

"Hi," Carolyn mouthed back, letting her hand drop to her side. She felt like she was in a movie scene. It was the type where the rest of the world falls away, leaving only the two main characters, but this time, they weren't lost in their love for each other. They were both, she suspected, trying to work out what on earth to say next.

Completely oblivious to her mother's discomfort, Isla was soon doing what she did best—demanding money. "Can you get me a drink and a packet of crisps when you go to the bar? I didn't bring any spends."

"Do they accept card?" Carolyn asked absently, before realising that Isla was settling in. She shook her head, freeing herself from an uncharacteristic stupor. "I thought I was just picking you up. And don't say spends, you're not in prison."

Isla shrugged. "Yeah, but then I got chatting. Can we stay for a bit?"

"I don't know, I—" came out before the blonde she'd spotted Isla chatting to earlier was thrusting her hand in Carolyn's direction. If this was Jenna, she suddenly had another situation to assess. "Hello," Carolyn said with a quick up and down appraisal. "We haven't met."

"No, but I know who you are from Jax. I'm Jenna. It's nice to meet you."

Carolyn shook Jenna's outstretched hand, not yet having decided if the feeling was mutual but now wondering what Jax had said. "I hope she was kind."

"For once, she was. I'm intrigued by any woman Jax holds in such high esteem."

That was a good sign. She still hadn't come over, though, and was now stood with her hands on the back of a chair talking to some of the players. "High esteem, hm?"

"Yes, I told her Isla had come to training before Christmas and she remembered you straightaway. In fact, I know she wanted to have a quick chat with you." Jenna tried to beckon Jax over, but she still had her back to them.

"Oh?" Hopefully it wasn't to chase them out of the football club. This was Jax's territory, but it was also Isla's, and whilst Carolyn didn't want to make anyone uncomfortable, she knew they were going nowhere. It would descend her small household into a warzone when it had only just recovered from New Year's Eve.

"I know you were on the committee before, and we were wondering whether you'd consider coming back."

Before Carolyn's relief could fully realise itself, Jenna was listing all the reasons it was a perfect fit, but she seemed to be missing one vital piece of information. Carolyn put out a hand to halt her, and Jenna ran an imaginary zip over her mouth.

"Just to be clear, Jax wants me to rejoin the committee?"

"Yes. Of course. Why wouldn't she?"

"No reason." Or at least no reason that Carolyn was going to tell Jenna, given she most likely knew nothing about what had passed between them. Then again, maybe she did, and it just wasn't a big deal to Jax anymore. As Sylvia had pointed out, almost five years had gone by, and it wasn't like they'd ever actually been in a relationship. Near misses may not factor highly on Jax's list of people she never wanted to see again. "I'll have that chat with her first, though, just to make sure."

Jenna clasped her hands together. "That sounds a lot like a yes."

"It's a maybe. I did enjoy being on the committee before and I made good friends through it but let me have a think." Carolyn gave Jenna a quick squeeze on the shoulder, having warmed to her enthusiasm, and offered her a smile.

"Okay, great. Hang on, I'll just grab Jax."

It shouldn't have been a surprise based on their initial interaction that Jenna quickly pulled Jax away from what she was doing. Carolyn barely had time to look down at the floor and tuck more hair behind her ear before they were face to face, and she desperately hoped she didn't look as nervous as she felt.

"Good to see you again," she said, meaning it but unsure how convincing she'd made her delivery. Had her plan to channel those strong and confident vibes come off in the face of the only person in recent memory who'd almost made her crumble? "You look really well."

"So do you." As soon as Jenna had left them alone, Jax smiled. "It's a bit of a surprise to see you again. Well, not a surprise, because I knew you were back, but..."

"I know, don't worry. I wasn't expecting to see you, either, until Isla told me Jenna was only filling in whilst you were away. I did check. I wasn't sure you'd want to..."

"I know. I'm sorry about Jenna ambushing you. She said she'd let me speak to you before she asked about you taking over as chair."

As chair? Jenna hadn't mentioned that, she'd just asked about rejoining the committee, and Carolyn had assumed in some nondescript role. "You want me to be the new chair of the club?"

The shrug was unconvincing, despite what Jenna had said, although Jax was usually one to say if she had a real problem. Loudly and sometimes with expletives. "Maybe not when Jenna hit me with it on New Year's Eve, but I've had a few days to consider. I think you'd be a fantastic chair and we always worked well together before. A lot has happened since then and I know we can't go back to five years ago, but I had started to hope that with a fresh start, it could work. We're clearly going to be around each other either way, so..."

They were leaving a lot of sentences half-finished, but it wasn't difficult to read between the lines. Especially with someone you'd once known so well. "If you're sure."

Jax smiled again. "I am. Do you think we should properly clear the air and catch up, though?"

"I'd like that. Very much." Even if it did all feel a bit too easy.

"I'll be up at the leisure centre on Tuesday night for under-eighteens training because Becky's asked me to talk to some of the other girls about dual signing for the senior squad. Do you fancy meeting me in the café for a coffee first?"

Carolyn nodded. "Okay. Thanks for dropping Isla home the other night, by the way. That was very kind of you."

"You're welcome. Any time."

Speaking to Jax this way, like she was on heirs and graces, was so at odds with how relaxed they once were with each other that Carolyn struggled to return Jax's smile. She'd tried not to think about it in Manchester but that had become harder and harder now they were back. There were too many reminders, too few distractions, and Isla was right about how much time Carolyn had spent on her own or with Sylvia. The past week, knowing she'd have to see Jax again, had made it impossible.

"I've missed you," she admitted, deciding that being a strong and confident woman meant also telling the truth even when you were terrified of the reaction. What was it Brené Brown always said about vulnerability?

Jax's smile faltered for the first time. "I've missed you, too. You're home now, though. I guess that means we don't have to miss each other anymore."

Their eyes met and Carolyn tilted her head slightly, her stance softening. "I guess it does."

# 5
## JAX

Drumming her fingers on the little chrome table she was seated at, Jax couldn't help but glance periodically at the door. She was back to feeling uncharacteristically on edge. Nervous. Unsure of herself. Perhaps a little excited again, too?

She diverted her attention to the swimming pool below her, visible through full height panes of glass. Even so, the whole café stunk of chlorine, and you could hear the cheers and splashes of tubby youngsters trying to drown each other in the deep end. She couldn't help but laugh when one of the lifeguards, only a few years older, tried to assert authority and lost his flip flop. Watching him fish it out whilst jeered at by preteens reminded Jax of exactly why she only coached adults. Or, at least, over sixteens. She didn't have the patience, or the ability to dial down her language.

When he'd finally retrieved it and slunk back to his chair on the side of the pool, the fun was over, and so was the distraction. Jax needed a new one, so wandered to the vending machine and sized up her options. It was an easy decision when she spotted a share-size bag of Maltesers. They were one of Carolyn's favourites, and as Jax ripped open the top, lobbing a couple in her mouth, she wondered what else she remembered. Isla's birthday, the twenty-ninth of January. Carolyn's tradition with her mother-in-law of receiving a bottle of Champagne every year on that date. Her supposed allergy to dust, which she used as justification for paying a cleaner. Her definite allergy to reality television, which she used as justification for not having a set in the living room. The way she admonished Jax for what she called 'being coarse' even though she threw her head back and laughed every damned time.

Jax flopped into her chair and threw in another Malteser. Man, that laugh. Deep, warm and real, just like Carolyn. She loved coaxing it out of her, but reminiscing was doing nothing for the nerves. Or the excitement, and Jax had meant it when she'd said they should put the past behind them. Carolyn had made her decision and Jax would continue to respect it.

If she shared any of Jax's nervous excitement when she arrived, Carolyn didn't show. She entered through the double doors by the little coffee hatch, all perfect posture and poise. Her hands slipped into the pockets of a long black coat, which was open to reveal a low-cut V-neck sweater in merle grey, and she walked with the confidence of a woman who knew she looked like a million bucks.

Carolyn removed her coat and sat down. "Still no luck getting floodlights put in at the club, then?"

"We gave up on trying to collaborate with the men to make that happen so we're still holding winter training here."

"That's a shame," Carolyn replied, reaching into the bag of Maltesers in front of her and taking one without asking. She popped it into her mouth and sucked it slowly.

Jax met Carolyn's eye, watching her try not to smile. She'd be expecting a protest over the chocolate and maybe it was meant as an icebreaker, but Jax was still a little off balance to be in Carolyn's presence. Even with the numbing smell of chlorine,

Jax had just caught the notes in her perfume and there was an odd chemistry experiment taking place in her brain, which was trying not to acknowledge just how attracted she still found herself even after all this time.

"You look great," she said, her faculties not having quite caught up. "Really great."

"Maybe divorce suits me."

Divorce? Jax took a pause to gather herself, and her feelings. Splitting up wasn't final but divorce was. "I'm sorry to hear that."

"Are you?" The smile on Carolyn's face dissolved as fast as her Malteser and she reached into the packet to take another. Was that not the response she wanted? Or was it just not the one she expected?

"Of course. I'll always wish you'd picked me instead of him," Jax admitted, her heart firmly pinned to her shirt where she'd always kept it. "But when that didn't happen, I still wanted you to be happy. I wanted things to work out for you."

Carolyn stared at the little ball of chocolate pinched between her thumb and forefinger. "You know it was never about picking *him*, though? You do understand that's a huge oversimplification?"

They'd always been straight talking with each other, sometimes to the point of brutal honesty, but Jax had still not expected them to get past the guarded chit-chat stage quite so soon into their reunion. "It sometimes felt that way but yes, I know it's an oversimplification. I always got that your life was more complicated than mine. You had daughter and a husband. You're also straight..."

Carolyn had nodded agreement through all of that, until the last bit. Her eyes shot up to meet Jax's again and her smile returned. "I think we both know that can't be true." She finally popped the Malteser into her mouth and wiped the chocolate from her fingers using a napkin from the middle of the table.

"And without the existing partner and the child, who will always come first in every decision I make, I would've acted on my feelings for you in a heartbeat."

"But you did have the partner and the child, and you made the right choice for yourself at the time. I get it." Jax shrugged, surprised to find that she meant every word. She was nothing if not pragmatic and Jenna often teased her for a lack of romantic spirit, but she'd learned at a young age that ideals and expectation only led to disappointment. The real world wasn't a fairytale. "So, that's the past. What's happening now?" She had a thought and tore a bigger hole in the top of the Maltesers packet. "In the spirit of this being a share bag, we can have a chocolate for each update. What do you reckon?"

Carolyn chuckled. "I reckon that it's a deal. You go first. Tell me something happy."

Resisting the urge to put this catch up at the top of her list, Jax defaulted to the biggest piece of news in her life over the past year. "I got promoted to Creative Director." She took a chocolate and crunched it rather than sucking, not wanting to hold up the conversation. "What about you, are you working since you moved back?"

"That's fantastic, well done. And yes, only just. I'm going to locum for a little while until I decide what to do next. After the stress and chaos of the pandemic, I could use a change of pace. Something with a better work-life balance."

"I can't even imagine what it was like."

"Heartbreaking, at times. So many people not getting the care they needed because we were swamped, and we'll be seeing the effects for a long time. For now, I'm enjoying covering maternity leave in a posh village surgery dealing almost exclusively with wealthy pensioners."

"Gout and dementia. What a treat."

Carolyn laughed again but Jax hadn't quite found the sweet

spot yet. "Just think. If I'd taken a different path, I could be a private consultant by now. Or have found a cushy little job shaping health policy for the government."

"Oh please," Jax chided, leaning back in her chair and pretending to size Carolyn up. She didn't need to, because they already knew each other too well. "We both know you'd hate that. You'd end up with a house full of stray cats or delinquent kids so that you had someone to care for."

"That's true. Apart from the cat bit..."

"I, on the other hand, would be quite happy to boss people around and make the rules all day."

"I expect you do now." Unlike Jax, Carolyn leant into the conversation, resting forward on her elbows and taking another chocolate. She shot a smile to acknowledge she hadn't technically earned one this time.

"I'll admit that I miss getting stuck in and actually creating stuff. It's funny, when you think about it. You spend ages becoming good at something, which gets you promoted to a position where you no longer do it. I've been taking on a few side projects, though. Just to keep my hand in." Reaching into the pocket of her coat, which was over the back of her chair, Jax grabbed her phone. She tapped through her latest work and pulled up one of her logo designs. "Do you remember Abi? I did new branding for her gardening business when she relaunched after Covid."

"Looks great. You're very talented." Carolyn leant further forward and pinched to zoom in. "And yes, of course I remember Abi. She's still here too, then?"

"There's been a lot of turnover but Abi will never leave The Blues."

Sitting back and grinning, Carolyn crossed her legs as she appraised Jax. "Sounds like someone else I know." She took the

Maltesers packet, rested it in her lap, and ate another. "So, who else is on our committee these days?"

"*Our* committee, huh? You've decided you're happy to be nominated, then?"

"I think so, yes. I just need to know who's going to be voting. You'll obviously have to fill me in on what they're like."

"Oh, obviously." And it wouldn't take long because there wasn't much to tell. "There are only three of us. Me," Jax said, gesturing up and down herself. "I'm amazing."

"As I already know."

"Becky had an automatic place on the committee as manager of the under-eighteen team, but I also got her to take on the secretary role. I expect you've met her a few times since Isla's been training with her. She's very organised and a big asset. Then the last member of our sad little crew is Jenna, who you met on Sunday. She's treasurer."

Carolyn frowned. "Will we get on?"

"I'm sure you'll disagree occasionally because you both need to be right, but yeah. Jenna's very determined and I think you'll actually end up loving her. Incidentally, she's also Abi's girlfriend."

Her features softening, Carolyn nodded. "Okay. I trust Abi's judgement."

Jax folded her arms. "Oh, but you don't trust mine?"

"No, absolutely not. I'll never trust your judgement again after you let that useless woman on the committee." Carolyn clicked her fingers. "What was her name? She had a daughter who played with Isla for a while but soon gave up, and then a younger son with the boys club." Becoming frustrated, she clicked her fingers in another burst. "You must remember. I think her husband was involved on their committee. Cocky. Short."

Jax reached into the bag still in Carolyn's lap and took

another chocolate whilst she tried to think who they were talking about. "Oh, you mean Greg and his wife! Yeah. They split not long after you left, and she recently remarried. He's chair of the boys club now and he's still a pain in the ass." She popped the Malteser in her mouth and bit down on it hard, imagining it was Greg's tiny brain, and Carolyn laughed.

"I remember you didn't get on with him. From this display of aggression against your Malteser, I presume nothing's changed."

"No. He wants the clubs to merge and I'm dead against it." Wriggling forward, Jax pointed at Carolyn, who continued to look amused at how animated she became at the mention of Greg's name. "I need to know your position. Are you on my side?"

"I agree. They've been floating the idea of merging for years but it's only to further their own interests."

"Exactly." Jax threw her hands in the air. "See, this is why I love you."

Realising what she'd just said, she felt her face warm and a little buzz in her chest. She hadn't meant that she loved Carolyn, just her outlook on Greg's plans, but it was a bit too close to true for comfort.

Mercifully, Carolyn didn't even bat an eyelid. Instead, she continued to pump Jax for information about all the new personalities around the club, until Jax's phone vibrated across the table. It was Becky, and their eyes both shot up to the clock above the coffee hatch.

"Crap, I need to get downstairs. Can you bring my coat?" Jax asked as she hit accept, pressed the phone to her ear, and pushed out her chair in one smooth move. "Hey, Beck. Sorry, we lost track of time. I'm just coming." She jogged across the café towards the door, ran down the stairs, and slid the device into her pocket. Then she coughed as the cold air hit her lungs. On the far end of the pitch, Becky had the under-eighteens gathering equipment, and Jax waved as she ran across the astroturf.

Becky gathered them all and Jax spluttered through her spiel about joining in with senior squad training, how welcoming they were, and how it was a good way to manage the step up to adult football. "Anything you want to add, Becky?"

"No, I think you covered it all. Eventually."

The girls laughed and the group dispersed, by which time Carolyn had made it to Jax's side and held out her coat. "You've convinced me of Jenna and Becky's professionalism, but I'm not sure I want to work with you."

"It's your fault for distracting me," Jax replied, snatching her coat.

Carolyn laughed. "Another thing that never changes." She picked up a bag from the floor. "I suppose we'll see you tomorrow. My daughter doesn't need any of your rousing speeches, she's already determined to get into the senior squad."

"And she's in it for Sunday, but don't tell her that because I don't put the team out until Friday. Becky also needs to process her registration when we get home and it's dependent on league approval." After slipping into her coat, Jax held up her crossed fingers. She'd already decided she wanted Isla based on her training performance last week. A place in the starting lineup was a while away but she could begin by getting some experience from the bench.

Her eyes dropping to the floor, Carolyn squinted a little. Then she righted her expression. What was that? She couldn't have been too shocked to learn that Isla was good enough. "Thanks both." She turned and waved. "See you."

It was a cool goodbye but then the weather was literally freezing and they weren't alone anymore, so Jax shook it off and helped Becky with the training equipment, hoisting a bag of balls over her shoulder. "I think she's onboard. If Isla's coming Sunday, we'll all be there so we can vote her in."

"Your charm has worked again," Becky replied as she picked up the rest of the kit. "You'll have to tell me how you do it one day but for now, take me home and warm me up."

"Steady on, buddy. You'll give people the wrong idea."

# 6

# CAROLYN

"This is exciting," Sylvia said, hugging her coat tight around herself.

Carolyn frowned. "Is it?" Because from where she stood, it was only cold and damp.

She'd long since resigned herself to spending her Saturday mornings on the side of a football pitch but was struggling to find enthusiasm for repeating the experience on a Sunday. Hopefully, now Isla was a little older, she wouldn't want her mum there every single week and Carolyn could go back to enjoying a day of rest. Sundays were meant to be her chance to stop, go for a jog, and prep for the new week. Not watch a horde of angry women fling themselves in the mud. She'd leave that kind of thing for her ex-husband to enjoy on the internet.

"Yes," Sylvia replied with a nod towards the clubhouse. "There are some lovely looking chaps over there. Perhaps we can find one to take your mind off the heartbreaker." She leant sideways and whispered, "Is he here?"

"No!" Carolyn raised a hand to her forehead, slightly taken aback but unable to resist a little laugh. She really should've expected this.

"It's not someone from the football club then? I presumed it must be. Either that or work. I couldn't imagine when else you'd find the time to meet someone."

"Not that you've given it a lot of thought, of course."

"Oh, of course!" Silence persisted between them for only one or two seconds before Sylvia said, "So, just to be clear, it's not someone from the football club?"

Carolyn laughed again and shook her head. "You're incorrigible." There was a little grunt, signalling that Sylvia was unhappy with the response. She wouldn't get any more information, though. Carolyn was relieved to be on good terms with Jax and enjoying reconnecting. It was more than she'd hoped for that Jax seemed open to having a friendship again and she didn't want to push her luck. "I've spoken to them, we've cleared the air, and it's all been put behind us. On that basis, it really doesn't matter who it is. Enough."

"Spoilsport."

"My love life isn't a sport." Not that she *had* a love life, but that was beside the point, and Carolyn returned her attention to watching the match. Despite losing the feeling in her extremities, and wishing she was enjoying lunch in a warm restaurant, she would never have missed Isla's senior team debut. They were down to the last twenty minutes, and she was bound to come on soon. Jax wouldn't have asked Isla to come if she didn't intend to play her.

Sure enough, five minutes later she was warming up on the side of the pitch, and Carolyn felt an anticipatory pang of nerves tickle her numb fingertips. She knew how much this meant and desperately wanted it to go well. The team were already three-nil up so the pressure was off, but Isla would feel it regardless. Not that she would let her game face slip. Neither of them would make that mistake today.

"Come on, Isla!" Sylvia yelled when Isla replaced Becky in

the centre of midfield. Then she turned her head and more quietly asked, "What's happening?"

"Isla has just been switched on in place of her under-eighteens coach. I think she's injured because she's limping."

"You should go and find out. Maybe they'll take you on as the team doctor."

"Hmm," Carolyn mumbled, not finding that a remotely inviting prospect.

"She's young to be a coach. Don't you think?"

"I suppose." She'd cooled towards Becky since Tuesday night. It was churlish to be jealous and if Jax had found someone else then Carolyn was happy for her. It didn't stop the feeling from persisting, though, however little right she had to that emotion when she was the one who'd turned down Jax.

"Pretty," Sylvia continued. "Very interesting hair."

That wasn't helping, and Carolyn shuffled from foot to foot before opting not to reply. Instead, she settled in to watch Isla, shouting as much encouragement as possible. Isla had a nervy start but it didn't take long before she looked more settled and started playing some of her usual penetrating passes.

"My dad would have loved to watch this," Carolyn noted, suddenly struck by another sort of sadness altogether. He had sparked her interest in the game and, by extension, Isla's. Whilst Carolyn didn't enjoy losing all of her weekends to football, she'd loved watching Tottenham from the terraces as a child. She'd also loved watching him share everything he knew, and enthusiastically telling anyone who'd listen that Isla would play for England one day.

Sylvia wrapped an arm around Carolyn's shoulder and gave it a brisk rub. "We'll just have to cheer extra hard for him when Isla scores a goal."

"That's a lovely thought but Isla doesn't score many goals. She's racked up a fair few assists, though."

"I haven't the faintest clue what that means, my dear. I only watch football for the chaps in little shorts and these women are all very nice, but they don't quite cut it. You just tell me when to cheer."

Carolyn laughed, once again grateful for Sylvia's presence in her life, and on this sideline.

By the time the referee blew the final whistle, the cold had penetrated her bones and only a bath would thaw them out. Isla had played well on her debut, though, and that made the discomfort worthwhile.

"Well done, sweetheart," she said as Isla trudged towards them, her shin guards in hand and her mud stained socks at half-mast. "I'm so proud of you."

"I was terrible."

"What?"

"I only played fifteen minutes and I missed a tonne of tackles."

"You're being far too hard on yourself. I told you this would be a big step up and you did very well indeed to get as much time as you did, given you're still only sixteen. Show a little patience."

With a big *harumph*, Isla led them in the direction of the clubhouse. Then she disappeared into the changing rooms and left them standing on the concrete outside.

"That was charming," Sylvia noted with a quick chuckle.

"Sorry. She isn't being especially gracious today."

"Was she bad, between you and me?"

"No, she wasn't," Jax replied. She'd crept up on them from behind and dropped a large bag of balls next to Carolyn's feet. "Hi. I'm Jax, Isla's coach." She extended her gloved hand to Sylvia, who gave it a demure shake. "Pleased to meet you."

"Likewise. Thank you for clarifying. Perhaps you could convey the same to my granddaughter."

"I'd be happy to, but first I need a drink to warm myself up."

"A woman after my own heart. Let me buy you one. Will you join me in a whiskey?"

"That sounds perfect."

Sylvia needed no more invitation to head into the bar with Carolyn and Jax trailing behind her. She rubbed her hands together, surprisingly enthused by her surroundings. "This is wonderful."

"For the second time that afternoon, Carolyn found herself asking, "Is it?"

"Yes. So much character, and the chaps are over at the back. See?"

When Sylvia pointed to the men by the pool table, Carolyn couldn't help but laugh. She really did have a one track mind. There was a man Carolyn recognised, though, and he seemed to have clocked her too because he was coming towards them.

"Oh god," Jax muttered, turning her back. "Greg. Hide me."

He didn't want Jax, instead holding out a hand to Carolyn. "This is a lovely surprise. Someone said they'd seen you on the sideline."

She shook it, despite a little confusion as to why he was being so familiar. They'd met a few times but didn't know each other well.

"It's Greg, isn't it?" Carolyn asked, taking a step back to restore the distance between them.

"That's right. I chair the boys club, although I expect Jax has shared that news."

"You haven't come up." She got in quick with the harmless lie. Jax was hot headed on the subject of Greg, when they needed to treat him with a lighter touch. "That's useful to know, though, because I've just agreed to take over as chair of the girls club. There are a few things we may need to discuss but not now."

"Oh, no. Not now. I expect you just want a quiet drink to celebrate your win. Can I buy you one?" he asked, gesturing to the bar with the half-empty pint glass in his hand.

"I'd like a drink, Greg," Sylvia cut in. She looped her arm through his and guided him towards the waiting bartender. "Do you like whiskey? I wonder if they have anything nice and expensive."

Carolyn chuckled as she hung back and watched Sylvia at work. "I think Greg got more than he bargained for."

"And I thought she wanted to have whiskey with *me*." Jax let out a short, sharp sigh. "I won't deny, I'm a little hurt."

"What would make it up to you?"

After consideration, Jax turned to whisper, "Can I have a chocolate bar?"

"You want me to buy you a chocolate bar?" Carolyn laughed again and leant a little closer. Then she whispered, "What type?"

"We only stock three kinds. You pick."

"If I get you a bag of Maltesers, will you share them again?"

"Will I have a choice?" When Jax grinned, Carolyn couldn't help but return it.

Her heart rate picked up as their eyes locked, and it raced further still when the door opened behind them. Carolyn stepped backwards and placed a hand on her chest, looking anywhere other than Becky's direction.

"Are you ready to do the big vote?" Becky asked, throwing her bag onto a chair. Jenna's landed on top of it when she entered the clubhouse, too.

"We need to," Jax replied, nodding at Greg. "She's started telling people she's our new chair already."

"Okay, let me just grab us some drinks and chocolate."

Becky headed for the bar, but Jax stayed close. "Sounds like you're off the hook."

"Doesn't it just," Carolyn muttered, fingering the chain

around her neck. "Although I'm sure Isla will still have a use for my debit card. We always agreed she'd start earning her own money when she turns seventeen, though, so it might finally get a reprieve."

"Are you talking about Isla getting a job?" Jenna asked, distracted from the conversation she'd just started with one of the other players. "Because she asked me if I'd give her one earlier."

That was Isla all over, and it was no surprise that she'd found time to apply for a job working for Jenna. The thought amused Carolyn. "And will you?"

"Well, I do need a new Saturday receptionist. She seems like she might be good at it so I'm considering giving her a trial. Doesn't it mean she'll have to stop playing for the under-eighteens, though? Becky won't be happy."

Another win, although Carolyn was less happy with herself that she'd immediately seen it that way. Becky had been nothing but supportive of Isla, and she knew it was unfair. "I think Isla's quite keen to make the step up to playing adult football and she was always going to struggle to play two days in a row. Something has to give, as I've already told her, between sports, work, schoolwork, and starting to think about university applications."

At that, Jenna chewed her lip and glanced down at the floor. "Um."

"Um?"

"I think you should probably speak to her about that. It's not my place to say."

"I will ask her, but what's the gist?"

"That she's not sure she wants to go to uni. Sorry."

Carolyn frowned, unsure why Jenna looked so worried. If Isla wanted to explore other options to university, that was her prerogative, so long as she didn't plan to spend the rest of her life on the sofa aimlessly drifting. The bigger concern was her unwillingness or worse, fear, to say anything.

"You don't have anything to apologise for," Carolyn assured, offering Jenna a smile. "We've had a lot going on lately and few chances to talk properly, but I'm going to make sure she knows that I'll support her whatever she chooses. And if she gets a job with you then all the better. She can see how a business runs and start earning her own money. A few days of hard work would do her good."

"I told you," Jax whispered, nudging Jenna's shoulder with her fist.

"What did you tell her?" Carolyn's frown was back, but it was more quizzical this time.

"That you aren't a snob."

"Is that how I come across?"

"I mean, you're a well-dressed, well-educated, middle-class doctor who drives around in a Lexus. It's not a big leap."

Carolyn laughed. "Say what you really think."

"Thanks, I always do, and this wasn't tough to work out. I know that your dad grew up in a working-class part of London, left school at fourteen, and worked his ass off to send you and your sister to college. Given he's your hero, I figured you wouldn't mind if Isla was like him."

At the mention of her dad twice in one afternoon, Carolyn shuffled, her new smile fading as quickly as it came. "He passed away last year. It would be lovely to think that Isla is anything like him and that it isn't only his love for football she's inherited."

Before she could process that emotion, she was hit with another. Jax wrapped her in a warm hug, her team hoody soft against Carolyn's cheek as she stiffened but then let herself sink into the embrace. It had been a long time since she'd hugged anyone but Isla, and her eyes prickled with tears at the unexpected show of comfort.

"I'm sorry," Jax whispered.

"Thank you," Carolyn whispered back, breaking all contact when she saw Becky walking towards them. She took another step backwards and tucked her hands into her pockets. "Anyway, we should probably get on with this vote so I can find Isla and have a chat with her."

They proposed, seconded, and redundantly thirded the nomination. Then Jax broke apart the KitKat Becky had just bought her and handed a stick of it to each of them.

"The covenant of the KitKat," she said, bashing each of their sticks with the end of her own.

Carolyn chuckled and took a bite, licking the chocolate from her fingers. She'd missed Jax's sometimes wacky sense of humour. "You're a lunatic."

"But at least I'm always myself."

That was true, and Carolyn nodded. "If I want honesty, I know where to go." Not to mention warmth, integrity, and compassion.

"I don't mean to drop you right in it, but we could do with organising our first committee meeting. Soon."

"Well, how about Friday? Is that *too* soon?"

Jenna sucked her teeth before nodding. "I need to cut Abi's aunt's hair first. She's only round the corner from here, though, so it's not a problem."

"I can as well," Becky said with a huff. "Need to be up early for the under-eighteens match. It's an hour away and they've also asked to bring kick off forward, so I was planning a quiet evening given I'm not getting a lie in."

Usually that piece of news would be a threat to Carolyn's laid-back Saturday morning schedule, too, but Isla had already made plans to get a lift with someone else. "I presume we're meeting in the clubhouse?"

"Or," Jax suggested with a little raise of her eyebrows. "We could host at our house where it'll be a bit quieter, and Greg won't interrupt us every five minutes."

At the reminder that it was *our* house, meaning hers and Becky's, Carolyn felt a now familiar jab to her heart. Being in the home they shared didn't sound like a lot of fun. "We could go to the pub if it's going to cause you any bother."

"It's no bother."

Maybe it wasn't for Jax, but Carolyn's agreement came accompanied by a forced smile. One she expected she'd have to replicate on Friday evening.

## 7

## JAX

"You're going to a lot of effort for a committee meeting," Becky pointed out as she stood in the kitchen doorway and watched Jax put the final touches on her charcuterie board.

"Just making the new chief feel welcome."

"Hmm." Swinging off the frame and then pulling open the fridge door in one smooth motion, Becky produced two bottles of lager. They did upmarket but only to a point and the Chablis was there purely for Carolyn's benefit. "You don't have the hots for her, then?"

At that, Jax's fingers slid over the packet of salami she'd been trying to prise open and it fell to the floor with a slap. "What?"

Becky shut the fridge and set both beers on the table. "Just an observation. First you spend so long catching up that you miss your talk with the under-eighteens. Then in the clubhouse you were practically glued to her side and kept finding any excuse to touch her. Now you're raiding Marks and Spencer's delicatessen aisle and I'm pretty sure that's your best perfume."

Damn. She really had been paying attention. It was always the quiet ones you needed to watch. Jenna was still utterly clueless, but Becky had rumbled Jax with dazzling efficiency.

"Of course I have the hots for Carolyn," she admitted, trying to joke it off as she bent to pick up her salami packet. "Don't you?"

"No. For a start, she's old enough to be my mother." Becky pulled out a chair and sat, hitching up her knee and hugging it. "You, on the other hand, have got it bad. What gives?"

Pausing with the salami packet clutched to her chest, Jax considered lying, but she was actually glad to have a confidante. "Can you be discreet?"

It was a rhetorical question, because Becky wasn't a gossip, and Jax flung the packet onto the worktop before grabbing her beer instead. She twisted off the cap and explained the basic history of how they'd met through the football club, become friends, and grown closer. Then Becky stopped her as she reached the crux.

"Wait, so this isn't a new crush?"

"No, it's an old one. She was married, though, and had a kid. I knew I had feelings for her, but I'd never be that jerk."

"And did she know?"

"No. I hid it pretty well and I never told anyone. Not even Abi, who's been one of my closest friends for years. It only came to a head when she told me she was moving to Manchester. She was really emotional about it, and I couldn't hold back anymore. So, I asked if the reason she was struggling was because of me. Well, us."

"And what did she say?"

Jax shrugged. "Nothing at first. I think she was a bit stunned. You could almost see it registering on her face as she had an *oh shit* moment. Then she finally admitted that the idea of leaving me hurt like hell and she had feelings too."

"Wow."

"Yep." Jax paused to take a few sips of her drink, hoping to numb the pain of remembering what had come next. "For a hot moment I thought she was going to leave him. She kissed me and it was ecstasy, but as with all highs, it didn't last. She pretty quickly decided that she wouldn't split up her family. Which I got, even if it didn't help me feel any better, because I was faced with a woman who I was crazy about, and who had feelings for me too, but who I knew I wouldn't get to be with."

Becky tilted her head, her face creasing with sympathy and probably a hefty dose of understanding. She knew what a broken heart felt like. "I'm sorry."

"Me too. It sucked for ages. At least if we'd tried and fought or something I could've squared it more easily, but we didn't. We got on great right to that last kiss, which was amazing by the way, and then we broke contact until she showed up here again."

"So, what's going on between you guys now?"

"Nothing." It was the honest answer, and yet it niggled on Jax. She shuffled uncomfortably and took another sip of lager. "Well, we *still* get on great, and clearly I can't disguise the fact that I fancy the crap out of her, but we're just friends. Or, at least, we're becoming friends again. I think."

"But she's single now. And so are you."

Jax frowned. She presumed Carolyn was single. She wasn't with her husband anymore, but actually that didn't mean there wasn't someone else. "I never asked." And even if she was single, Carolyn had agreed they would leave the past alone. She wanted to move on. Not back. "It doesn't really matter. She hasn't given me any indication that she wants more than a friendship."

"Mmm."

When Becky offered no other follow up, Jax pressed. "Come on. Don't just *mmm*."

"I don't have anything else to say yet, but I'm watching with interest and I'll report back."

"You do that."

Jax was about to get up and return to her meats when the

doorbell trilled. Why Jenna had bothered ringing it, though, was anyone's guess, because she opened the door for herself and walked straight in.

"Do you think I'll be a good mum one day?" she asked without any preamble, heading for the fridge and pulling out a beer.

"Hello Jenna. Nice to see you. Yes, we're both well," Jax replied, finally setting out her salami. "Do you want a drink? Let me fetch you one of my best imported Belgian lagers even though you're meant to be doing Dry January…"

Jenna looked down at the bottle in her hand. "Oh. Thanks." She set it on the table unopened and then shuffled out of her coat, hooking it over the back of a chair. "Sorry, I'm just having a crisis and I need your help."

"You want to ask two childless single people about parenting?"

"No, I want to ask Carolyn. You two are useless. Isn't she here yet?"

She was due a little late because she'd been held up at work and was coming straight from there, and Jax knew this because they'd been texting each other sporadically throughout the day. "Expecting her any minute. In the meantime, you'll have to put up with us."

Jenna peered over Jax's shoulder and sneaked a grape. "This is fancy. Why have we never had nice food before?"

"Because I like Carolyn better than you," Jax replied, hearing a car pull up outside and hoping it was her. She wiped her hands on a cloth, set her board in the middle of the table, then frowned as both Becky and Jenna began to pilfer it. "Please don't eat everything before she even arrives. And use plates." She grabbed a couple from the cupboard and set one in from of each of them. "You say I'm useless for parenting advice, but I have to put up with you. Surely that qualifies me?"

"I'd say so," Carolyn agreed, appearing in the kitchen doorway and running a hand through her hair. "Sorry. The front door was ajar, so I came straight in."

"Was it now?" Jax asked, glaring at Jenna and feeling her point was well and truly made. Then she returned her attention to Carolyn, offering to take her coat and pour her a glass of wine.

"I wouldn't say no to a small one," she replied, setting a black leather satchel by the fridge. "And some food, if there's any left. I've not had time to eat anything. Then you can tell me why you're giving parenting advice. What have I missed?"

"Jenna wants to know if she'll be a good mum one day, but she hasn't explained why yet." Returning from the hallway, where she'd just hooked Carolyn's coat on a peg, Jax busied herself uncorking the wine and pouring a glass whilst she half listened to Jenna's explanation. It was hard to find much enthusiasm, though, when she was far more interested in finding out about Carolyn's day. Especially considering she'd come in a striking indigo trouser suit which drew Jax's attention no matter how hard she tried to divert it back to the conversation. Becky was right and she had it bad.

"Not long after we got together," Jenna explained as she snapped a breadstick into hundreds of pieces, half of which spilled across the table. "Abi was really clear with me that she wanted kids someday. She said she'd reached the age where she didn't want to get into a long term relationship where it was off the cards."

"That's sensible," Carolyn noted, taking the wine glass with a little mouthed "thanks" when it was handed to her.

"I agree. Expectation setting. I told her I'd also love to have kids one day, so it was definitely on the cards if things work out."

"But you're now worrying about whether you'll be a good parent, as everyone does."

"Exactly. I always told myself I'd give my children all the security and love I never really had growing up, but what if I can't? Like, what if I just don't know how because I spent my whole childhood moving between my mum's place and my grandparents, and never feeling like I was wanted anywhere? I have all these visions in my head of me and Abi taking our kids to the beach, and the zoo, and reading bedtime stories, and going to school plays. It's a fantasy, though. I know it wouldn't be that easy and what if I'm not up to it?"

Jax's stance softened and she regretted teasing Jenna. She really did have a problem, deserving of a nice lager, a grape, and the mess she was continuing to spread across the table. "Shit. What's brought all this on tonight?"

"I was at Abi's aunt's place, and she asked if I had time to quickly trim her neighbour's hair whilst I was there because she was struggling to get out where she had a newborn. Abi cooed over the baby whilst I did the cut, and she was just such a natural. It got me thinking about how much I love being part of her family and how they've practically adopted me, and then I got sad, and started thinking about it all. I don't want to let any of them down, you know?"

"Buddy, none of Abi's family is ever going to feel let down by you. I promise. For some reason they love you. Don't ask me why."

Carolyn gently smacked the top of Jax's arm with the back of her hand and shook her head derisively. "I think what Jax is trying to say is that you deserve to be loved and accepted by Abi's family and they'll be there for support if you choose to have children. For what it's worth, no one knows what they're doing to start with. There's no manual and everyone makes mistakes. You'll make some too, but you'll work them out."

"Yes. What Carolyn said. My sister has five kids, the first one came along when she was only nineteen, and she's made hundreds of stuff ups over the years. Those boys knows she loves them, though." Jax pulled out her phone and brought up the last family picture from her Christmas trip to Nebraska, sliding it over the table to Jenna through the sea of crumbs. "They even know their cantankerous, smart-ass aunt loves them. You'll be a great mum. I promise."

Jenna picked up the phone and laughed, probably at the disparity in size. All five of Jax's nephews now dwarfed her and in the picture, they were holding her horizontally whilst she tried to stop her hat from falling off. "Did *you* never want kids of your own?"

"Nah." Jax picked up her phone when Jenna slid it back over the table, and bashed off the bits of breadstick without complaint. "I was only fourteen when my first nephew was born, and my sister had to come back and live at home with us because her boyfriend shot through. I ended up helping a lot, until I moved over here in my early twenties, and at the time I was glad to be out of it all."

Carolyn pulled out a chair and sat down, crossing her legs and pinching a loose thread from her trousers. "You wouldn't have changed your mind? Even if you'd met someone who desperately wanted them?"

She continued to look down into her lap, fiddling with her seam. Was this about Isla? Proof that things wouldn't have worked between them given Jax didn't want children? Because that was entirely different. "I think if I had ever met someone who already had kids, yes. But small babies? I'm not so sure. I've learned I'm a lot better equipped for when they can talk and want advice or to kick a ball about. Less so with crying and nappies."

Carolyn let out a little laugh. "And Becky?"

"And Becky what?" Becky replied, still working her way through the charcuterie board. She bashed her hands together and finally engaged with their conversation, which Jax knew would be a tough one for her. She thought she'd found the person she'd marry and start a family with until last year.

"You don't want babies?"

"I'd love them." She pushed back her plate and let out a small sigh. "But this is a sore topic for me right now. I don't know if Jax mentioned, but I ended up living here because a seven year relationship broke down and I had nowhere else to go when he cheated on me and set fire to all our plans, so…"

Carolyn frowned. "I'm sorry. I didn't know that." She pointed from Becky to Jax. "So you're her… what? Sorry, I'm confused. I'd presumed you were together."

The amount of laughter from both Becky and Jenna was borderline insulting and Jax folded her arms. "No, Becky is just my lodger. Glad the idea is so funny, though."

"Sorry," Becky spluttered, a hand over her mouth. "But you're… no." She shot Jax an indiscernible look, but her intentions soon became clear. "I'm single, and so is Jax. Jenna is the only loved up person in the room. Or so I presume."

"Oh gosh." Carolyn laughed again, a hand on her brow. "I'm sorry." She relaxed back in her chair and grabbed her wine to take a few sips. "How embarrassing."

That was also borderline offensive, and Jax placed a hand on Carolyn's shoulder. "Hey, why is it so embarrassing that you assumed Becky and I were together? I'm starting to get a complex here."

Carolyn placed her hand over Jax's and gave it a little squeeze. "I didn't mean it that way. I just shouldn't have assumed. And you have to admit, Becky is rather too young for you."

That was rich. There were twelve years between them, which was exactly the difference between Jax's forty and Carolyn's fifty-two. "You think, do you?"

"Yes. Stop sulking, pass me some paper from my bag so I can take notes, and sit down so we can start this committee meeting."

Jax grumbled but did as she was told, delving into the satchel and pulling out a pad, then sitting down next to Carolyn and awaiting her next instruction. It made Becky and Jenna titter again, and she barely dared ask, "What's so funny now?"

"Nothing," Jenna replied, picking up a breadstick and actually chewing it this time. "I'm just so happy we've finally found someone who can put you in your place. You know some of the players are genuinely scared of you?"

"No they're not! They were desperate for me to come back after Christmas to get away from *you*. I'm not at all scary."

Carolyn had taken a pen from her pocket and begun scribbling notes on the top of her page but absently reached under Jax's chin to give it a little stroke. "That's right. You're a pussy cat, with the correct handling." When Jax purred, she chuckled and withdrew her hand. "Now, what's the priority for this meeting? I notice we didn't circulate an agenda."

Becky had been watching the interaction closely, her lips pursed, and shook her head slightly. "My fault. I wrote one but forgot to send it. I can pull it up on my phone, though. Hang on." She tapped through the device until she found the list. "First item is finances. Jenna has brought the club accounts up to date and I gathered together all of Greg's invoices, and they show a projected loss this season. It's not a huge deficit, only around five hundred pounds, but we still need to plug it."

"On to fundraising, then," Carolyn said as she scribbled on her sheet again. "I actually have a proposition here."

"You're going to give us five hundred pounds?" Jax asked, earning her another gentle whack.

"No. But I had a chat with Isla after the game on Sunday about her next options and in an effort to prove I support her choices, which is apparently still in dispute, I would like to task her with organising a fundraising event. Under supervision, of course. But it'll show I have faith in her, give her some experience of running a budget, and hopefully secure us some money in the process. What do you all think? I will of course take full responsibility for any problems."

They all agreed that it sounded like a great idea, and Carolyn moved them on swiftly to the next related point, which was Greg and the proposed merger. The mention of his name had the usual impact on Jax's stress levels, and she got up to retrieve Jenna's discarded drink.

"I say we have him murdered," Jax suggested as she threw the cap into the bin. "How much extra fundraising do you think it would take?"

Carolyn shook her head again. "I agree he is a little slimy, but he could be a useful ally. You need to calm down and think strategically."

"Yeah, Jax," Jenna teased, still enjoying how efficaciously Carolyn cut her down to size. "You're not in charge anymore. Listen to the boss."

"I *am* listening to the boss," Jax shot back, well aware that they needed to try to work together. She just wasn't going to entertain the idea of a merger.

"Good," Carolyn replied, setting down her pen. "Whilst you're pacing, can you grab my bag for me?" She reached around for Jax to hand it to her and pulled out a little pouch. From the pouch came a pair of dark blue plastic rimmed glasses, which she perched on her nose. "I want to read you an email he sent me today."

She could read anything she liked in those glasses, and Jax suddenly found her anger for Greg superseded by another warming feeling—lust. Were they new? In any case, it was a very becoming look for Carolyn, and Jax was in thrall as she scrolled through her phone to find the message.

"Dear Carolyn," she read aloud. "I hope you don't mind me contacting you privately, but I know Jax regularly chooses to ignore my emails and I saw your address had been added to the club website. I still feel that it would be helpful for us to meet and discuss how the two factions of the club can work together, especially given our shared interest in the clubhouse. There are a number of matters to discuss, including finding a new manager for the bar, which has been running on part time staff and volunteers since reopening after Covid. I would be happy to buy you dinner and look forward to us successfully working together in the future. Please just let me know when you're free." She set the phone back on the table and removed her glasses, chewing on the end of the arm. "So?"

"I knew he fancied you," Jenna said, leaning forward and grabbing another grape. "The way he was sucking up to you and your mum on Sunday."

"My mother-in-law, but yes, I got the same impression. Regardless, I think his points are valid. We can't keep ignoring him and we do need to work together."

Jax still hadn't made it past the thought of Greg with his hands all over Carolyn, and she was having to very literally bite her tongue to keep her anger about the club from spilling over with the addition of irrational jealousy. She had no right to an opinion about Carolyn's dinner companions, however much she hated the idea of anything happening with Greg, but she did have a right to voice her concerns about getting too close to him from a committee point of view. Again.

"I don't ignore his emails," she said, trying to uncurl the fist at her side. "I told him I wouldn't be answering whilst I was away and I dealt with them when I got back. He always wants to make me out like I'm unreasonable and uncooperative, just because I don't agree with his ultimate aim to merge the clubs. That's what this is really about. He thinks he can schmooze Carolyn, charm her onside, and then eventually get what he wants." And if he also coaxed her into bed during the process, he'd probably see it as a bonus, but Jax wouldn't say that aloud.

"I know you're not unreasonable," Carolyn assured, pushing Jax's chair out a little further and encouraging her to sit down. "But reacting to him so obviously just plays into his hands. Maybe it would be better if I dealt with him for a while."

Jax slumped onto her seat. "I guess I don't have a choice."

"It'll be fine. I won't accept dinner, but I will offer to meet him in the clubhouse after the game on Sunday. How's that?"

They all confirmed agreement, Jenna and Becky more readily than Jax, and then rattled through the other items on the agenda. Mainly it involved approving requests for equipment, or initial plans for the big summer tournament, and Carolyn pushed them along apace.

When they reached the end, she declared their first meeting a success, but Jax was less sure. She still felt uneasy about Greg, but knew it was partly personally motivated, so decided to keep her mouth shut.

"Well done, boss," she said instead, at least happy to praise Carolyn unreservedly. "I think we can all agree we made the right choice for chair."

"From what I understand, I was your only choice, but I'll take it." She gathered up her papers and slotted them into her bag. Then the returned her glasses to their pouch and tucked them into her pocket. "I hate to dash but I need to collect Isla from her gran's. She's atoning for missing dinner last Sunday by letting Sylvia cook her another meal. You can't beat a teenager's logic."

"I need to go as well," Jenna said, looking up from the phone she'd begun tapping at. "It looks like I have to work in the morning because someone's just emailed in sick. Do you want to ask Isla to come in and see me tomorrow afternoon? It's the barbershop on the high street."

"You're still poaching my best midfielder, then?" Becky asked with a sigh.

"Sorry. Business is business."

"I'll pass it on," Carolyn agreed, waiting until Jenna had put on her coat and then following her to the door. "See you all Sunday. And Becky, I hope your leg is better. I noticed you were limping after the last game. I know a good physiotherapist if it's still a problem."

They let themselves out and Jax shoved the remaining piece of salami into her mouth. "That went well."

"Mmm," Becky replied with a little raise of her eyebrows.

"Don't *mmm* again."

"Do you want my verdict?"

Jax bashed her hands together and sat a little straighter. "Go on then. Hit me with it."

"I think she totally still has feelings for you, even if she doesn't realise it again. Did you see how much she relaxed when she found out we weren't a couple? I'd noticed her being a bit weird with me suddenly since you guys reconnected, but she went back to how she was before Christmas when I dropped that in. She even just asked about my injury, which she'd completely ignored on Sunday."

When Jax went to reply, Becky held up a finger to stop her. "One piece of advice." She waited for Jax to clamp her mouth shut and pretend to zip it. "Don't turn into a jealous jackass over Greg. She isn't interested in him."

"As if I would!" Becky gave her a look that said *who are you kidding*, and Jax had to concede. "Fine. I hated the idea of Greg creeping on her."

"Really? You hid it so well. Carolyn's right, though. Let her

## 8

# CAROLYN

"Are you ready?" Carolyn asked, smiling as Isla entered the kitchen on Sunday morning with not only her kit bag, but her laptop and a large pad of paper. She'd agreed enthusiastically to helping with the fundraiser and wanted to show off her ideas to the rest of the committee after the match. The question was whether the committee were prepared for the all-round assault of hearing every detail.

"I've come up with a theme," Isla replied, dumping everything by the central island.

"A theme for what, exactly?"

"The all-ages club night. That's what I've settled on. It presents the most opportunities for add on services. For example, I can also run a raffle, and maybe even arrange a profit split with the bar for all the customers I'm bringing in. Jenna said yesterday that it's integral to her business. She has deals with all sorts of suppliers, so if someone comes in for say a beard trim, she can also upsell them beard creams and combs and stuff. That'll be part of my job."

She'd returned home high on enthusiasm for that, too, and Carolyn struggled to suppress another smile. She loved this side of Isla, so full of passion and ready to take on the world. "I'm sure you'll be excellent at it. Have you told Becky you won't be playing next Saturday?"

Isla frowned. "No, not yet. I was going to ask if I can still train. Do you think she'll say yes?"

"I'm sure she'll be happy to have you."

For now, though, they had yet more football to worry about. Carolyn picked up the laptop bag and swung it over her shoulder, then took one final sip of coffee and collected the pad of paper before ushering Isla out of the house and onto the drive. It was a relatively mild day for the end of January, and the sun shone high in the sky, causing Carolyn to squint as she popped open the door of her Lexus.

"Are you coming?" she asked when Isla lingered on the porch with her phone in hand.

"Yeah. It's Dad. He's asking again when I can visit. I've told him there's no game in a fortnight so I could go then, but it'll mean missing work when I've only just started."

She hadn't seemed at all keen to go even before work became an issue, and Carolyn had yet to determine why. They'd never reached the bottom of what had happened at dinner a couple of weeks back, and it had returned to the forefront of her mind.

"Would you like me to speak to him?" she asked, tucking the laptop and pad behind her seat.

Isla finally joined her, dumping her kit bag in the passenger footwell and buckling her belt. "I can handle it. Maybe I'll ask him to visit me, instead. After all, I don't see why I should be the one who always has to travel to Manchester, and the only time he comes here is when he's passing through for work. Especially when it's my birthday next week."

That was true, except she'd cut him off for football last time, which didn't strengthen her case for wanting him to hang around longer. "I'm sure if you made proper time for each other and planned something, he'd come to visit. He can always stay with your gran. She'd like to see him as well, no doubt."

"I'll ask him later," Isla decided, zipping her phone into the side pocket of her bag. "Right now, I need to focus on the match and my presentation."

Amused that it had now turned into a full presentation, Carolyn smiled again. "Okay, sweetheart." She pulled off the drive and drove them across the estate, towards the ring road. "Since we're vaguely on the subject of your birthday, I was going to shop whilst you're playing today. Is that okay? I won't have any other time before your party on Friday and we need supplies."

"Sure. Thanks," Isla replied absently, staring from the window. "Oh, I moved the party to Saturday, though."

"What? But your birthday is Friday."

"I know, but now I'm working on Saturday. I can't be up late the night before."

That made a lot of sense and Carolyn couldn't argue, so she didn't bother. It made no real odds to her whether the party was Friday or Saturday.

They carried on in silence until they reached the clubhouse drive, and Carolyn slowed as she crunched over the gravel. Jax was stood in the middle of the car park chatting to a large woman in a lurid tracksuit but turned and waved furiously when she spotted them.

Carolyn wound down the window as she pulled up, and Jax leant on the chassis to peer inside. "Congratulations on the job. I hope you're prepared for the hell of working for Jenna."

Isla only raised half a smile, opening the door and chucking her bag out of it. "She says far worse about you." She walked towards the changing rooms, turning back briefly to raise her hand in goodbye.

"Is she okay?" Jax asked.

"I think so," Carolyn replied, glancing after her. "Just a little trouble with her father. I'm off to the supermarket to try fixing it with snacks."

"Ooh, snacks. Can I put in a request?"

Carolyn laughed. "Go on then. I hope you know I wouldn't do this for anyone else, though."

"I feel so special. Will you get me some chocolate chip cookies? The big ones with three types of chocolate. I've been craving them all morning but the village shop don't stock them."

"Far be it for me to argue with your cravings. I'll see you in the clubhouse later. Good luck."

Carolyn wound the window up and waited until Jax had moved out of the way before performing a three point turn and heading back down the drive.

Three supermarkets later, she'd finally collected everything on Isla's list. The back seat of the Lexus was piled high with crisps, pretzels, cakes, biscuits, soft drinks and, of course, Jax's cookies.

The game was almost over when she pulled up in the club car park again. She hopped out and tried to unwedge Isla's laptop and pad from behind her seat, where they'd been trapped by a four pack of Diet Coke bottles, managing to free them just as the referee blew his final whistle.

She scanned the pitch, checking to see if Isla was dirty and had played, or clean and had remained on the bench. Given how turbulent her mood was today, she needed the boost of some decent game time, so it was a relief to find her caked in mud.

Carolyn went straight through to the clubhouse so she could wait for everyone to change, placing Jax's cookies on a table alongside everything Isla would need for her presentation. Then she ordered a coffee and settled in to watch some football on the myriad of screens. When her coffee was delivered to her, the lure of the cookies became too much, and she ripped open the top of the packet to take one as an accompaniment. But just as she raised it to her lips, she heard a cry of "Traitor!"

Jax pointed at Carolyn from the doorway, and she tucked the cookie back in the packet.

"I wasn't doing anything," she lied, bashing the crumbs from her fingers. "Just checking they were fresh."

"And I thought I could trust you. This is the ultimate betrayal."

"I'm so sorry. Will you ever forgive me?"

Jax moved out of the doorway and sat down next to her. "It depends. Will you feed me one quickly? I've got mud on my hands." She held them up and wiggled her mud stained fingers to prove her point.

"What on earth have you been doing?" Carolyn asked as she pulled the cookie back from the bag and tore off a piece. She put it in her own mouth, causing Jax's eyes to widen and her mouth to drop open. It was convenient because when Carolyn tore off a second piece, she could slide it right in.

Jax covered her mouth with the back of her hand, trying to chew and talk at the same time. "I fell over on a patch of hard frost by the storage shed."

Carolyn laughed as she noted the brown stains on the knees of her tracksuit bottoms. The left one had ripped, and a little blood was soaking through. "Oh, no. Are you okay?"

"Try for more genuine sympathy next time."

"Sorry. But isn't it typical that I'm not watching the one time there's something really worth seeing."

Jax glowered. "Our friendship is on thin ice right now. You'd better feed me more cookie."

Laughing again, Carolyn ripped off a bigger chunk of cookie and slotted it into Jax's mouth. "How did Isla do?"

"She played half a game because Becky's still struggling with her hamstring and set up Jenna's equalising goal. She's had a good afternoon."

That was a relief, although she didn't look as happy as Carolyn expected when she came through the door of the clubhouse mere seconds later. Even the offer of a cookie didn't raise a smile.

"Jax said you had a great game and got an assist. I'm sorry I missed it."

Isla slumped into the chair opposite. "Yeah. It was fun."

"Once more with feeling. What's wrong?"

"Nothing. I'm just tired. Can I get on with telling you what I planned for the fundraiser now so we can go home?"

It was unlike her to want to rush home. Carolyn still had a feeling this was to do with Marcus, but now wasn't the time to get into it. "Of course. I was meant to be speaking with Greg today, though, so you may need to hang around a little longer."

"Who's Greg?"

"He's your mum's opposite number on the boys committee," Jax answered. "He also does a lot of the day to day running of this clubhouse and the hall."

"Does that mean I'd need to go to him to book it for the fundraiser? And if I want to ask about a split of bar profits?"

"Yep. You probably won't get the split of bar profits, though. This clubhouse is owned by the community, and run by a joint committee from all the clubs that play here. It relies on bar profit and contributions from the clubs to stay open."

"Oh. We shouldn't ask for that anyway, then. Good to know before I suggested something that made us look bad."

At least someone was interested in supporting good diplomatic relations, and Carolyn smiled. "Jax doesn't get on with him very well but we're trying to improve the working relationship, so yes. That's probably a good idea."

Jax shuffled and let out a small huff. "I'm trying, okay? Like you asked. I still don't trust him but Becky pointed out that I *do* trust you, so I'll let you handle Greg however you think is best." There was a pause before she muttered, "Even if I have to watch him try it on endlessly."

Was that the real problem here? Or part of it. There was no way Carolyn would let anything happen with Greg, Jax's archnemesis, even if she did suddenly change her mind and start fancying him. She wasn't cruel and their friendship meant more to her than doing as Sylvia or Isla had suggested and getting back in the dating saddle. It would also end any chance of more between her and Jax, and she wasn't going to be the one to make that decision.

"Isla, do you want some money for a drink?" Carolyn asked, delving into her pocket for some loose change. She also found a packet of antibacterial wipes she'd been carrying religiously since the pandemic. "Get Jax a coffee too, would you? She takes a splash of milk and three sugars."

Isla took the opportunity to spend yet more of her mum's money without any hesitation, counting it in her palm as she wandered towards the bar.

"Let me look at your knee," Carolyn said, turning to face Jax.

Jax rolled up the leg of her tracksuit bottoms, then placed her foot on the edge of Carolyn's chair.

"What's the verdict, doc?" she asked, letting out a quiet but discernible *mmm* when Carolyn's hand gently stroked up and down her calf. "Are you going to have to amputate?"

"Yes. Sorry."

Jax held her eyes tight shut. "Okay, just be quick."

Carolyn chuckled, her fingertips tickling the back of Jax's knee. She sat forward in her seat and inspected a little closer, at least trying to make it look like she was showing a professional interest and not just finding any excuse to touch her. "On second thoughts, I think we'll let you keep your leg. I'm just going to clean out the mud. Hold still." She took her hand away and pulled a wipe from the packet, then gently dabbed the blood and dirt. "Does that hurt?"

"A little but I'm being a brave soldier."

"Yes you are," Carolyn agreed, taking a fresh wipe to finish the job. "I think you deserve a reward for that." She threw the wipe onto the table and then gestured to the packet. "If you clean your hands, you can have another cookie."

Jax leant forward too. "I preferred when you were feeding them to me."

"Oh, so that's why you fell over. It was all an elaborate ploy to have me take care of you and feed you cookies." Carolyn hooked her hand around the back of Jax's leg again so she could rub the side of her knee with her thumb. She caught Jax's fingers curl into a loose fist from the corner of her eye and wondered where Jax would be touching her right now if they weren't in a room full of people they knew.

"Clever, huh?" Jax replied. There was a pause and she bit her bottom lip momentarily before whispering, "I stopped short of asking you to kiss it better."

"Wise," Carolyn whispered back. "I could hardly do that in here. People would talk." Anywhere else, though, was fair game.

Jax had a glint in her eye as it met Carolyn's, implying she had an equally flirtatious reply, but before she could deliver it, Isla returned with a can of Fanta in one hand and two bags of crisps in the other.

"They're bringing your coffee," she said, oblivious to how fast Carolyn's hand had just withdrawn from Jax's leg. She dumped her crisps on the table, set down her drink, and grabbed her pad from beside Carolyn's chair. "The others are doing food prep at the moment so I'm just going to show you two my ideas. Okay?"

"Of course," Carolyn replied, relaxing back in her chair and crossing her legs. "I'm looking forward to hearing all about it."

"Me too," Jax seconded, picking up the packet of wipes from the table and finally dabbing her hands. When they were vaguely clean, she delved into the cookie bag.

Isla held up her pad and flipped the cover to reveal the first page. "So," she began, pointing to the word 'disco'. "At first I thought we'd do a disco because it's family inclusive and also really community minded, but then I realised discos are lame and how we package this is very important. That's why we're going to advertise it as an all-ages club night. Thanks to Jax for mentioning that you used to be big on clubbing, because it gave me the idea."

Jax hung Isla a high five. "Always happy to help."

"It made me realise that tonnes of parents were once young people who liked to go out, but then they had kids who ruined their fun. This will be a chance for them to dance to old music and bring their children along. A true family event, and more money for us because they'll have to pay for everyone from toddlers to grannies."

The thought of Sylvia raving to drum and bass in the middle of the hall next door amused Carolyn and made her smile again. It was a good idea, though, and she nodded her appreciation. "Excellent. I like it so far."

"Ticket sales are where I envisage making the most money, but I also want to run a raffle and I'm going to sell various accessories. Glow sticks, for example. You can buy them cheaply on eBay and we can add a big markup. It'll fit with the early nineties club music I plan to play." Isla flipped over to the next page of her pad. "However, when theming, I wanted to tie the event together with sports. I'm proposing we make it a sporting heroes night with a prize for the best dressed. We don't make any extra money from that; I just thought it would be fun and on brand."

She'd listed examples of some of her sporting heroes, including Jax, and Carolyn laughed. "All good, and extra points for the blatant brown nosing."

Isla shrugged. "It was a joke."

"Hey!" Jax protested, reaching for another cookie. "I could totally be someone's hero. You're both so rude to me."

"You're on a par with Sally Gunnell, are you?" Carolyn asked, folding her arms in challenge. "Or Millie Bright?"

"No, but there is such a thing as a Grassroots hero. If it weren't for coaches such as me and Becky, where do you think the likes of Millie Bright would've started?" Jax pointed her cookie at Carolyn, then sat back wearing a satisfied grin. "Please continue."

"I don't have anything else to say," Isla replied, gesturing to her laptop bag. "Unless you want to see the preliminary figures I put together. If you're happy with my plans, I need to find a date, book the hall, and start working out the details."

"Well, it all sounds good to me. I think you've done a great job so far."

"Me too," Carolyn agreed, warmed by how supportive Jax was being of Isla. The two of them seemed to be getting on like they were also old friends.

"Thanks." Isla flipped the front page back down over her pad and slid it onto the table. "Can we ask Greg about the hall, then?"

They could, if he ever arrived. Carolyn turned to crane over her shoulder, making sure he wasn't loitering or playing pool, but he was still nowhere to be seen. Then she pulled out her phone and checked her emails. Nothing.

"Have you been stood up?" Jax asked with a lingering air of smugness.

"Looks like it. What a shame. We might have to ask another time."

"Yeah, that's such a shame." Jax hoisted herself out of her chair, wincing when she tried to straighten her knee. "I need to go because I'm meeting a friend for dinner tonight but well played today."

Carolyn had to quickly clear her frown as she wondered who Jax was meeting. It wasn't her place to ask, though, so she got up too and started collecting Isla's things. "We should go, as well. Lots to sort for the new week. Do you want a lift home?"

"Nah, don't worry. It'll be fine once I start moving. Text me later and let me know if you hear from Greg."

"Will do."

They bundled all of Isla's things into the Lexus, trying to slot them around the party supplies, and then headed out of the village as the sun set in a blaze of orange over the town. Isla was quiet again, back to staring out of the window, and Carolyn found herself in a similarly reflective mood. She was enjoying how easily she'd fallen back into a friendship with Jax. It was almost more fun to be around her now, knowing that the energy between them was attraction and not trying to deny it. Confusion and, eventually, guilt had always marred the experience but now Carolyn was free to be herself.

"I'm sorry I wouldn't let you invite the ladies to your party," she said as they pulled onto the drive.

"It's okay. Probably not space anyway."

"No. What if I got Jax and maybe a couple of the others along, though? As my friends, so it's not odd."

"Really? Does that mean you'll also go out for a while?"

Carolyn considered and ultimately agreed. "Yes. I'm sure I can trust you to be on your own for a few hours."

"Thanks Mum." It perked up Isla's mood again and she even gave Carolyn a peck on the cheek before bounding out of the car.

A few hours later, once they'd eaten and tidied, Carolyn relaxed at her central island with a glass of wine. Isla was upstairs in her room, and it was surely late enough that Jax would have finished dinner.

She went to text but changed her mind and hit the call button. Then she drummed her fingertips on the worktop as she listened to the trill once, twice, three times. Maybe Jax was still out with her friend and they'd gone on somewhere else, but just as Carolyn had decided to give up and wait until tomorrow, the call connected.

"I'm starting to think you can't keep away from me," Jax said lazily, and Carolyn imagined her at the kitchen table sipping a lager.

"I called to thank you for earlier, but I can retract it and hang up. How was your dinner?"

"Good. I was just catching up with an old colleague who might want me to do a bit of freelance branding work."

At that, Carolyn smiled with relief. "Not a hot date, then?"

Jax laughed. "No. Why, were you jealous?"

"Oh, of course," Carolyn joked, despite it very much being true. She clasped the ring hung on her chain and raised it to her lips. "Are you busy on Saturday night?"

"I could be. Jenna wants to go to the pub, but we do that all the time so make me a better offer and I'll consider it."

"I usually like a challenge but in this case, it's more throwing myself on your mercy. I was going to ask if you'd come to Isla's birthday party for a bit. She thinks so much of you, and it'd be a sort of concession for not letting her invite the entire team."

"I'm a booby prize?"

Chuckling a little, Carolyn played with the chain, running it through her fingers. "For Isla, yes, and all the better if you can bring Jenna too, but I've promised her I'll stay out of the way for at least part of the evening, and I thought you could keep me company. As my daughter keeps pointing out, you're my only real friend here these days. You have lots, though, and I expect you'd prefer to spend your evening with them, so..."

She didn't really think Jax would want to spend the evening with anyone else. In fact, she hoped desperately that Jax would jump at the chance to entertain her, even if it meant spending part of the night with a bunch of teenagers.

"I'm your only option? Wow, what a flattering proposition. This just gets more and more enticing." Jax was back in play mode and pretended to sigh. "Is there anything at all in it for me?"

"Come on Saturday night and you'll find out." Carolyn ended the call, then pressed the phone to her chest and smiled at her own flirting skills. She sometimes didn't recognise herself around Jax but in all the best ways.

# 9
## JAX

"You owe me a drink," Jenna grumbled, trudging along behind Jax like a sulking child. She had on a big raincoat despite only a light drizzle and tucked her chin into the collar.

Jax strode up the driveway of Carolyn's house, past the Lexus she'd just blocked in, and knocked on the front door. "Stop complaining. It's only one drink before you meet Abi for dinner."

"But it's raining."

"Barely, and we're going inside." Whilst waiting for someone to answer, Jax slicked back her rain misted hair and then straightened out her leather jacket. The weather was a little milder than it had been, and she was taking the opportunity to wear something sexier than an oversized mountaineering coat. She'd paired it with skinny jeans and a shirt, open to show just a hint of her best red underwear. "I thought you liked Carolyn and wanted to kiss her ass?"

"I do like Carolyn, but I stopped going to seventeen-year-old's birthday parties when I was fourteen."

"Fourteen?"

"I was an early developer."

Jax laughed but it stopped dead when the door opened and Carolyn appeared, framed by the hallway light behind her. She'd definitely dressed for an evening out rather than playing chaperone. "You look fantastic."

Smoothing a hand over a deliciously revealing sequinned top, Carolyn stood aside to let them in. From beyond her came the sound of a stereo accompanied by chattering teenagers.

She closed the door behind them and then helped Jax out of her jacket, hooking it on a peg. "You look great, too. I love your hair like that. You don't usually wear it down."

"It's the rainy-day-in-England look." Jax smoothed her hair back again, then peered through the doorway into the living room. She really wanted a tour because she loved nosing around other people's houses. Even when there were noisy kids in them.

"Go on through." Carolyn gestured towards a different doorway at the end of the hall, bypassing the living room and encouraging them into the kitchen. "Would you like a drink? I've hidden the good stuff."

They both followed, weaving past a huge central island and out through patio doors onto a decked area with a hot tub inset under a pergola. Jax stopped and Jenna grumbled again as she almost bashed into her from behind.

"You have a hot tub?" Jax asked, her mind taking about five million leaps forward to imagine kissing Carolyn in a swirl of warm bubbles. It was entirely involuntary. "How am I only just learning this?"

There was a plastic chest next to it, which looked like it should contain gardening tools, and Carolyn produced two cans of lager from inside. "It came with the house. Sort of."

"What do you mean it came with the house?"

"The old owners were moving abroad and they couldn't take it with them so I made a very low offer to keep it. Goodness only knows why because I'll never use it. Isla said she would but so far she's been in only once."

Jax took both cans and explained that Jenna wasn't drinking. Then she smiled to find it was indeed the good stuff—craft lager from a local brewery. Not that she expected anything less because Carolyn had great taste in everything. "You have a hot tub and you've *never* used it?"

"No. Nor do I intend to." Carolyn led them back into the kitchen, where there were a few small groups of teenagers still hanging around chatting and joking. "Hang on a second and I'll let Isla know you're here. I expect she'll drop whoever she's talking to as soon as she finds out you've brought Jenna along."

"Jenna?" Jax asked, her pride a little dented. "So I'm not just the booby prize, I'm the *booby* booby prize?"

"The wooden spoon. Yes, sorry."

Jenna grabbed a can of Fanta from the work surface. "Don't take it too personally. Most people like me better than you."

"Hmm, well I think Isla does," Carolyn replied with a little eyebrow raise. There was a story, and Jax got the feeling that she wanted to spill it because she was meant to be fetching Isla but so far hadn't made any attempt to do so.

"What gives?" Jax whispered, setting down one can and cracking the ring pull of the other. "I can smell gossip. It's a skill I've learned from years managing a women's football team."

"There's no gossip," Carolyn whispered back. "I just have the impression Isla may have a little crush. Not a word to her or anyone else about it, though."

"Me?" Jenna looked quite pleased with herself, smiling as she wiggled her shoulders. "I don't know why I'm surprised." She made eye contact with Carolyn and quickly changed her tune. "Not that I would ever encourage it. She's a kid, and I am in a very happy relationship. I'm also her boss now..."

"I'll allow you to be flattered," Carolyn replied, collecting her own drink from the central island. She had a glass of bubbly so was clearly keeping the *very* good stuff for herself. "Besides, I may be wrong. She's just a little too interested and a little too enthusiastic whenever your name is mentioned."

They all went quiet when Isla entered, and her eyes searched them each in turn. "Someone said there were old people here. I presumed it was you."

So much for her crush, and Jenna took the comment personally. "I was going to say happy birthday but I'm not sure I want to, now. Can I use your bathroom? I need to go somewhere and get over that brutal attack."

"It's upstairs, first door on the left, and I meant like... old*er*. I'm glad you came."

She didn't sound very pleased they'd come, not that Jax cared too much. She was here for Carolyn and planned to whisk her off as soon as possible. "We won't cramp your style for too long."

"Yeah, don't worry," Isla replied distractedly. She bit her thumbnail and glanced over her shoulder towards the kitchen door Jenna had just exited through.

"Everything alright, champ?"

"Mmm. Would it be weird for me to ask your advice?"

Someone would probably make it weird, yes, but that didn't mean she shouldn't. "Shoot. You've got about ninety years of experience right here."

Isla looked at the doorway again, lowering her voice. "How do I make it clear I want to be more than friends with someone? I've tried everything but the message just isn't getting through and I kind of feel like tonight is my last chance."

Carolyn and Jax frowned at one another, and Jax tilted her head slightly. Was the crush really on Jenna? Surely Isla wouldn't ask her mum or Jenna's friend about this. Especially when she was here. Then again, she *had* waited until Jenna had left the room, so anything was possible.

"Um." Floundering, Jax turned to Carolyn. "Any ideas?"

Carolyn scratched her forehead, visibly uncomfortable. It was odd and sort of amusing to see her falter so thoroughly when she usually had everything under control, and her reply came out in bursts. "I think it depends upon who it is. Context is important. You might approach it differently depending on whether it's a girl or a boy. With some girls you would want to make sure it's appropriate first. Because some won't reciprocate, and even these days someone might not react as kindly as..."

"I think your mum's trying to say that straight girls don't always like being hit on by other girls."

Carolyn's frown deepened. "I suppose I was saying that, but now I think I've made it sound like there's something wrong with it, when for the record I absolutely do not have an issue with girls *hitting* on other girls. I have... was... am attracted to a woman, so there's no judgement here. But there are other factors to consider. Age, for example, might be a... thing."

"Something else to consider for sure."

"Yes." Letting out a huff, Carolyn placed her hands on her hips. She looked like she'd just run a marathon, or at least made it part way through and collapsed on the side of the road. "Have I helped at all?"

Isla only stared blankly. "You think I want to ask a girl out?"

Carolyn looked to Jax again, as if hoping she might jump in and provide some clarity. "Well, yes. Don't you?"

"No. I want to ask out Curtis, my friend from school. We met on my first day and we hang out *all* the time, but he just won't take the hint."

Letting out a delirious laugh, Carolyn's shoulders rolled forwards. "Curtis? Okay." She shook her head. "Well, you might have stopped me from rambling."

"I would have, but I was enjoying it. Good to know you're into women but I'm not. And since we're being totally honest, I should probably tell you that I already got a bit drunk when we went to one of my friend's houses and I made a fool of myself by throwing up *very* close to Curtis." Isla let out a brief sigh and shook her head, as if admonishing herself for the mistake. "So, have you got any real advice?"

"Advice about what?" Jenna asked, re-entering the kitchen and cutting off Carolyn before she could ask a million of her own questions. Jax expected that included finding out how Isla had managed to sneak a hangover under the radar.

"About how to let a guy know I want to be more than friends."

"I can't help with guys but it's probably the same as with women. Try the subtle stuff like touching his arm and making tonnes of eye contact. If that doesn't work, just tell him outright."

"The Jenna school of seduction is in session," Jax replied, looking forward to the moment they shot Jenna down a second time and she found out no one had a crush on her. "Is that how you won over Abi?"

"No, I got her drunk and had her pin me up against the wall of the clubhouse on your birthday, but I can hardly suggest that to a minor in front of her mum. Especially when it sounds like you've already tried it."

"No, you can't," Carolyn agreed. She drained half of her drink and set the glass down on the worktop. "Show us which one he is."

Isla led them to the patio doors. "That's Curtis," she said, hiding around the blinds and pointing to a group of lads at the end of the lawn. "The tall one."

Jax squinted. They were all tall, but one stood out. The boy in the middle towered at least a foot over his friends. Not only that but he was stacked for such a young guy. "He's huge. Are we sure he's only seventeen?"

"And black," Jenna added.

"He plays rugby," Isla continued, her eyes still fixed on Curtis as he laughed and back-slapped with his mates. "I've been to watch some of his games for the school and he's been to my football ones."

"Are we okay with that?" Jenna seemed to be having a conversation all of her own, and Carolyn turned to frown at her, folding her arms.

"Are we okay that he's black? I see, so not only am I a snob, now you've got me figured for a racist?"

Jax laughed because she knew Carolyn was just winding Jenna up, but Jenna didn't seem to have cottoned on. She stepped backwards, and her face screwed so hard that she was almost eating her eyebrows.

"What? No! I meant the rugby. Of course I don't think you're a racist. I'd never... I mean..."

Carolyn struggled to keep from smiling and it let her off the hook. "I knew what you meant. Luckily. And you have a point. I'm not sure how I feel about you dating a rugby player. We support football in this house, young lady." She unfolded her arms and went to the fridge, pulling out a half-empty bottle of Champagne and topping up her glass. "We should go out soon, whilst I'm still prepared to leave my daughter alone. I thought we could head into town. There's a cocktail bar with a live band on tonight. Dancing and drinking might take my mind off whatever's happening here."

Jenna laughed a little too hard. "You want Jax to dance? Now that I'd pay to see."

"Hey." Jax thwacked Jenna's arm and it sloshed a little Fanta onto the gleaming white floor tiles. "What's so funny about me dancing?"

"I have never once seen you dance."

"And I've never seen you take a shit. Doesn't mean it's never happened."

Carolyn stepped between them. "Now, now. Come on, children. There is an easy way to settle this."

She reached back to set down her glass on the central island, collected her phone, tapped over the screen, and then the music on the kitchen smart speaker changed to Whitney Houston's hit *I Wanna Dance With Somebody (Who Loves Me)*.

"You think you're funny, huh?" Jax mouthed to Carolyn, whose eyes glinted as she bit back a smile. Her teeth dragged slowly over her bottom lip and then she held out her hand.

They both knew some basic Salsa steps from practicing them together all those years ago and found themselves laughing and teasing each other as they tried to remember the old routine. It resulted in various staged attempts by Carolyn to stand on Jax's feet, but she wouldn't let Jax do the same because she was wearing a very nice pair of shoes, and no one messed with her heels.

"If you touch these, you're in trouble," she warned, as Jax placed her heavy booted foot mere inches away from her stylish blue stilettos.

"I still don't know how you manage to walk in those, let alone dance. Buy some flat shoes."

When they gave up on the Salsa and resorted to gyrating against each other, Isla had endured enough. She covered her face and let out a long, low groan, then strode over to the smart speaker and unplugged it at the wall.

"Hey!" Carolyn protested when they were left with only the music filtering through from the living room.

"Please leave," Isla begged, clasping her hands together.

"You're an embarrassment," Jenna added, shaking her head.

"Honestly. Poor Isla. And poor me for having to watch that when I can't even have a drink."

"Fine, we'll go out." Carolyn held up her hands. "I think Jenna's right about just telling Curtis, by the way. Especially if you're friends. He may not have any idea you want to be more than that." She moved towards the kitchen door. "And no alcohol tonight, it won't help. Call me if there are any problems. I mean any at all."

"There won't be."

"I'll have her home by eleven," Jax said, following into the hallway. It won a laugh from Carolyn, who was grabbing their jackets from the pegs by the front door.

"I don't care what time you have her home, so long as it's not in the next hour and she has some fun."

Jax opened the door and held it for Jenna and Carolyn to pass. She had a feeling she could manage fun, and possibly some other stuff that Isla didn't need to know about. The rules were for the teenager, not the adults.

## 10

# CAROLYN

The pavement was slick with water but even so, Carolyn clipped along it at pace. She had a feeling that if she didn't move swiftly, she might end up back at home, spying on Curtis and trying to gauge his intentions.

"I almost preferred the idea of her fancying Jenna," she said, raising her voice because Jax was struggling to keep up and had fallen half a stride behind. "At least nothing was going to happen there."

"How are you walking so fast in three-inch heels?" Jax replied, a little out of breath.

"Years of practice. My feet will be killing me later but that's the price you pay for vanity."

"You'd look just as good in flats."

"Is that your attempt to flatter me or make me slow down?"

"Bit of both."

"I hope you'll keep up with me better on the dancefloor." Because right now, it was a much-needed distraction. So was another drink.

"I don't think Usain Bolt could keep up with you right now." When Jax reached out a hand and grasped her wrist, Carolyn turned on her heel and came to an abrupt stop. "Do you want to go home? Because I'm happy to play chaperone with you instead if you'd rather we keep an eye on Isla and the giant rugby boy."

Her hand lingered, her fingers stroking the inside of Carolyn's wrist. It reminded Carolyn of what else had slipped out earlier and she wondered whether Jax had inferred she was the object of growing desire.

"Sorry. It's just thrown me a bit, but I'll try to relax."

"Okay. If you change your mind, let me know." Jax slipped her whole hand around Carolyn's and gave it a reassuring squeeze. At least, it was probably meant to be reassure her, but it only made Carolyn's heart beat faster. She turned her wrist and stroked her fingers over Jax's soft palm for a second or two, and then withdrew her hand and shivered, partly against the cold.

"We should go before we freeze to death."

They weren't far from the high street and soon reached the door of the wine bar. Lights flashed from inside and bathed the street in colour, the sound of a trumpet punctuating the chatter of smokers stood outside the pub next door.

A welcome heat radiated through the chill that had set into Carolyn's body. She slipped off her coat and scanned the room for a spare seat, standing on tiptoes to see over the throngs of people until she spotted a sofa at the very back of the room. "Shall we go over there?" she asked, pointing towards it.

"Yes. You claim and I'll get the drinks," Jax replied.

The rest of the space was filled with small round tables, edging a dancefloor, and Carolyn wove between them until she could throw her coat onto the seat, narrowly beating a group of men who nodded politely and accepted that she'd won.

It took Jax a good ten minutes to get served, but she eventually made her way over with two sparkling cocktails.

"Bellinis," she clarified, taking a sip and then nodding. "Mango. They're nice." Jax passed the other glass to Carolyn and then switched hers between each hand whilst wriggling off her jacket, throwing it on top of Carolyn's coat. When she sat down, she hitched up her leg and hooked her free arm over the back of the sofa. "Don't take too long over that. I want to dance."

"*You* want to dance? You're not just here for my benefit, then?"

"Oh, I'm totally here for you. I just want us to dance. You got me in the mood earlier."

Carolyn laughed, wondering how much to read into that. Knowing Jax, a lot. "Is that right? We'll have to see if you've still got the moves." She took a few sips of her drink and then set it on the little side table next to the sofa.

"Did you ever go out dancing in Manchester?" Jax asked, leaning in close to be heard over the din.

"Not really." Carolyn watched the rest of the crowd having fun and smiled to be back amongst them. "I should've made more of an effort really but all the friends I might have gone dancing with were here."

"Yeah? You didn't make any friends up there?"

"A few, but it was difficult. Don't forget there was a pandemic raging in the middle. It made meeting new people quite difficult."

Jax frowned. "Sounds lonely."

Carolyn shrugged and grabbed her drink to take a few more sips. "It was at times. I had Isla, though. We kept each other vaguely sane, but I had no hesitation in moving back as soon as I could."

"And she was happy to come with you?"

"We gave her the option to stay with Marcus or come with me. I don't think it was a very difficult decision for her, especially since her gran is here. They're very close and Sylvia is the only grandparent she has left. I think losing my dad made that hit home." It had sharpened Carolyn's desire to move, too.

Besides her sister in London, who she was also closer to again, Sylvia was *her* only remaining family. "You've never considered settling back in Nebraska?"

Jax recoiled in a way that made Carolyn chuckle. "No. I enjoy visiting but my life is here now. I really should write that Englishwoman I spent my twenties with and thank her someday."

"She did you a favour, huh?"

"I'm not sure I saw it that way when she left me, but yeah."

"Maybe *I'll* write her a thank you card. Or send her death threats."

"Haven't decided how you feel about me? Hmm, I've always had the impression you'll drop me the minute you find someone better to hang out with."

"Absolutely. Biding my time." Carolyn placed a hand in the middle of Jax's chest and pushed her back into the arm of the sofa. "I don't even like you, really." She went to take another sip of her drink, to find she'd almost finished it. "I suppose since you're all I have, though, we should dance. While you're *in the mood*."

Jax let out a theatrical sigh and set down her own glass. "I suppose we should."

They made their way to the dancefloor. Unlike in the kitchen, when Jax slid her hand under Carolyn's shoulder blade, she found her hips surge forward involuntarily as if they knew better than she did what they wanted. Who they wanted. How they wanted to move. Perhaps more alcohol had freed them up, but whatever it was, they'd taken on a mind of their own. A close hold became an even closer hold and Carolyn's gaze dropped to the figure of eight motion she'd started and Jax was now matching.

"We were always pretty good at this," Jax pointed out as the hand that had been resting under Carolyn's shoulder slipped down to the small of her back.

"What's that? Pretending to do a proper Salsa as an excuse to flirt with each other?" Because that's what it had always been, even if Carolyn hadn't acknowledged what they got out of it at the time.

Jax laughed. "Exactly how many drinks have you had?"

"Three or four. Why?"

"Because you're usually pretty subtle but that was..."

"True?" And she was tired of pretending that they weren't doing exactly the same thing tonight. They didn't need to lie or feel guilty because they could behave however they wanted. They could even get obscenely close if the mood took them, and Carolyn slipped a leg between Jax's, the friction of their jeans only adding to the heat between them.

"I think I like unsubtle Carolyn." Jax's mouth curled up at the side as she slid one of her hands even lower, tucking it into Carolyn's back pocket.

Carolyn liked this version of herself, too, and hooked her arms over Jax's shoulders, blood thumping hard over every erogenous area. Even the ones Jax wasn't caressing. It was a long time since she'd touched anyone this intimately and Carolyn explored further as they danced. She found the soft tuft of hair at the nape of Jax's neck and stroked it with the back of her hand. Then she felt the strong pulse under her fingertips as they travelled down Jax's throat, taking away a trail of perspiration. She circled over Jax's protruding collarbone, pushing aside the lapel of her shirt, and glanced the silky red underwear beneath. What were her breasts like? Smaller than Carolyn's, for sure, but it made her nipples harden when they pressed together.

She loved to have her breasts touched and they throbbed at the thought of warm hands roaming over bare skin. Nothing turned her on more. Carolyn closed her eyes, imagining Jax's hands cupping and massaging where she most desired them. All the while they ground against each other, until sweat was pooling in the small of her back, but when she let out a low growl of appreciation, Jax laughed, and the motion stopped.

She gripped tight on Carolyn's hips. "Are you still with me?"

Carolyn was very much with her. Too much with her, perhaps. "Hmm?"

"You were in a world of your own then. Were you thinking about all the places you'd rather be than here with me?"

She'd clearly meant it as a joke, but Carolyn was happy to reassure her. She raised a hand to stroke Jax's cheek, their hips moving again as the beat switched to a slower, pulsing rhythm. Her other hand slid up Jax's back, along her damp shirt. "I *was* somewhere else, but you were with me. Don't worry."

"Yeah? I hope it was somewhere nice."

"It was somewhere *very* nice. Maybe I'll tell you all about it later."

"My interest has piqued."

Every part of Carolyn had piqued with interest, and she closed her eyes again as she rested her head on Jax's shoulder. She tried not to moan when Jax's hands travelled up and down her back, her lips brushing against Carolyn's neck. It would be so easy to kiss her right now, but would Jax want that, really? It was one thing flirting and another to take this to the next level. What if she was worried about getting hurt again? It would be understandable, and Carolyn didn't want to push, so she just rocked in Jax's arms a little longer, until the band took a break and they were forced to do the same.

"Another drink?" Jax asked.

Carolyn nodded, her body cooling from the sudden absence, despite the heat of the crowd. "I'll meet you at our sofa."

She made her way through the crowd and sunk into it, blowing out a long breath and trying to return herself to the real world. It was tough, though, because her whole body glowed hot. She fanned the bottom of her top to circulate some air. Her hair was damp with sweat, and she tucked it behind her ear, her fingers still fussing over a few strands when Jax returned.

They talked some more, discussing the better parts of Manchester, whilst the DJ filled in. All the while, Carolyn was acutely aware of Jax's presence. The heat of her leg only inches away on the sofa. The smell of her perfume when she moved and it wafted from her wrists. The way her gaze was drawn forward and into Carolyn's cleavage whenever she touched her necklace.

When one of them got up to the toilet, the bar, or just to adjust their clothing, their legs ended up closer. Their arms began to brush together. It made Carolyn's hairs stand on end, prickling her skin. She ran her thumb over her fingertips, wondering if the rest of Jax's skin was as soft as the palm she'd stroked earlier in the night. She felt her other hand inch towards Jax's as it lay open on her lap until their fingers were touching. Carolyn moved her little finger along the side of Jax's thumb slowly, waiting to see if she would withdraw it.

She didn't.

Her hand tipped over and gently clasped Carolyn's, then she absently trailed her fingertips up and down as far as her wrist. Carolyn had a struggle to remember what they were discussing over the noise of the bar and her own thumping heart. Perhaps if she moved a little closer, it would help, and she shuffled to remove the sliver of distance between them. As she did, Jax turned her body slightly and hooked her free arm over the back of the sofa again, leaning in closer.

"Can you hear me okay?" she asked, the vibration of her voice tickling Carolyn's ear and sending a shiver down her spine. She licked her lips slightly, finding her mouth had run a little dry. "Do you want to dance again if it's too loud to talk?"

"No," Carolyn replied, suddenly aware that all the blood had rushed to two places—her face and her clitoris. "I can hear you fine now." She placed a hand above Jax's knee. "I don't think I can dance again. My feet are in bits. You'll just have to stay close like this."

"Oh, no. That'll be tough." Jax smiled and glanced to where Carolyn's fingers were rubbing into her leg. Then her gaze flicked up to Carolyn's mouth and she ran her tongue over her bottom lip. She looked like she was going to say something else as she leant forward, but she only smiled and raised her hand to Carolyn's cheek, gently stroking it with her thumb.

Carolyn's lips parted slightly and she kissed the pad of Jax's thumb when it glanced over them. She tried to make eye contact again, hoping to find some reassurance that this was okay, but Jax was preoccupied. Hooded eyes stared at Carolyn's mouth and all she could do was take a chance, if it was really that, because she could see that the desire to kiss was a mutual one.

She could feel Jax's breath on her. It tickled tantalisingly close, and Carolyn had to move her hand to the nape of Jax's neck again to steady herself as she trembled with anticipation. Their lips brushed together, and already her tongue was searching, flicking lightly against Jax's and tasting the mango from her cocktail.

The next time their mouths met, their lips and tongues made fuller contact and Carolyn gripped Jax's hair a little tighter as she exhaled with pleasure and relief. Her heart fluttered and so did her clit when Jax began to take control. She moved a hand to Carolyn's lower back, the other guiding her chin up into another kiss, and then firmly splaying across her cheek as their tongues massaged together. Carolyn moaned more conspicuously, allowing herself to sink into Jax and pressing forward so that their breasts touched.

It took the realisation that she was one step away from slipping her hand inside Jax's shirt for her to finally pull away, heavy eyed, breathing hard, and desperately hoping that Jax wasn't about to say that was a mistake. But before either of them could reply, they each seemed to realise that the band had stopped, the lights had come up, and people were beginning to leave.

"Exactly how long were we kissing?" Jax asked, looking down at her watch.

She was making jokes rather than running for the door, and that was probably a good sign. "We should probably head home."

"We should," Jax agreed without making any move to do so.

Instead, her eyes fixed on Carolyn's mouth again and she smiled before lingering over one more kiss. They were at risk of getting caught up in it, though, so Carolyn placed a hand on Jax's shoulder to reluctantly prise her away.

"You're a bad influence on me."

"I'm pretty sure you started it."

Carolyn was pretty sure she did too, so she only shrugged and stood, grabbing her coat. "Shall we get a taxi?"

"We can try, but that means going to the other end of town and it'll be busy. Shall we just walk? It'll only take fifteen minutes. Unless your feet are shredded."

They *were* shredded, but Jax was right. Carolyn hooked on her coat and then flicked her hair off the collar. "I can walk. You might just have to hold my hand."

Jax laughed and sat forward, wriggling into her leather jacket. "Oh, really? I'm not sure how hands and feet are connected but you're the doctor, so…" She stood and slipped her palm around Carolyn's, giving it a gentle squeeze and then entwining their fingers.

"I don't have time to explain all the medical reasons but you'll just have to take my word for it," Carolyn replied, struggling not to smile as her chest contracted at the simple intimacy.

They spilled out with the rest of the crowd, only to be met by more drizzle. A light mist of rain clung to Carolyn's hair and face, and she pulled her coat tight with her free hand as they made their way up the high street. By the time they'd reached the last pub, though, larger blobs of rain had begun to fall, and they ducked under an awning meant for smokers just as it came down in torrents.

"Crap," Jax said, letting out a shot of laughter and looking left to right. She held Carolyn's hand a little tighter. "That was bad timing. We might need to run."

"I can't run in these heels!"

"Then there's only one thing for it," Jax decided, crouching slightly and holding her hands out behind herself. "Get on my back."

"Don't be ridiculous!"

"Well if you can't run in those heels, you don't have a lot of choice, unless you want us to freeze or drown."

Carolyn peered out from under the canvas awning, barely holding back the sheets of rain hitting the pavement in front of her. She had a feeling they were going to freeze or drown either way, but found herself agreeing. "Okay. I won't hurt you, though, will I?"

"Now who's the one being ridiculous?"

Jax crouched again, this time next to a bench, and Carolyn put a foot on it to give herself a lift. She bent her leg once, twice, three times, and then found the courage to fling her arms around Jax's neck as a pair of hands wrapped under her knees to hold her in place.

"What on earth am I doing?" she whispered next to Jax's ear, closing her eyes and clinging on for dear life.

"Are you okay?" Jax replied with a little laugh.

"Ask me again in a few minutes."

At that, Jax took off and Carolyn let out a little squeal as rain pounded the top of her head, pushing the hair into her eyes. She squeezed them shut again and listened to the thud and splash of Jax's boots on the concrete for what felt like both seconds and hours, but was probably a few minutes, until the pounding ceased and Jax's breathing echoed against the Perspex walls of the bus shelter where she'd just stopped.

"I need a breather," Jax said, panting and then blowing her top lip to spray the water from it. She had a river running over her face, along her nose, and down her chin, until it plopped onto the ground. "How are you now?"

"Wet," Carolyn replied, noting a similar torrent but going the other way, down her back and soaking into her top. She'd buried her face to protect it but her hair must look an absolute state, matted to her head and dripping over her ears. Even so, she couldn't help giggling, and nor could Jax. "Thank you for carrying me." She pressed a kiss to Jax's cold, wet temple, and held it there.

"That's okay, it's your turn to carry me now." Jax crouched again and gently dropped Carolyn to the ground. Then she straightened and turned, pretending to limber up with a hand on a torn movie poster, a dim light flickering above. They were on the edge of Carolyn's estate now and away from the perpetual noise of the town centre, only accentuating Jax's heavy breathing as it misted in the cold and damp of the bus shelter.

"As appreciative as I am, there is not a chance that would work." Carolyn shivered as another trickle of frigid water ran down her back and soaked into her bra strap. "I'll pay you back with a nice warming brandy when we get home. So long as they haven't found my stash."

"I'm surprisingly warm right now. It's one of the benefits of running, especially with the extra effort of having someone clung to your back." Jax took a step forward and clasped

Carolyn's hand, rubbing a thumb into her palm. "You're freezing, though. We should keep going. I've caught my breath now."

She may have caught her breath, but Carolyn had just lost hers. She stroked her fingertips up the inside of Jax's other hand, nodding her agreement, and smiled when their fingers entwined again. "I almost don't want to go home and our night be over."

Half of Jax's mouth curled up and she tilted her head, shuffling closer. "Me either. It doesn't have to be over, though. I thought you'd offered me a brandy?"

"I should offer you a warm bed, too. You've been drinking so you can't drive…"

"Yeah?"

"Mhm. The sofa bed, obviously, you couldn't… we couldn't… in my bed. With Isla there." But Carolyn hoped she'd made the implication clear enough. She wished she could take Jax home to her own bed, but it was across the hall from Isla's, and that was a definite no-go tonight. Isla wouldn't go into the living room, though, if she knew Jax was sleeping in there.

In case there was any doubt as to her plans, Carolyn moved Jax's hands onto her hips, then cupped her cheeks and smoothed the drops of rain from her lips with her thumb. "How do you feel about us getting out of these wet clothes, making up the sofa bed, and then having that brandy together? Unless you just want to go to sleep, of course."

"Well, I am very tired." Her eyes fixed on Carolyn's lips, Jax's head inched forward.

"It's all the running."

"Absolutely. And the dancing."

"That's true," Carolyn agreed as their mouths danced so close they were almost touching. "I've asked a lot of you already, so I'd understand if you turned me down. For the drink, I mean. You might not even like brandy anymore. Or want to risk the hangover."

Jax's lip twitched again. "No, I definitely still like brandy. And I'm not worried about a hangover. It's given me one before but it's always been worth it." Their eyes finally left each other's lips and met in one final question. This time, though, it was candid and straightforward. "Carolyn, are you sure you want to do this? Because I desperately want to kiss you again, but I also know I'd rather walk all the way home in the rain than be a one night stand. You mean too much to me. If you're going to break my heart, please back away, because I'm not sure I have the willpower to do it."

Carolyn slid her hand down to Jax's chest to find their hearts were beating just as fast as one another. She had thought about it. In fact, she struggled to think about much else when they were together, and she knew the answer. "I've always been sure of you and I'm so incredibly tired of fighting against the urge to be with you. Will you please just kiss me again?"

She did. Slow and tender, her fingertips curling into Carolyn's hips as if she needed to brace herself to keep from consuming her all at once. Jax's lips were cold but her tongue was warm and soft as the kiss deepened, a little urgency spilling over into a desirous grunt when Carolyn's hand slipped around her neck and gripped her hair. Their breathing grew heavier and the heat in Carolyn's core warmed her from the inside out as Jax grabbed her ass to draw her closer, massaging and rubbing until Carolyn became aware of her hips rolling into the touch. They were back on the dancefloor only this time, Jax's hands were right where Carolyn wanted them, and her smile broke the kiss.

"Now that I've answered your question," she whispered, pausing for Jax to nibble on her bottom lip. "Can I take you home?"

Jax laughed, her eyes still dark and her hands still roaming over Carolyn's butt. "Fine. I suppose we really should make sure the place is still standing."

She hadn't been wanting to think about that, and Carolyn groaned, her head hitting Jax's shoulder. "Whatever we're met with, just keep thinking about the brandy we're going to enjoy later, and we'll get through it."

## 11

## JAX

Jax sniggered as she watched Carolyn fumble with the lock, water dripping off the bottom of her coat and plopping into a puddle on the porch. The key slipped across the door and Carolyn laughed, taking it in both hands and eventually threading it into the correct position. They weren't *that* drunk, but they also weren't sober. With the added hinderance of darkness and a rainstorm it had turned into quite a task.

"Got it," Carolyn confirmed as the door popped open. She threw the keys just inside the hallway and then removed her coat, shaking it out and spraying Jax with water.

Jax raised her hands in front of her face. "Hey, I'm stood right here."

"Sorry. I'm just trying to give my floors a chance. Can you take off your jacket too? And your shoes?"

"Are you always this demanding when you want someone to undress?"

Carolyn's laugh was a dirty one that Jax had never heard before. She didn't have time to reply, though, before the door flew wide open and Isla appeared in the hallway.

"What time do you call this?" she asked, folding her arms.

Jax removed her jacket and passed it to Carolyn. Then she looked down at her watch, but she couldn't see the time because the face was obscured with blobs of rainwater. "I thought we didn't have a curfew so long as your mum had fun?"

"Are you drunk?" Isla shook her head with mock outrage. "This is unacceptable, young lady."

Carolyn took a step forward and threatened to give Isla a wet hug. Then she laughed again and hooked her coat next to Jax's. "Why is it so quiet? Where are your friends?"

"They left almost an hour ago. It's gone midnight."

After peeking her head around the living room door, Carolyn turned back and frowned. "Am I in the right house? It's clean."

"Of course it's clean, and it's a good job because from the state of you both I'd say Jax needs to sleep on the sofa bed. She can't drive home like that."

Jax had still been stood on the doorstep but took a step inside and unlaced her shoes. Then she looked up and smiled at Carolyn, who was trying to keep from laughing. "What a good idea. Why didn't we think of that?" She slipped off her boots and left them to drip on the door mat. "Don't suppose you have a dry T-shirt or something I can sleep in? Your mum has already made it clear that she doesn't want me in her house when I'm wet." At that, Carolyn made eye contact and bit her lip, trying not to laugh again. "Isn't that right?"

"Absolutely," Carolyn agreed, clicking the door shut and turning the lock. "I'll get you a towel and a T-shirt from the utility room and we can hang your clothes to dry."

"Whatever." Isla yawned and hooked her hand around the banister. "I'm going to bed because we've got a match tomorrow. In case you hadn't remembered." She directed her last comment at Jax. Then she bounded up the stairs, stopping halfway and pointing at them each in turn as she added, "Don't stay up too late."

"We won't," Jax replied, hoping it was a lie and following Carolyn into the kitchen whilst unbuttoning the shirt clinging to her torso. "What shall I do with this?"

"Give it to me. Your jeans, too."

"Do you want my underwear?" Because that was a very tempting proposition right now, and not just because every single item of clothing on Jax's body was drenched. She threw her shirt at the central island, watching as Carolyn's eyes fixed on the tattoo just above her right hip bone.

"A star? That's original."

"Yeah. I bet your seventeen-year-old self was far more sensible."

Carolyn turned and peeled down the back of her jeans slightly. Peering over her shoulder at the faded heart above her right buttock, she said, "Marginally. But my eighteen-year-old self wasn't." She pulled the jeans back up and folded her arms. "Come on then. I thought you were taking everything off?"

Jax pretended to fumble over the top button. "My fingers are too cold to unbutton my jeans." It was a relief to find they were back to bantering freely with each other. Things had taken a serious turn in the bus shelter and she had worried momentarily that it might be awkward when they got home. "Can you help?"

Carolyn let out a laugh and took a few paces forward, then went to work on the button. "Funny how they could unbutton your shirt."

"I know," Jax replied, lowering her voice and checking over her shoulder. "But my hands are suddenly only good for one thing."

"What's that?"

Trailing her fingertips up Carolyn's side, Jax whispered,

"This". Then she brushed the wet ribbons of hair from Carolyn's shoulder with the back of her other hand and placed a kiss at the base of her jaw. She tasted a little salty and it tingled Jax's lips. "What do you reckon, doc? Is it serious?"

With the final button undone, Carolyn smoothed Jax's jeans off her hips. "Do you want my professional medical opinion?"

"Sure."

"Give me your wrist." She slipped her fingers around Jax's wrist and gently felt her pulse. After three or four beats, Carolyn shook her head. "Very fast. Any idea what could be causing a reaction?"

"No. It's been doing that all night."

"Hmm." Letting the wrist drop, Carolyn stepped away and picked up Jax's shirt. Then she strode across the kitchen towards a door at the back of the room and disappeared inside. When she returned about ten seconds later, she had a fluffy white towel, a T-shirt, and a pile of bedding, which she set down on the central island. "First things first, get changed. You're shivering."

Jax peeled the jeans from her legs and they slapped to the floor. Then she walked towards Carolyn and reached around her to pick up the towel, laughing when her body unclothed and in close proximity made Carolyn blush. "Are you okay there?" she asked, dabbing the moisture from her neck and the ends of her hair. "You're playing with that chain around your neck like you always do when you're nervous."

"I'm not nervous I'm..."

"Turned on?"

She didn't answer but she didn't need to.

Jax loosely folded the towel now that she'd finished with it and set it on a stool. Then she scooped up her jeans. "I'm not sure these are going to dry before the morning."

"We can probably put them in the tumble dryer on a low

heat." Armed with something practical to do, Carolyn dropped the chain and set off with purpose towards the same door as earlier.

This time, Jax followed. The small utility room was warm and smelled of cotton fresh laundry detergent. There was a washing machine next to a dryer on one wall and opposite that was a work surface, propping up two baskets of fresh clothes and bedding.

The only light came from the kitchen behind them but Carolyn didn't bother adding to it, instead popping the dryer straight open and inviting Jax to throw her jeans inside. Then she twiddled the controls and the machine hummed into life.

"It's cosy in here." Jax shivered as her body finally began to warm up, a fresh covering of goosebumps prickling her skin. "Maybe we should get you out of your wet clothes, too. You know, whilst we're in the right place..."

She tugged on the bottom of the sequinned top, and Carolyn raised her arms to allow Jax to wriggle it over her head. It released a second scent, this time of perfume. The utility room was becoming a sensory paradise of all things Carolyn and Jax was enjoying a long inhalation until she was confronted by spectacular breasts in a lacy navy bra and her breath hitched. When Carolyn chuckled, they jiggled, and Jax found her head drawn towards them.

"Are *you* okay?" she whispered, clearly delighting in having had a similar effect on Jax. "I'd never noticed how much you like my cleavage before."

"Like hell you hadn't," Jax whispered back, her fingertips tingling and her lips parting slightly with urgency to feel the soft flesh in her mouth. "There are a lot of things I admire about you: intellect, sense of humour, your compassionate nature. But right now your body is top of the list. In fact, it's making me a little faint. Every time I look at you, all I can think about is kissing you and running my hands over your skin. Do you think there's any cure?"

Carolyn let out a low giggle that made Jax's chest contract with affection. It was so unlike her. "I don't know. How long have you felt this way?"

"I'm afraid it's chronic. I've had these symptoms for years."

Carolyn grasped Jax's wrist again. "Let's see how this is doing."

It took every bit of restraint Jax possessed to keep up their little game and not just pin Carolyn back against the dryer. If this was anyone else, they'd be fucking by now, but she didn't want to just fuck Carolyn. She was enjoying playing with her. Hearing her laugh, and watching her come undone with little blushes and unspoken admissions of her attraction.

"What's the verdict?" Jax asked, as Carolyn's palm slid down over the back of her hand.

"I think I can help you," she replied, wearing a devilish smile as she cupped Jax's hand over her left breast and held it there. "Any better?"

Carolyn's nipple was hard and Jax rolled it between her thumb and forefinger through the lace, her clit twitching when Carolyn pressed down, encouraging a firmer caress. Then she left Jax to roam freely over her curves and pulled her in from the waist, their kiss harder than earlier. She exhaled against Jax's mouth as hands travelled over every inch of the bra, a thumb rubbing into her nipple again and pinching it until she let out a low groan.

"I'm beginning to think you like me touching your breasts almost as much as I do," Jax said when it broke the kiss. She pressed her lips to Carolyn's neck instead, sucking and nipping whilst Carolyn tried to get out a breathy reply.

"I could have you do this all night." She clawed across the bottom of Jax's back with her fingertips when her bra was undone and the fabric fell away. Then she arched, pushing her right breast into Jax's waiting mouth.

Jax was very happy to do this all night, too, except that her legs were beginning to tremble where Carolyn was rubbing her butt and hips, circling closer to where she ached for touch. She wasn't sure how much longer they could remain upright and she backed Carolyn against the dryer for stability but knew it wouldn't keep them vertical for more than a few minutes.

"I wish I could take you to bed," she whispered, before submitting to another lusty suck on Carolyn's neck. Carolyn was still in her jeans and Jax finally let her hands drop from her breasts to unbutton them. She slipped her fingers inside, rubbing just once down the front of Carolyn's underwear so that her hips bucked forwards.

"We really should've made up the sofa bed before we started this," Carolyn replied, pushing her jeans down and kicking them into the corner of the utility. "I'd take you to my bedroom but I can't promise I'll be quiet enough."

Jax went to reply but her mind had just tripped up on all the noises Carolyn might make and it forced her to take an executive decision that they would just have to make up the sofa bed now. She intended to spend as much of the night eking out those pleasurable sounds as humanly possible, and the utility room could not be their final destination.

"Hurry then," she urged, taking Carolyn's hand and guiding her back into the kitchen.

Carolyn let out another giggle, grabbing the bundle of bedding and clothes on the way past. When she reached the living room door, she raised a finger to her own lips to shush them, but she was the only one making any sound. Jax was quickly on the other side and pulling off the sofa cushions.

The room fell dark when Carolyn shut the door, but she illuminated them by turning the dimmer and bringing up the inset ceiling lights slightly. It created a glow in an already warm and inviting room. The lounge was tastefully decorated in muted beige tones but the sofa added a touch of colour: blue with patterned throw pillows. When Jax had pulled out the bed from it, she could see the space more clearly. In front was a fireplace with a marble surround and mantel, lined with family pictures. In the corner was a wing chair and bookcase. Then on the wall opposite the window was an old drinks cabinet.

"This place is nice," she noted, about to also make the point that there wasn't a television but deciding against the distraction. She didn't want to stop Carolyn from her work of laying a fitted sheet over the mattress, especially given she was on all fours as she tucked in the far corner. Her butt was an underrated and often overlooked masterpiece, and Jax tilted her head as she enjoyed it. "However, this place isn't as nice as your ass."

"I'm relieved it turns you on more than my soft furnishings. I would've been *really* worried about your wellbeing if that weren't the case." Carolyn shook out a thick fleece blanket, her breasts wobbling as she smoothed it in front of herself and folded over the top. "Will you be comfortable here?" she asked, leaning over the side to grab a couple of the throw cushions. "And warm enough?"

Jax knelt on the edge of the bed, expecting it to sag but finding that it was firm memory foam. She should've known it would be quality. "Why don't you get under the covers and test it for me?"

Letting out a little chuckle, Carolyn wriggled under the fleece. She laid on her side and pulled it up to her chin. "It's lovely under here. Maybe I'll just stay and you can have my bed."

"There's only one problem with that."

"What?"

Jax lifted up the side of the blanket and shuffled under it, facing Carolyn and stroking her hip. "I was in the middle of my treatment," she replied, struggling not to return Carolyn's amused smile.

"Oh yes."

Carolyn rolled onto her back, taking Jax with her. Suddenly between Carolyn's legs, resting with an arm on either side of her head, Jax lost any ability to play the game. Her hips pressed into Carolyn's and all that kept them apart was two flimsy pieces of fabric, which did nothing to hide how hot and damp they each were.

Jax bypassed Carolyn's mouth and went straight for her neck again, sucking and nibbling as they ground together, her clit pulsing with every thrust. She could've laughed at the predictability of Carolyn placing a hand on each of her cheeks to guide her head back to her breasts, had Jax not been so aroused and desperate to consume them.

She explored every inch of their surface, now uninhibited by the bra and able to take each of Carolyn's nipples into her mouth, swirling her tongue around them so that Carolyn groaned and arched her back again. Jax repeated the action over and over, until Carolyn was writhing under her and clawing her back, digging her fingernails in hard enough to leave indentations.

Crimson flushed up Carolyn's chest and neck, as red as the bra she deftly unhooked and threw across the room. Their breasts touched, flesh on flesh for the first time, and Jax rocked them together as she slipped her tongue into Carolyn's hot mouth. Then she worked all the way down, from Carolyn's chin to her throat, her collarbone and briefly over her breasts again. Jax noted a satisfying squirm as her tongue swirled around Carolyn's navel and licked around her last remaining item of clothing.

She could smell the desire as Carolyn lifted her hips and

allowed her underwear to be slipped down her legs. Carolyn grasped handfuls of the sheets in anticipation of what would come next, her breathing shallow as Jax worked her way back up, kissing from ankle to knee. She repeated on the other side, then blew across the damp thatch of hair between Carolyn's legs so that she growled and tilted her hips again.

Carolyn looked up with a little surprise when Jax wriggled her forward slightly and knelt by the side of the bed. It soon turned back to pleasure, though, another raspy moan urging Jax on when she used the more stable position to claw over Carolyn's breasts with her left hand whilst slipping inside the fingers of her right.

Jax smiled as she repeated the figure of eight move they'd danced earlier over Carolyn's G-spot, finding a rhythm and a pressure that had her twisting the sheets. Then she dipped her head to suck gently on the inside of Carolyn's thigh, sweetness and salt bursting on her tongue.

"You're a desperate tease," Carolyn said breathlessly, her legs trembling the closer Jax flicked to her clit.

"I know," Jax replied, blowing again and enjoying another squirm. She was drenched to her wrist and knew Carolyn was on the brink, but it was too much to resist remaining in this state, bringing her close to the edge and then backing off a little.

She rubbed her hand more firmly into Carolyn's nipple and finally ran her tongue over Carolyn's swollen clit. Then she did it again, and again, swirling the tip and then the flat in ever quickening succession until she could feel Carolyn tighten around her fingers, her back arching one last time and a hand clamping over her own mouth to muffle the sound of her cry.

When she lay still, Jax withdrew her hand and wiped it on the edge of the sheet. Then she sat on the bed, laughing because Carolyn seemed to be lying in some sort of post coital coma, her eyes closed and her breathing still laboured.

"I think your hair got the sheet wet," Carolyn whispered finally, wriggling to move out of the wet patch under her ass.

"No, that was all you."

"Really? That's a relief."

"It's a *relief*?" Whilst levels of lubrication were not always an accurate indicator of sexual arousal, Jax had still never been with a woman who'd experienced relief when she made them so wet.

"Yes. It's been a few years since I've had sex. Menopause..." Carolyn shrugged and then pulled herself up to sit against the throw cushions. "I wasn't sure how my body would've changed."

Jax crawled over the bed, adjusting the pillow behind her back as she settled in beside Carolyn. "Well, I'm glad I could help you conduct a little experiment."

"Sorry, it's not a sexy topic."

"I don't know, I found all of that *very* sexy." Jax pressed their lips together again, until her smile unwittingly broke the kiss.

"What are you laughing at?" Carolyn whispered.

"I'm not laughing, I was just experiencing intense happiness."

"Oh. I suppose that's allowed. Shall I get us those brandies?" Carolyn smoothed her hand up the goosebumps on the back of Jax's arm. "You're so cold that you're shivering again." After another lingering kiss, she rolled off the bed and walked over to the drinks cabinet. From it she pulled two glasses and a bottle, then poured them a couple of generous measures, handed one to Jax, and took a slow sip.

Jax shuffled to get comfy, careful not to spill any of her drink, and held up her arm to make a space for Carolyn. "Are you coming back?"

Carolyn set her glass on the arm of the sofa and crawled her way up the bed, nestling into the crook of Jax's arm, wrapping

Jax's hand under her breasts, and pulling the blanket up over their legs.

"Are you any warmer?" she asked, resting her head sideways and smiling when Jax dabbed yet another kiss to her hair, which was beginning to dry in wisps.

"A little." Jax took a sip of brandy and it burned down her throat. She didn't often drink spirits but Carolyn was right and it was having a warming effect. "This is perfect."

"Mmm. I should hope so, it's expensive stuff."

"I meant us, not the brandy, but good to know where your priorities lie."

Carolyn raised her hand from Jax's arm to her cheek, stroking it with her thumb. "I knew what you meant. Besides, brandy's never a particular priority of mine. Chocolate, on the other hand…"

"I know how you feel about chocolate. I'll never compete."

"Sorry. Maybe if you combined the two?"

Jax stroked her thumb into the underside of Carolyn's breast. "Now there's a thought. Maybe I'll take you to Belgium or Switzerland and cover you in melted chocolate."

"Cover *me* in melted chocolate? But I want to eat it. Maybe if you were to take me to Belgium or Switzerland and buy me chocolates from all the finest chocolatiers, I might let you also cover me in chocolate and lick it off."

"It's a deal. When are you free?" Carolyn laughed again but didn't reply, and Jax was about to do the same, but then she had a change of heart. "I think we should actually go."

"Are you serious?" Carolyn asked, turning to rest forward on her hand. She wore a quizzical look, but then it turned to a smile. "I haven't been anywhere since before the pandemic. It would be nice to get away for a couple of days. Would that be crazy?"

"Probably, but you only live once. We could relax and spend some time alone."

"Alone with several hundred thousand Belgians or Swiss people?" Carolyn laughed when Jax wore a derisive look and shook her head.

"Alone in that no one we know will be there. It means we can do whatever we like without the risk of being busted."

"Like eating chocolate…?"

"Yes, like eating chocolate."

Carolyn considered for two or three more seconds. "Isla tells me there's no football next weekend. Unless you've already made other plans, would that work?"

Jax hadn't even registered that they had a free Sunday yet, she hadn't quite got that far, but if Isla said so, it must be true. "Sounds like it."

Carolyn bit her lip. Then she nodded. "Okay, let's do it."

"Yeah? I'll look at transport and accommodation tomorrow evening."

"We should get a little drunk more often."

"I'll be happy to get a little drunk again. Maybe we should go to Belgium. You know how I feel about their lagers." Jax once again struggled to keep the delight from showing on her face and it was making Carolyn's attempts to kiss her again difficult. "I might need a minute to get my mouth to cooperate. It keeps doing this weird thing whenever you're around."

"Smiling, you mean?"

That was it.

## 12

# CAROLYN

Carolyn pulled the duvet around herself like a cocoon. Maybe when she emerged, it could be without the throbbing headache. *Bang, bang, bang* was all she could hear as the blood thundered over her temples. What was even the time? And when had they finally made it to sleep? All she knew was that the dawn had begun to break when she'd submitted to uncurling herself from Jax's embrace and going to her own bed.

She rolled over, still holding the covers tight, and peered through one eye at the blurry green numbers on her alarm clock. Then her eyes shot open when she realised that the banging noise wasn't in her own head, it was coming from the door. It was already eleven and Sylvia was here to bring Isla's birthday gift, eat brunch, and watch the football match.

Carolyn scrambled to free herself from the duvet and then made the second realisation: she was completely naked.

"Muuum," came the croaky voice from the other side of the door. Apparently they'd both enjoyed a lie in.

"Hang on a minute. Let me just put clothes on," Carolyn replied as she dropped the duvet to the floor and pulled underwear from a drawer.

"Are you only just getting up?"

"Can you go and let your gran in please?" Still fumbling to hook the clasp on her bra, Carolyn made the third and final realisation. "Oh, Isla!" she called out, stopping the slow trudge of heavy footsteps down the landing.

"What?"

"Don't forget Jax slept on the sofa. She might still be here."

"Of course I remember, I'm not the one who got *drunk*. Some of us are just tired from working all day yesterday and then being an amazing hostess."

Drunk wasn't the only thing she'd got, and Carolyn smiled at the memory. She'd completely let go in every way possible and had loved every minute with Jax, but now they were sober again and she wasn't sure what happened next. They could escape again in a week's time but until then, she had to figure out how to navigate normal life in this slightly altered state. Starting with facing Jax in her kitchen without anyone noticing something had changed between them.

She heard the door slam shut. Then it banged again and her heart thudded. The first time would be Sylvia arriving, and she hoped that the second wasn't Jax leaving without saying goodbye.

After pulling on a sweater and tugging on a pair of jeans, she rushed down the stairs to find the only person in her kitchen was Sylvia.

"Oh," Carolyn said breathlessly.

"Well, you could look a bit more pleased to see me."

"Sorry. I am, it's just... where's Isla?"

Sylvia was sat on a stool at the central island and poured herself a mug of coffee from the cafetiere. "She went outside with your friend to fetch a birthday card from her car. It was apparently forgotten last night."

At that, Carolyn took a deep breath and centred herself.

Then she padded across the kitchen and poured herself a mug. "Good."

"Do I know this person? She looks familiar."

"It's Jax. You remember, Isla's football coach? You met at the last match. We went out for a couple of drinks last night to escape Isla's party." Carolyn took a sip of coffee, hoping it would mask her fatigue for a while. "We had a few too many, though, and it was pouring rain, so she slept on the sofa."

"A good night, was it?"

The best in a long time but Carolyn had to dial down her enthusiasm. "I think Isla had fun." Although she hadn't asked, and that probably needed fixing. They'd been too preoccupied to enquire much about Isla's evening when they got in last night. "She even cleaned up after herself, so I'm calling it a success."

"Looks like you both had some fun." There was a mischievous expression on Sylvia's face as she peered over her mug. Then she set it down and reached into her handbag, pulling out a compact mirror. "Come here, darling."

Carolyn frowned as she set down her coffee and rounded the central island. It turned to a look of horror, though, when Sylvia held up the mirror and revealed the large purple bruise on her neck. "Oh my Lord."

Embarrassment turned her face a similar colour and she snapped the compact shut. Then the front door clicked open and she panicked, floundering as Sylvia unwound the silk scarf from her own neck and tied it around Carolyn's in a haphazard fashion. They were still fussing with it when Isla entered the kitchen, thankfully focused on her gift.

"Jax got me pizza vouchers. That was cute, right? Maybe I can take Curtis."

"Absolutely," Carolyn agreed, her eyes rolling skywards when she realised that she'd also forgotten to ask anything about how things had gone with him. Her mother of the year award was hanging by a thread. "Does that mean you managed to work things out?"

"They have a date," Jax answered from her position by the doorway. She'd changed back into her own clothes, her shirt a little damp around the collar. "I've just been hearing all about it."

"A boy?" Sylvia enquired with her shoulders scrunched. "This is exciting. Tell me everything."

"Whilst you do that, I'm going to shoot." Jax thumbed over her shoulder with one hand, the other in her pocket.

"You won't join us for a bite?" Sylvia asked, running her top lip through her teeth and glancing to make sure she'd successfully mortified Carolyn.

"I'd love to but I need to get home and changed so I can set up for the match."

"I bet you would. Another time, though, I'm sure. We'll see you in a little while."

Carolyn glared at Sylvia momentarily and then followed Jax into the hallway, shutting the kitchen door behind them to get a little privacy. They still didn't have much of it, though, because she knew Sylvia would be trying to hear their conversation.

"How's the hangover?" she asked in a hushed tone as Jax grabbed her jacket.

"I don't have one, which is a nice surprise. Good job we got distracted from that brandy, huh?"

Carolyn laughed. "On multiple counts. You remember everything that happened, then?" She hadn't meant to sound quite so worried when asking that, and yet it made Jax frown.

"Of course I do," she whispered even quieter than they'd already been speaking. "You really think I wouldn't remember having sex with you?"

It wasn't so much whether she remembered it as whether she regretted it that interested Carolyn, but before she could clarify, Jax answered by delicately kissing her.

Taken a little by surprise, although she was unsure why, she felt herself blush. "It's going to take some getting used to, being kissed like that."

"Kissed like what?" Jax asked, smiling with her lips still poised only a few inches from Carolyn's.

She meant with so much care, and in a way that caused butterflies deep in the pit of her stomach. It was a sensation she'd not experienced in a long time. Almost five years, actually. Give or take.

Carolyn returned the kiss instead of answering Jax's question, then heard movement in the kitchen and decided they were probably pushing their luck. "I suppose I should let you leave. We can talk more later, once Sylvia has grilled me."

"Why's Sylvia going to grill you?"

Carolyn pulled down the scarf, revealing the evidence of their passion. "Because you weren't so gentle last night. It's a good job she spotted it before anyone else."

Jax covered her mouth, her eyes widening. "Wow. Sorry. I think we got a little carried away somewhere around four o'clock this morning." She opened the door and took one step over the threshold. "I'd offer to kiss it better for you, but... maybe not. See you in a couple of hours and bring garlic?"

Carolyn laughed at the sight of Jax bearing her teeth, impersonating a vampire, and shut the door on her. Then she leant back against it and took a deep breath, preparing for whatever would face her in the kitchen.

"Mum!" Isla yelled.

"What?" she asked as she re-opened the internal door.

"Did you tell Gran she couldn't give me a car?"

"Yes."

"Did you know she was going to give me the money from the car instead?"

No, Carolyn didn't, and she had to admire Sylvia's exploitation of a loophole. "That was very generous of her."

"It's not for now," Sylvia clarified, laying her palms flat on the central island. "I know you have a job and you're earning your own money but as your mother very sensibly points out whenever your future is mentioned, we live in an uncertain and ever changing world." Carolyn thought for a second that she was going to follow up her statement with something sensible, but she should've known better, and laughed when Sylvia added, "You might get fed up with that ever changing world and need a holiday."

Sylvia had half understood the principles underpinning the decision and that was good enough for now. Any more would have to wait until Carolyn had slept for more than a few hours. "Thank you. Shall I make us brunch? What would you each like?"

Isla hummed for a few seconds. Then she glanced up at the kitchen clock. "I don't know. I'm not actually sure I'm hungry and I don't like to eat before a game. Maybe I'll just head upstairs and get ready."

"But we're not leaving for an hour-and-a-half."

"I know, but—"

"She wants to message this Curtis," Sylvia finished. Then she shooed her hands towards Isla. "Off you go." Needing no more invitation, Isla bounded up the stairs, and Sylvia turned to face Carolyn. "I want to speak with you privately, anyway. Tell me everything."

Carolyn took another sip of coffee and wondered quite how far to go. Knowing Sylvia, she'd be quite happy to hear every little detail, but there was such a thing as oversharing.

"I spent the night with Jax."

"Yes. I gathered that, dear. How long has this been going on?"

The real answer to that was about six or seven years, but Carolyn stuck with an answer that wouldn't lead to so many questions. Hopefully, Sylvia wouldn't have a clue that Jax was the person she'd been referring to as 'the heartbreaker' for weeks on end. "Only since last night."

"Too many drinks or are there feelings involved?"

"There are feelings. Jax is wonderful and we get on so well."

"You and I get on well but we've never jumped into bed."

Carolyn laughed. "I'm very attracted to her. This is the first time I've had such an intense chemistry with anyone in a long time and I'm enjoying it. I'm just not sure how Isla will react when she finds out. What do you think?"

"I really haven't a clue, my dear. But if you're happy then I hope she'll accept it just fine."

The implication that Sylvia also accepted it 'just fine' was an odd sort of relief. "I don't plan to tell her anything until we've worked out what's going on between us. I trust you'll be discreet?"

"Oh, the soul of discretion! You have some fun, darling. Try not to worry too much about Isla for now. I have the sense that she'll be preoccupied with her own romance for a while, anyway."

"What did she tell you about that?"

Sylvia wafted a hand. "You know how it is at that age. Curtis is wonderful. Their first kiss was wonderful. He's taking her out next weekend."

Carolyn smiled over her coffee. That all sounded very relatable and she couldn't wait to hear more about it from Isla.

## 13

## JAX

"You're alive then?" Becky asked absently from her place on the sofa. She had her feet up in a pair of fluffy slippers, a fleece draped over her team tracksuit as she watched last night's Match of the Day.

The sight of so many layers made Jax shiver. She regretted wearing only her leather jacket. "I might grab a hot shower before the game."

"Washing off your sin?"

Jax leant on the inside of the door frame and tried to look innocent, despite Carolyn's neck attesting that she wasn't. "Don't know what you're talking about."

"Then let me spell it out. You spent your Saturday night with a woman you claim to just be friends with despite having once been completely in love with her. Then you've only come home the morning after, in a dishevelled state and wearing the same clothes you went out in. Spill." Pausing the catch-up service, Becky turned and hooked her arm over the back of the sofa. "Come on. I know there's gossip."

For a moment, Jax considered fobbing her off, but she could do with talking to someone. "We kissed."

"*Just* kissed?"

"Well, no. Okay. It went further than kissing."

"And?"

"And we're spending next weekend together. I think." That was the plan, but they'd made it whilst drunk. Would Carolyn still want to go with the benefit of sobriety and the chance to consider all implications? Surely so, given she seemed to have no regrets this morning, and Jax forgot about the shower for a second in favour of looking at Eurostar times.

"A whole weekend together?" Becky asked, shuffling over to let Jax sit. "That's major progress."

"I know. If we'd just met then I'd say it was too soon to go on a trip but given the circumstances, and the fact that it's the only way we can be alone…"

Jax left the thought hanging because Becky would get the gist and she'd just loaded the schedule for Friday night trains. They were heavily booked already, which was no surprise, but there were still enough seats if they acted quickly. The cost was higher than it would've been in advance but that didn't bother Jax. She had rent money coming in now, and it would easily cover the unexpected expense without needing to go anywhere near savings.

"Thank you for moving in and upgrading me from four stars to five," Jax said as Becky peered over her shoulder to get a better look at the hotel options she'd moved on to viewing.

"I'm glad someone's love life benefited from mine crumbling."

When Becky grabbed the phone from her and took over scrolling, Jax sat with her hands suspended mid-action. "Hey!"

"Go and have your shower. I've got this under control."

Jax grunted as she hauled herself back off the sofa. Her legs hurt like hell from dancing. Then again, it could be the result of carrying Carolyn on her back in the pouring rain.

She left Becky to wriggle back into her original position and did as suggested, showering away the salt and grime of sweat and rain. It was the first time all weekend that she'd considered tactics for the game and she was uncharacteristically behind, drawing positional dots in the steam of the shower door. By the time she was clean, she had her team worked out, and hoped Becky wouldn't be offended by one particular choice.

"I'm thinking of starting some of the youngsters," Jax said as she re-entered the living room, now in her team tracksuit but still towelling her hair. "What do you reckon?"

Becky continued to scroll the phone. "You mean you're thinking of starting Isla?" she asked distractedly. "I wonder how she'll feel when she finds out her mum is getting her sexual favours."

"No," Jax replied, throwing the towel at Becky and knocking the phone to the floor. "It's nothing to do with that. We're playing the bottom of the league team who have barely scored a goal all season. It'll give all the kids a confidence boost and rest the likes of you and maybe Abi who are struggling with injury and fitness."

"You're dropping *me* for Isla? Ouch." Becky rolled sideways to collect the phone, and Jax frowned.

"It's not like that."

"I know. I'm only kidding. It's a good idea and I could use a rest. You don't need to look so worried."

She was trying not to, but Jax had a lot on her mind. Top of it was making sure Carolyn still wanted to go away because, despite reassuring herself, the notion that this might all end up too good to be true still niggled somewhere in the back of her brain.

The only way to end the worry was to confront it. That meant drying her hair and getting to the club, and so it's what Jax did.

When she arrived at the ground, early even by her own standards, she was the only one there. Becky had refused to leave until necessary, so Jax went to sit in the changing rooms alone, transferring her ideas from the shower to her little whiteboard. She'd just finished when she heard the first sound of footsteps outside the door.

"You're early," Isla noted as she entered wearing a big grin.

"So are you. It's almost like you knew you were starting today."

"I'm starting? No way! This is such a good birthday weekend."

"Yeah? What else has happened since I saw you two hours ago?"

"Curtis is coming to watch." Isla beamed as she flung her bag at the bench. "I didn't think he would because we only saw each other last night and we're not officially going out until next weekend, but he wanted to see me play with you guys."

That explained why she was so early, and excited, but Jax was happy for her. "Good day to be starting, then? You can thank me by putting through some of those awesome passes to Jenna."

"I am going to have the best game of my life."

Not doubting that for one second, Jax laughed. It stopped dead, though, when Carolyn wandered into the changing rooms. This wasn't usually her domain and Jax hadn't expected them to speak until the game was done. It caught her a little off guard and she had to make sure her smile was appropriate. Not that Isla was at all cognisant of anything happening around her that didn't involve Curtis or the football game she was about to play.

"He's here," she announced, tapping through her phone.

Before either of them could reply, Isla had bounded back out of the changing rooms, and Carolyn chuckled. "I think it's safe to say our advice worked last night."

"I'd say so. It looks like everyone had a good time, huh?"

Carolyn held her hands out to either side. "I'm stood in a smelly changing room just so that I can see you, so I'd say the answer must be yes. I've often thought what a job you've done, lowering my standards."

"Oh, I see. Last night was about lowered standards." Jax stood up from the bench so they were face to face. "It'd be useful for me to understand which orgasm was worse than the last," she whispered, trying to keep a serious face. "At what point did you hit rock bottom?"

Carolyn adjusted the replacement scarf around her neck. It was a Tottenham football one, at odds with her usual look, and the memory of why it was there caused Jax's hand to creep into Carolyn's again. She was doing a poor job of playing it cool but the truth was, she didn't want to.

"Will you be wearing that in Belgium next weekend?" Jax asked, stroking her fingertips up Carolyn's wrist and back down again.

"It depends, how far are you planning to go when you lick the chocolate from me?"

"Now there's a question," Becky replied, causing Carolyn to jump and pull back her hand, pressing it to her chest.

Jax's heart was experiencing similar spasms. "Bloody hell, Beck. A little warning?"

"You should be thankful it was me and not someone else, if you're trying to keep this a secret."

"It's clearly not much of a secret," Carolyn pointed out, her hand still rubbing her chest.

"I guessed there was something going on between you guys. Sorry. Jax wasn't blabbing about you or anything, and I won't tell anyone else. I can help you and make sure Isla is okay and stuff while you're away next weekend, though, so there are some benefits."

Carolyn's demeanour softened and her hand dropped to her side. "That's kind, thank you. I don't think it's so much that this is a secret as we would probably like some privacy." She turned to face Jax again. "Is that okay with you? Just so that we can figure ourselves out."

That was exactly what Jax wanted. A low pressure way to explore her feelings for Carolyn, without the likes of Jenna interjecting with an opinion every five minutes. "Yes, please. Beck, if you want to be helpful, can you just go and stand on the other side of the door for two minutes?"

"Yes boss." She saluted and exited, shutting the door behind herself.

"I really wasn't being indiscreet," Jax confirmed in a hushed tone so that no one outside could hear.

"It's fine. I ended up telling Sylvia what happened, anyway, and I'm not trying to gag you. I would just prefer we stay under the radar until I'm sure what this is and can have a proper conversation with Isla. It's one thing me seeing someone, she's all for that, but you're her coach."

"And a woman, which she probably isn't expecting."

Carolyn bobbed her head. "I don't know, I let slip that I was attracted to a woman and she didn't seem to care. But there's some history between the two of us that overlaps with a time I was married to her dad, and I'm not sure how she'd feel if she found out about that. Besides which, it's really great that she seems to like and trust you so much, but it could also make her feel like I'm pushing in on all the friendships she's building with her teammates." She squeezed the top of Jax's arm, as if she needed to reassure herself and keep from ending up in an endless loop of supposition. "I don't know. In any case, I want to tread carefully. With her, as well as you. I'm very conscious of what you asked me last night and I don't want to hurt you any more than I do Isla."

"I remember what I said, but I also know there are no guarantees. I want to try, though, and see what we are to each other. It's always a risk but I think I'd regret it more if I walked away and didn't take the chance."

"Me too." Carolyn moved her hand to Jax's cheek. "Last night was a very good start." She dropped a lingering kiss on Jax's lips. "And I'm looking forward to seeing what happens. For now, though, we're early because I finally heard back from Greg and he wants help interviewing a potential new bar manager, so I should go."

"I hope he had a good excuse."

"He did. Surprisingly. I'm giving him the benefit of the doubt. Besides, I'm quite excited to get stuck into my chair duties and interested to see who he's found."

So was Jax. She had a feeling whoever this person was, they would be young, pretty, and female. "There was me thinking you just arrived early to see more of me."

Carolyn laughed and leant in close, their lips almost meeting again. "I wanted to see you, too. I have to confess I was a little worried you may have changed your mind." They kissed again and then she stepped away, tugging at her scarf to show the love bite. "Can you stick to the chocolate next weekend, though? I have no idea how I'm going to hide this at work tomorrow."

"A slip with some dentures? A run in with a walking frame? You fell on a fish from the tank in reception?" Jax continued to reel off more and more ludicrous suggestions, until Carolyn had to kiss her to make them stop.

"No," she said, going in for one last kiss. "Behave."

Jax laughed but didn't say anything more because she wouldn't make promises she couldn't keep.

## 14

# CAROLYN

Carolyn closed her case and then paused with her fingers still on the zip. Had she packed her toothbrush? Yes, she must have done. And even if she hadn't, they sold toothbrushes in Belgium. She still had no idea where they were going in any greater specificity than that. She'd agreed a budget with Jax and then left her to plan. The week had been a hectic one and they'd barely spoken since, besides a brief exchange at training drop off on Wednesday evening, and the thought of their reunion made Carolyn's stomach do a little twirl.

"Are you sure you'll be alright?" she asked Isla, who was resting back on Carolyn's bed texting Curtis, as she'd been for the best part of the past week. "Your gran is only a few minutes away if you need anything and Becky also said you can call her if you run into any problems."

Isla finally looked up from her phone. "I'm seventeen, not seven, and you're only going away for two nights. I'm pretty sure I'll survive. To be honest, it's a bit of a relief."

"A relief?"

"Yes. That you've finally got a friend to do this stuff with. Old lady city breaks."

Old lady city breaks? When had she been foisted into the category of 'old lady'? Let alone Jax. "That's just charming. I'll tell her you said that, shall I? Maybe I can slip it in right before she picks the team next week."

"Do your worst. I don't think she'll drop me after I scored that great goal, on top of two assists."

Carolyn grumbled and lifted her bag from the bed to the floor. She needed to go but not before confirming one last thing. "How are things going with the rugby playing Romeo?"

"Very well, thank you." Isla had resumed her tapping, her head buried in her neck as she stared intently at the screen. "We're using the vouchers Jax gave me for dinner tomorrow and he's just asked if I'll be his date for V-Day, too. Isn't that cute?"

"Adorable, but don't forget to call your dad about next weekend. He's coming all the way down to see you, like you asked, so it might be nice to make some plans besides dinner with your gran and football. Okay?"

"Okay."

Despite some concern that she'd return on Sunday to find Isla in exactly the same position, Carolyn had to leave. She was meeting Jax at the train station to catch their connecting train to London, so they could make a late Eurostar booking. "I'm off now. Not that you'll notice."

"Have fun. Bring me back a box of chocolates."

"I will," Carolyn replied as she carried her case onto the landing. "Love you."

"Love you, too."

It was only a fifteen minute walk to the station so Carolyn had decided to make it on foot to save having to find parking. The weather was mercifully dry for the first time that week but back to near zero temperatures, so she wheeled her case with one hand, the other tucked in her pocket for warmth. When she reached the station, Jax was waiting on the platform, and waved furiously to attract her attention despite there being no crowd.

Carolyn stopped and smiled, her stomach giving another little flutter as she tried to work out how their greeting should go. In the end, Jax made the decision for her when she went straight in for a kiss.

"Are you excited?" she asked, still close enough that their breath misted together.

"Yes," Carolyn answered as she leant in for another kiss and it finally moved her brain into weekend mode for the first time. She took her hand from her pocket and slipped it around Jax's soft, surprisingly warm palm. "Are you finally going to tell me where we're going?"

"Belgium...?"

"I know Belgium, but where?"

"Oh. Brussels. I decided that since we don't have long, it was best to go somewhere that's easy to get to. Don't want to waste time on any more travelling than necessary. Is that okay?"

It was very smart and given how tired she was tonight, Carolyn wholly approved. "Exactly the logic I would've used, and I've somehow never been to Brussels, only Bruges, so all the better."

The train pulled in behind them and they boarded, using the forty minute journey to catch up on each other's weeks. When they spilled out in London, the platform was far busier, and Jax took Carolyn's hand again to keep them together as they made their way towards the underground to transfer to St Pancras. They were cutting it fine and had to rush to get through security, joining the boarding queue with only minutes to spare.

"If this is your idea of excitement, I'd like to remind you that I can't run in heels," Carolyn pointed out as Jax lifted their bags into the overhead storage. The train was packed but they had a cosy little spot at the back of the carriage. It looked very enticing for a doze.

Jax lifted up the seat arm and slid in, next to the window. "I forgot we would be slowed down by those things."

"Those *things* are expensive and very stylish."

"They also look impractical and uncomfortable. Are you really going to walk around the city in them all weekend?"

"No, they're for dinner wear, but I didn't want to risk squashing them in my case. I do have a pair of flatter ankle boots for sightseeing."

"I still say a pair of sneakers would be *more* comfortable but it's a start." Jax patted her pockets. "Have you seen my passport?"

"No. Sorry, Jacqueline. I haven't." Carolyn sat down and sniggered when Jax shot her a daggered look. "What? I'd forgotten your full name, it never really occurs to me. I think because it suits you so badly."

"Gee, thanks for the reminder. As if I didn't already know how badly it suits me. Everyone always thinks I go by Jax because it's more gender neutral or something but it's not that at all. I just don't have any other viable choice. Even my middle name is terrible."

"It's not terrible. Neither name is bad, for someone else, but I agree that they don't suit you. It's like the few times colleagues have tried to call me Caz and it makes me shudder. I'm sure there are some lovely people named *Caz* but I'm not one of them. It just doesn't fit."

"I shouldn't accidentally call out Caz in bed later, then?"

"Oh, yes? You think we're sleeping together tonight, do you?" This was probably a redundant argument given Jax had already clarified she should book only one room, but Carolyn was enjoying their play. It made up for a thoroughly dull week.

"I don't know," Jax countered. "I haven't decided whether I

want to give you multiple orgasms again this weekend. I suppose I'll see how I feel. How nice you are to me."

Carolyn blushed a little at the memory of those orgasms. Then she snuggled against Jax's shoulder as the train pulled off, still desperately tired and hoping she might get at least one of them if she could manage a little rest. She smiled when a kiss dropped on her head, then closed her eyes and drifted in and out of sleep for most of their two-and-a-half-hour journey.

When she woke fully it was because Jax had kissed her head again, then given her leg a gentle wobble.

"We're here," Jax said, closing the lid on her e-reader. "Earth to Caz."

"Call me that again and I'll murder you in your sleep," Carolyn mumbled back, rubbing her eyes and then cricking her neck as she tried to return herself to reality. "What's the time?"

"Just after eleven local time. My phone rolled forward an hour for the difference when we passed through France."

"Oh." That meant they'd struggle to find an open restaurant, and Carolyn's stomach grumbled. "I'm a little hungry, though."

"I thought you might be." Jax produced a baguette from by her side, stuffed with fresh ham, cheese and salad. "They came through with food earlier so I got you something."

The nap had done wonders and now that she also had food, Carolyn could feel her mood lifting. "Are you going to look after me like this all weekend? You should be careful because I might get used to it."

"That's my plan. Get you hooked on all the care and attention, then ask for something in return."

"Oh, no. What?"

"I might have also checked out a bar we can head to before we find our hotel. It looks like a total tourist trap but it sells over two-thousand different beers. Are you up for it or are you too tired?"

Carolyn smiled. "I'm sure I can manage one." Besides, they were here to enjoy themselves, not just spend it all in a hotel room. Her excitement began to build again as she got up and waited for Jax to lift down their cases. "Have you found anything else for us to do this weekend or do we need to Google later?"

"I've pre-Googled and have suggestions. We should probably visit the main square whilst we're here, and find the Mannekin-Pis."

"The what?"

"The Mannekin-Pis. The Pissing Boy. It's a thing, apparently. And he has a sister, found near the bar we're going to tonight."

Chuckling, Carolyn wheeled her bag down the carriage. "You're really hitting me with all the romance, aren't you?"

"That comes after," Jax replied, helping Carolyn down onto the platform, where a shot of cold air went right through her and she shivered. "There's a chocolate museum with melted chocolate samples a short train ride away. I figured that would appeal to us both. I also got a recommendation from a colleague of good places to eat tomorrow and Sunday."

"Now we're talking." Carolyn unwrapped her baguette and took a bite while Jax pulled both of their cases towards the exit. "How do we get to this bar of yours?"

"We walk. It's only five minutes away. Maybe ten in those shoes."

Ignoring the latest assault on her footwear, Carolyn continued to admire Jax's organisational skills. She really had thought of everything so far, and it was nice to have someone taking charge for once, especially with so much thought for what she might enjoy. On all recent holidays, she'd been at the bottom of the pile.

"Thank you," Carolyn said as they walked over the cobbles, agreeing her shoes were wholly impractical when she almost rolled her ankle. She righted herself and took another bite of her baguette, which was surprisingly high quality. It tasted like it'd come out of a Parisian patisserie and not from a train.

"What are you thanking me for?"

"For being wonderful. Mostly."

Carolyn finished her sandwich as they made their way the short distance to Jax's bar. She was right and it did look like a tourist trap but that was okay because they *were* tourists. Besides, they'd have no better time in a locals bar than here.

She bundled her wrapper and stuffed it into her pocket, then pushed open the door, walking under the image of a large pink elephant. It must be something to do with the branding but she didn't like to ask.

Inside there were barrels that had been fashioned into tables and she spotted one or two vacant. Carolyn let Jax select their drinks whilst she took the cases to one and waited, slipping onto an old wooden stool. She peered up to find there were beer trays stuck to the ceiling, and running right around the top of the wall was a shelf lined with bottles. It was quaint, rustic and, most importantly, warm.

"I have no idea what I just ordered," Jax shouted over the din as she set a glass of pinkish beer in front of Carolyn. "I think it's cherry. If you don't like it we can swap."

Carolyn took a sip, surprised to find she enjoyed the tang. "It's actually nice. I could get used to drinking lager if it tastes like this."

"They have a lot of fruit flavours. But then, they have a lot of everything. I may have to come back three or four hundred times. Is that okay?" Jax dragged a stool from the other side of the barrel, close enough that when she sat on it, their legs had to slip together. Then she wrapped her hand under Carolyn's knee and leant forward so they could hear each other without shouting.

Unlike last week, Carolyn had no hesitation in placing her

hand over Jax's and stroking the back of it. "All the culture and history of a capital city and you want to sit in a bar drinking beer? Not that I should be surprised. You are American, after all."

"Says the woman who wanted to come here to eat chocolate. And waffles. Which, by the way, locals don't put chocolate on. Sorry."

"At least I'll be able to order them because I know enough French to get by without resorting to pointing and Google Translate."

"You think, do you? I can't wait to watch you order dinner tomorrow night."

Jax laughed a little and then lingered over a kiss. It was another thing they were doing freely now, but it still gave Carolyn butterflies every single time. She reached around to gently stroke the back of Jax's neck, pulling her in and deepening their next kiss. When she finally pulled away, Jax was wearing a decidedly dopey smile.

"I love kissing you," she said, leaning in to do it again. "I also love that I don't have to pretend about how crazy attracted I am to you anymore."

"And I love that you think you were hiding it. We were both flirting pretty outrageously, Miss *Ouch I've Hurt My Knee Please Feed Me Cookies*."

"Yeah, I got a lot out of that. Your attention *and* cookies."

She'd had Carolyn's attention since New Year's Eve, one way or another, and the focus only became sharper the more time they spent together.

They finished their drinks and Jax resisted the urge to buy more, deciding that they should probably find their hotel and check in because it was almost midnight. It was only another short walk through the city centre streets but before they could make it, Jax was intent on showing Carolyn Jeanneke-Pis, the pissing girl fountain, inset on the wall adjacent to the bar.

"It's... interesting," she surmised, tilting her head and trying to work out why this was a tourist attraction. It was just a statue of a small girl, only about half a metre tall, urinating into a basin.

"It's only been there since the eighties but the original Manneken-Pis has existed since the sixteen-hundreds. You wanted culture, you got culture."

Carolyn laughed. She was also getting cold, and pulled her coat tight around herself. "I appreciate it. Could you get me into a heated room, next?" And maybe a warm bath. Something to wash away the dirty feeling that always came with travel, before slipping into crisp white hotel sheets. It sounded like bliss right now.

Jax obliged, guiding them out of the alley, past more bars and restaurants, and onto a busier road with a hotel on the corner. She led Carolyn into a stylish foyer with a gold reception desk and checked them in, then through a high ceilinged bar area and into the lift.

"I hope this will meet with your standards, ma'am," Jax said as they rode it up to the fifth floor. "It's only a junior suite but I was pushing the budget if you wanted five stars."

That was rich. Jax was hardly one for slumming it, any more than Carolyn. "Please. I know the cost of that designer coat you're wearing. Let's not pretend you don't also like a little luxury."

"Hey, I'm just a simple farm girl from Nebraska. Raised on corn. Tippin' cows. I don't know what no five stars is."

Carolyn folded her arms and glared at Jax's hammed up Midwestern accent, which belonged in an episode of The Simpsons. "Really, because I could've sworn you grew up in the *city* of

Omaha where your parents ran, and still run, a successful car dealership."

"Three, actually." Jax shrugged when the lift pinged and the doors opened. Then she looked down at the key card in her hand. "I think we need to go left."

She wheeled the cases down the hallway until she reached their room and buzzed them in. On the far side was a sofa, with a television attached to a dividing wall, splitting off a super king size bed. There was also a writing desk, a coffee table, and small area with drink making facilities set over a minibar. All were finished in high end walnut and sleek chrome.

"Well, for a simple city girl whose parents only own three car dealerships, you know what a nice hotel room is," Carolyn said, peeking into the bathroom to find there was a sink set into marble, a double shower cubicle and, crucially, a large bath. "Do you mind if I warm up in this?"

"The toilet? No, but I'm not sure you'll fit."

"I can't keep track of who you are tonight. Country girl, city girl. Creative Director, comedian."

Jax pulled the bathroom light cord to fully illuminate the space. "I'm always a comedian. It's part of my persona. Are you taking a bath?"

"Yes."

"And can I help you undress?"

There wasn't really much choice in the matter because Jax was already removing Carolyn's coat. She stepped out of the bathroom to hook it on a peg, then returned to help peel off her sweater, followed by unbuttoning her jeans.

"I see your fingers are working again," Carolyn pointed out, squirming a little when Jax slowly pulled down her zipper.

"You must have cured me."

Carolyn slipped the coat from Jax's shoulders. She felt the

sudden urge to have Jax out of her clothes too, but still wanted the bath. "You're coming in with me."

"*Am* I?" Jax asked, pulling her coat back over her shoulders. "What if I don't want to?"

Carolyn shrugged and turned to run the taps, making sure that Jax could see her breasts as she bent over. "Fine, don't come in."

She found some bubble bath in an assortment of toiletries next to the basin and poured in a liberal glug. Then she wriggled out of her jeans and kicked them across the room towards Jax, who was stood with her coat wrapped around herself.

"Will you make me a cup of tea, though?" Carolyn asked.

Still motionless, Jax watched as Carolyn unhooked her bra and discarded it. Then she audibly swallowed when Carolyn slipped off her briefs and put her hands on her hips.

It snapped Jax from her stupor and she hurriedly cast off her coat, followed by her sweater, T-shirt, boots, jeans, and underwear.

"Sorry, what did you say?" she replied when she was completely naked.

"Never mind."

Carolyn had lost her appetite for tea. There were suddenly far more important things on her mind, like getting off the cold tile floor and into a pool of bubbles. Preferably with Jax wrapped around her. It wasn't even about sex, although she was aroused. The strongest desire was to be held. To sink back into Jax's arms and enjoy the warmth and intimacy of it. The affection of butterfly kisses on her shoulders. Whispered words in her ear. Another person's heartbeat and a loving embrace.

Not that she'd say no if an orgasm followed.

## 15

## JAX

Jax woke on her back with blonde hair tickling her chin. Carolyn had slept flopped across her body like a weighted blanket and Jax kissed the top of her head, smiling when she wriggled and let out a few grunts.

"What time is it?" Carolyn mumbled.

Jax looked over at the clock on the bedside table. "It's ten-thirty." And they'd been wrapped around each other for at least ten solid hours, if you counted the time they'd spent in the bath. Carolyn still smelled of floral bubble bath, her skin soft and smooth as their legs slipped together. "I guess we should get up at some point but it's not enticing."

Carolyn grunted again. "I know. If we'd just wanted a dirty weekend, we could've done it closer to home. I suppose we should find brunch and then head to the chocolate museum."

It had come to something when even the prospect of a building dedicated to chocolate didn't fill her voice with excitement, and Jax laughed. "Have we finally found something you enjoy more?"

"I get the impression that you're surprised."

"I'm not surprised at you, I think I'm a bit surprised at

myself. I feel like a teenager sometimes when I'm around you, all hormones and desperation, and it's a long time since I've wanted to spend this much time in bed with someone." Jax stroked the hair out of Carolyn's face as she propped herself on an elbow and peered up with bleary eyes. She loved seeing Carolyn laid completely bare when she was usually so well put together. It was like getting to the soft caramel encased in a hard chocolate shell. "You look very beautiful right now."

"I look a mess," Carolyn countered, dipping her head to dab Jax's chest with kisses.

It rattled the chain around her neck, which was the only thing she never seemed to take off, and Jax clasped the ring it held. "Have you always worn this on your chain?"

"No. When we were clearing out my dad's house, we found some jewellery belonging to my mum. We agreed that I'd take her engagement ring and my sister had her wedding ring. I put it on my chain for safe keeping before we'd even left the house and then never took it off. You'll think this is morbid but I'm sure it's as much to remind myself that I'm the next generation to go as to remember them. It's a cliché but life is short."

"I don't think it's morbid. But I do now feel guilty for lying in so late when I promised you chocolate."

Carolyn laughed. "You make it sound like lying here together is wasted time but it's not. I am hungry, though, which means we probably should get up."

They submitted to doing so, dressing and then heading out in search of food. Armed with more sandwiches and a coffee each, they then boarded another train and headed a short distance out of the city to find the chocolate museum.

"When do we get to the actual chocolate?" Carolyn asked as they wandered the galleries, past endless screens about the history of cocoa and sustainable production.

Jax pointed to a stand at the end of the corridor. "I think

that's an interactive bit. They're dotted around. You get to mould chocolate."

"Do I get to eat it?"

Jax smiled, amused by how little Carolyn was concentrating. She was ricocheting from one display to the next without a care in the world for once. "Yeah, I think so."

They reached the station, where a shiny brunette was demonstrating how to mould chocolate shells by hand. Then she let everyone try one.

"This is more like it," Carolyn said as she ate a second.

"Why do I feel like I'm the only one taking this seriously? Some of the info is actually pretty interesting. You can read about how Belgian chocolate came to be so good."

Carolyn placed her hand in Jax's. "Sorry. I'm just feeling a bit frivolous this weekend."

"Yeah?" Frivolity was something Jax could get on board with, and she tugged Carolyn forward. "Come on, then."

"Where are we going?"

"You'll see."

Carolyn knew there was melted chocolate on the tour but Jax hadn't told her exactly how much. She'd only found out herself because she'd read the TripAdvisor reviews on the train, and she had a feeling that the finale would satisfy Carolyn's desire for frivolous indulgence.

When they reached the doors to the last room, having passed by the rest of the exhibition, Jax stepped behind Carolyn and covered her eyes.

"Are you ready?" she asked, nudging the door open with her foot.

"Wherever you're taking me smells incredible," Carolyn replied, inching forward.

"That's just me."

Jax removed her hands to reveal a large, windowless room

with vats of chocolate around the perimeter, ranging from white to dark. There were dozens, all available to sample. Theoretically, that should be with the tiny cups provided, but there was no one making sure you didn't take too much.

"Oh goodness I've died and gone to heaven," Carolyn whispered. She reached behind herself to take Jax's hands, wrapping them around her waist. "I'm not sure how we're getting this back to the hotel room, though. What's your plan?"

"For the licking part?" Jax cuddled in tight and pressed a kiss to Carolyn's temple. "I think you're sweet enough. I just want you to enjoy yourself in here."

"That's possibly the cheesiest thing you've ever said to me but I'm too distracted to tease you. Which flavour do you want to try first?" Carolyn raised both of their hands to point at the Ecuadorian dark. "Do you like dark chocolate or are you more of a milk person? Not that I'm sure why I'm asking. You're American so you haven't a clue what chocolate is meant to taste like. You just eat sweetened grit."

"Um, excuse me? I've noticed a few of these jibes since we started seeing each other. Have you figured that I like your boobs enough that I won't object too strongly?"

"That's largely my understanding of the situation, yes. Am I wrong?"

Jax let go of Carolyn and picked up a couple of the little paper cups. "Not entirely. Besides, I have to agree that I prefer British chocolate. And Belgian." She held one out for Carolyn to take. "I like dark but not too dark. Maybe a seventy-percent. I see they have a one-hundred percent over there and that sounds bitter as hell. I'll save it for my sister when she's lamenting that Obama isn't still in office."

Carolyn laughed. "I might try it. I also miss Obama. I can see why she's bitter about it."

Jax followed to the darkest chocolate vat and watched as

Carolyn opened the tap to release a little into her cup. She stuck her finger in and licked it off, then coughed and banged her chest with her fist.

"Bit much?" Jax asked, rubbing her back.

"I don't think you'll like it. Here," Carolyn said, taking the clean cup from Jax's hand and walking back a few vats to pour some of the seventy-percent. She stuck in her finger again and this time held it up to Jax's lips.

Jax smiled and took a loose grasp on Carolyn's wrist, then slowly lathed her finger clean. "This one's good."

"The chocolate or me?"

"Both."

They continued in a similar vein until they'd sampled at least a dozen different chocolates and even Carolyn was complaining she was queasy. Then they finally submitted to leaving, heading out through the shop to buy Isla a gift.

Armed with a big box of chocolate shells that had cost more than some cars, they made the trip back to the centre of Brussels and decided to wander around a few of the obvious tourist sites, somehow finding the appetite to eat waffles from a street vendor before returning to the hotel to rest for a while and change for dinner.

"Is the restaurant you picked upmarket or casual?" Carolyn asked, holding up two dresses. She raised them alternately.

"Relaxed," Jax replied from her place on the bed, legs crossed over and her hands cradling the back of her head. "It's more of a café that does healthy options and a lot of vegan stuff. I figured it was a good shout for today after we spent the whole afternoon eating chocolate and waffles. But there's a brasserie for tomorrow night, before we leave. That's a bit more upmarket."

"You're right, that is a good shout. My body is screaming for some vegetables. How do you always think of everything?"

Jax shrugged. It didn't take a lot of working out. "I guess I'm just thoughtful. What can I say?"

"Your modesty also astounds me."

Carolyn opted to remain in her jeans rather than changing, partly due to the sub-zero temperatures. Then she fixed her make up and decided to check in with Isla, who couldn't get her mum off the phone fast enough because she was about to go on her date with Curtis.

"I guess no one needs you but me." Jax forced a sigh and then rolled off the bed.

"You *need* me, do you?"

"Yes. Desperately. I need you to order us some nice food in the café so that I don't embarrass myself."

Carolyn laughed as they made their way for the door. "I'll resist any more jibes about your nationality. For now."

Everywhere Jax's colleague had recommended was within a ten minute walk of the hotel, quite purposefully because she didn't want them to spend their entire weekend travelling. It was another example of what a considerate person she was, especially when it came to Carolyn, but she did still intend to get her own back just once.

When they reached the café, they were taken to a quiet corner. It was a clean, modern place, with a parquet floor, high ceilings, and strings of bulb lights overhead. Very metropolitan and also, incidentally, very Dutch. Not that Jax had chosen to point that out to Carolyn.

"Are you ready to order?" she asked, selecting a wheat beer and a salad bowl from the menu.

"I'll just have what you're having," Carolyn replied, turning over her menu and pushing it forward. "You've chosen well so far."

Jax told Carolyn her order and then sat back, waiting for the waiter to come over and for Carolyn to place it. In French. Then she tried to contain her smile when the waiter made the correction, and Carolyn blushed.

"Didn't I mention?" Jax asked when he'd gone. "This is a Dutch speaking café. Well, Flemish, but that's basically Dutch, right? It's one of the things I love about this place. They don't *just* speak French. I thought you'd already have figured that, though, being English and knowing absolutely everything. You wouldn't want it pointed out by an American."

Carolyn folded her arms. "Well played. I'm sorry."

"Me too." But Jax knew Carolyn could take the joke, or she wouldn't have done it. They called a truce and by the time the food arrived, it was all forgotten.

Carolyn smiled over a bowl of salad that was bigger than her head. "I'm so glad we did this. I've missed travelling."

"Me too. Damn pandemic."

"It wasn't just the pandemic. I struggled to get Marcus and Isla to go anywhere that didn't involve a pool." She picked up a roll and broke it in half. "Do you mind me mentioning him?"

"No, of course not. You were together for most of your adult life and you have a daughter. I'm pretty sure he's going to come up." Besides which, Jax was sort of curious. They'd never discussed him much and she still had no idea what had finally split them up. She'd been too busy enjoying the spoils. "Do you mind me asking what happened in the end?"

Carolyn shrugged. "I think you know most of it. Our marriage wasn't in a good state even before we moved to Manchester. We were throwing ourselves into work and I was getting my emotional needs met by you, apparently." She set her roll down and picked up her beer glass instead, resting back in her chair and taking a sip. "We were in our early twenties when we got together. We're not the people we were then, and nor should we be. Many couples are able to navigate that together but there's not enough common ground between Marcus and I anymore. I've known it for a long time, I just wasn't prepared to admit it because I was afraid of the upheaval. Manchester was a last ditch attempt to move on as a pair, try to make it work, but it was mostly for Isla's benefit."

"I guess it's quite a lot to ask that you'll want exactly the same things in every phase of life."

"Yes. Marcus is already talking about early retirement, his payoff for all of those long hours, but we're in very different places. I can't imagine retiring. I love working and I'm a long way from wanting to give it up. The final nail in the coffin, though, was when he went back to the office in a break between lockdowns and met someone else. It fizzled out pretty quickly but it wasn't long before another came along."

He'd cheated? Jax felt as though all the air had just been knocked out of her. It was an odd sensation to be so pissed with the guy for betraying Carolyn, even though it had ultimately contributed to her being single again. Apparently, the protective instinct won out over anything else. "Wow. I'm sorry."

"Don't be. We both know I'm not squeaky clean on that score. You and I may never have slept together but in a way, isn't emotional cheating worse? It's why I could never be too hard on him. Especially given how much of a state I was in when we first moved. I missed you and deep down knew I wanted to be elsewhere, which is hardly conducive to making a marriage work."

Even so, when you'd uprooted your whole life, it was a pretty harsh blow. "You're more forgiving than me, that's for sure."

Carolyn shrugged again and set her glass back down. "Honestly? It was a sort of relief. A way out. Besides, I had other things to worry about in the end because work was so stressful during the pandemic and my dad became ill. None of this must get back to Isla, by the way. I don't want her to know about the affairs."

Jax reeled at everything Carolyn had been through. She

couldn't even comprehend it all, or how she remained so seemingly unfazed. "Of course. Anything personal you share with me will always be confidential, whether it's Isla or anyone else."

"Thank you. Isla knows a version of the truth. She thinks we grew apart but that we're friends, which isn't a lie. We just want different things. We'd always discussed seeing the world, or heading back to Ibiza for a fun, spontaneous trip, but Marcus has decided he'd rather play a bit of golf and wind down. That's perfectly acceptable, it's just not for me. I still want passion and excitement."

"Seeing the world like heading to Belgium on the spur of the moment and eating great food?"

"Yes, and passion like incredible sex on my sofa bed." Carolyn laughed and finally dug in for a forkful of salad. "What about you? I've resisted the urge to ask whether there's been anyone new. Partly because I think I'll be horribly jealous."

Jax scratched the back of her neck, unsure how much to share. "One or two flings but nothing serious. The pandemic wasn't good for my love life. A girl has needs, though."

"A girl definitely has needs. I've become very good at satisfying them for myself. So good that I instinctively packed my vibrator without even thinking about the alternative this weekend."

"Is that so?" Jax asked, interested on various levels. She leant forward, an elbow on either side of her bowl. "Tell me more."

"More about how lonely I've been?"

"No, more about how you've been owning your own pleasure. I think that's a more positive spin. You say you have your vibrator with you?"

Carolyn set her fork down and also leant forward. "Yes. Does it bother you?"

"Why on earth would it bother me?"

"Bother is the wrong word. It doesn't make you feel insecure?"

"No. I think it's very sexy that you know your own body and how to pleasure yourself." Jax lowered her voice when a waiter walked past. "Maybe you can give me some tips later. Show me what you like."

"Really?" A little warmth coloured Carolyn's cheeks, and she began to finger her necklace again.

Jax took Carolyn's other hand and held it on the table, stroking a thumb gently over her soft skin. "Mmm. Did you enjoy last night?"

"I would've thought that was obvious. Did you?"

"It was okay." Jax smiled so Carolyn knew she was joking.

"Oh, I see. Couldn't match up to those flings. Well, you'll have to forgive me. I'm a long time out of the game and I've never been with a woman before you, so..."

"Here come the excuses."

"Watch it. I wasn't at all worried about that until now but I might change my mind."

Jax squeezed Carolyn's hand. "I'm teasing. You have absolutely nothing to feel insecure about. I'm the one who should be worried."

"Let me guess? Are we following the narrative that I'm a cock hungry straight woman who you'll never satisfy?"

Jax spluttered at Carolyn using the word 'cock'. There was something so jarring about it. "No. So long as we're also not following the narrative that as a woman who has exclusively been in sexual relationships with men, you must be insecure about your performance with a woman. I will allow you to be a little in awe of how good I am in bed, though. I like that part of the story. You should at least pretend that you're finally experiencing a technicolour of sexual ecstasy after years of colour-blind, boring, and ultimately unfulfilling sex with men. It's only polite."

It finally won Jax the laugh she'd been after for weeks, and she delighted in watching Carolyn struggle for breath. When she'd finally regained the ability to speak, she'd turned Jax's knuckles white from gripping her hand so tight.

"I don't even know what to say to that," Carolyn confessed, still laughing and dabbing the tears from under her eyes. "But of course, out of politeness I will make you feel like a sex god at all times."

"It's all I ask. I only wish we didn't have to go home tomorrow so you could worship for longer. I'm already wondering when we'll be alone again."

"Me too. I've had a great time. I'd like to say we could do something next weekend, but I'm meeting up with an old friend and then having dinner with Marcus on Saturday. He's coming down to spend time with Isla and watch her match, and we agreed it would be a good idea to do something together. The Monday is Valentine's Day, though. Would you like to be my date?"

Jax was more than happy to be the passionate and exciting antidote to a weekend with Marcus. "I would love to be your date."

## 16

# CAROLYN

Carolyn peered through her bedroom curtain at the water lashing onto her pergola. The weather was certainly not making her any more enthusiastic about heading out to dinner.

"Is it bad there, too?" she asked, returning her attention to Jax.

"It's bad everywhere, except for my bed."

"Is that right?" They were on video chat for at least the third time that week because it sometimes felt like the only way to be alone with each other, and Carolyn made sure Jax could see as she let the curtain drop and shimmied out of her trousers. She held the phone out to her side as she turned around and flicked through options in her wardrobe. "What shall I wear?"

"Absolutely nothing works for me."

Carolyn laughed, enjoying the attention. There was never any equivocation about how sexy Jax found her and she loved how it made her feel. Desired. Noticed. Appreciated. Exactly what she needed before facing an evening with her ex-husband. "I could wear my best black dress, but I was saving that for Monday. Or, at least, I presume I can wear it on Monday. Where are we going?"

Jax panned her phone camera around her bedroom. She was getting ready to go out too but had picked an outfit for the pub far more easily. "My house, but you can wear your best dress. I just didn't think a romantic meal in public was a great idea when people don't know about us, and it might get back to Isla."

"Good thinking. And how convenient that it's only a stone's throw from your bed."

"Wow. You know, I hadn't thought of that. But now you mention it..." The lewd smile on Jax's face implied she had thought about it, but it was another thing Carolyn didn't mind even a tiny bit. She'd had a lot of fun indulging in some mutual self-pleasure with Jax last Sunday morning before they checked out of the hotel, and she was looking forward to continuing their exploration at some point.

For now, though, she had to remain on topic and pulled out a navy dress she usually wore for work. "This will do. I don't know why I'm worrying over what I wear tonight, anyway."

"You go girl." Jax held up her hand as if expecting a high five, and Carolyn laughed again.

"I will *go girl*. We're leaving in ten minutes so I need to hang up and get ready, but I can't wait for Monday, and I'll try to keep my hands off you again tomorrow."

"I will also try but I'm not making any promises because Wednesday was a struggle. Call me later if you need to debrief, and if I'm back from the pub I'll answer."

Carolyn wished her fun with Jenna and Abi, then disconnected and set about a quick change. She wasn't usually tardy but had become distracted by the call, and now needed to make up time.

She had her dress half over her head when her phone rang again, and she wondered what Jax had forgotten to tell her. Jabbing at the accept button, she held the device in one hand

and tried to shimmy the garment down her body with the aid of the other.

"That was quick. Couldn't keep your hands off me for even this long, hmm?"

She was laughing until Sylvia's voice replied, "No dear, I'm quite capable of keeping my hands off you."

Having only the zip left to wrangle, Carolyn put the phone to her ear and ran her fingers through her hair. Thank the Lord this was only a voice call and Sylvia couldn't see the horrified look on her face. "Sorry, I thought you were someone else."

"I can imagine who. You can tell me all about it later but first, I'm in crisis."

"Are you okay?" The hand on Carolyn's head dropped to the centre of her chest, which suddenly shot through with panic.

"There's a power cut on this side of town. I've got dinner in an oven that is no longer running, and I'm illuminated only by candle and torchlight. Can we decamp to your house?"

Carolyn's heart thumped again, this time at the thought of Marcus in her house. There was something about the prospect of old and new mixing that felt oddly like contamination, and she'd rather go out in the driving rain. "I suppose we don't have a lot of choice. Are you going to be alright getting the food over here?"

"Yes, I'll call Marcus and he can pick me up on his way. Can you switch the oven on in preparation and I'll make a dash?"

"On his way? Isn't he staying with you?"

"No. Insisted on a hotel. Goodness only knows why, it's a waste of money."

Sylvia checked a few more details and then disconnected, leaving Carolyn to try to do the same. So what if Marcus was the first person she ended up entertaining at her new kitchen table? It was no big deal.

She continued to remind herself of that as she set out place mats and cutlery. When the doorbell chimed, though, she couldn't help a swell of nerves rising from the pit of her stomach. This was the first time they'd been together as a four since the divorce and she had no idea how it would go. Marcus occasionally dropped her text messages but they were all related to Isla and they didn't ever delve into each other's personal lives. It made her wonder what on earth they'd find to talk about.

"I'll get it," Isla yelled as she came bounding down the stairs with a lot more enthusiasm. At least someone was looking forward to dinner and, credit where it was due, Marcus had taken her point that she was the one making most of the effort to travel. Apparently, he was even talking about coming down for Isla's disco. Not that Carolyn dared call it that in front of her.

Thankfully, any awkwardness was allayed by Sylvia's worries about her food, which Marcus was carrying incorrectly. Carolyn chuckled as he tried to question how you could carry a tray improperly, only to find himself continually shushed. He really got it in the neck, though, when Sylvia realised he hadn't picked up the dessert.

"I thought you had it!" Marcus slid the potatoes into Carolyn's oven and then turned around and finally acknowledged her. "You look well," he said with a little shake of his head because Sylvia was still making her displeasure known. "Sorry about this."

"It's not a problem," Carolyn replied, finding it had helped her nerves. "You look well, too." A little thicker around the waist than the last time she'd seen him but otherwise, unchanged. It occurred to her only then that he looked like a taller, more handsome, and less slimy version of Greg. The thought made her laugh a little and put them both at ease. "Do you want a drink?"

"Yes. A large one."

"You're driving," Sylvia interjected, cutting between them and going straight for the hob. "So make it a small one."

"A small one, then. Please."

Carolyn grabbed a bottle of white from the fridge and poured them each a small glass, then a larger one for Sylvia because she looked like she could use it.

Chit chat followed. How work was going, on all sides, which now included Isla. She waxed lyrical about Jenna, and it led onto a discussion about the disco fundraiser. Then the conversation came around to football, as it so often did in Isla's company, but Carolyn had a feeling the game would be off given the storms.

"I wouldn't be surprised if it's cancelled tomorrow," she pointed out, knowing the pitch would most likely be waterlogged.

"Yeah, that's what everyone on the group chat keeps saying. Jax just put out a message that she should know soon. I can't believe Dad came all this way to watch me play and it won't happen."

"He came all this way to see *you*, not just to watch you play. Isn't that right, Marcus?"

He looked up from his phone, which he'd been tapping at intermittently. "Yes, of course. What would you like to do instead? We could go bowling, or to the cinema. I could even take you shopping."

Shopping? That was his usual suck up activity, but it would be nice to have someone else's debit card take a battering for a while, and Carolyn was all for it. "You wanted some work clothes."

"Yeah. I guess." It was unlike Isla to show no enthusiasm for a trip to the shops but it didn't seem to have shifted her disappointment this time. "I really wanted you to meet everyone, though, and introduce you to my coach."

"There will be other times, sweetheart. Maybe your dad can

meet Jax at the disc..." Carolyn stopped herself and quickly corrected to, "Fundraiser."

"Remind me the date for that?" Marcus asked, picking up his phone from the table again. When Isla gave it, he squinted. "I'll do my best, but it's Nancy's birthday that weekend."

Nancy? Carolyn's interested piqued. Was this the woman he'd been seeing pre-divorce or a new one from the post-divorce period? It made little odds, either way, but she was curious. "I presume this is your girlfriend? If we can still say that at our age."

"Yes." He paused to tap again, then shuffled to put his phone in his pocket. "Sorry, I'm being rude. She's just been asking me how it's going. I think she's a little intimidated by my accomplished ex-wife."

"As well she might be," Sylvia called over from where she was dishing out their food.

Carolyn dismissed the thought with a waft of her hand. "Don't be ridiculous. What does she do?"

"She's recently retired but she used to be a palliative care nurse. When her husband passed, I think it became harder for her to do that kind of work."

Carolyn tilted her head. "She's a widow? I'm sorry to hear that." Not to mention a little surprised. She didn't know what she'd expected, but a retired widow wasn't it, for some reason. "It sounds like she's very accomplished herself, so I'm sure there's no need to feel intimidated."

"Thank you. She'll be glad to hear that. Are you seeing anyone at the moment?"

Carolyn glanced opposite, to where Isla was busily sending messages to Curtis, and wondered how she was going to react. "Yes. I am."

Isla's head pinged up and she grinned. "What? Are you? That's amazing! What's his name?"

Faltering, Carolyn fingered the rim of her wine glass. She didn't want to lie but she didn't know what to say. It didn't feel right to mention Jax's name when they'd agreed not to tell Isla anything yet, so she opted for, "John." Then she turned to look over her shoulder and shot Sylvia a smile when the kitchen area went suddenly silent.

"Yes, John," Sylvia agreed, nodding and going along with it. "I remember you mentioning." She carried over two plates, setting one in front of Isla and the other in front of Marcus. "How are things going?"

"It's only been a few weeks but we're having a wonderful time. I don't want to say too much and jinx it." Not to mention dig a giant hole. "We're having a romantic Valentine's dinner tomorrow night, though, so I expect that's all three of us with plans."

Isla still looked like she'd just heard the best news of her life. "Oh my God, I can't wait to meet him. I'm so happy for you."

Marcus was less enthused, but he raised his wine glass all the same. "Me too. I hope you enjoy your evening."

Carolyn thanked him, and then Sylvia for what looked like another fantastic meal. She wanted to divert the topic now, though, and found anything to talk about that didn't mean adding to her own lie. They exhausted school, briefly touched on Nancy's retirement activities, circled back to work for a while, and then finally landed on Isla's future plans as the post-meal coffee was poured.

"What do you mean you don't want to go to university?" Marcus asked when he tried to make course suggestions and found out that she may not apply.

"I might take the money Gran gave me and start a business," Isla replied with a shrug. "Or pay for some other sort of course."

"And what does your mother say about this?"

"Her mother says she needs to follow her own path. We can't

spend her whole childhood teaching her she's a capable young woman who can achieve anything she sets her mind to, only to then turn around and set conditions upon what's acceptable. Personally, I can't wait to see what she's going to do with her life."

Carolyn raised her mug and gave Isla a little nod, not wanting to cause any friction but also knowing she'd hold strong on this. She'd allowed Marcus to send Isla to private school until she turned sixteen and accepted there were some advantages. This was different, though. He had strong views when it came to higher education and Carolyn knew that a lot of them were about status and expectations, which she intended to balance out so that Isla could make up her own mind.

"University is expensive," Carolyn continued, pausing for a sip of coffee. "It's not like when we went. And if you're not pursuing a career that requires a degree, I can see why she'd choose differently. Better to be out in the world earning money and experience, but she hasn't made a definite decision yet. We'll just have to wait."

"I suppose," Marcus conceded, still frowning but choosing not to push the point. Instead, he finished his coffee and then looked up at the clock on the wall. It was almost nine. "Since we left dessert at Mum's, why don't I take everyone for something in town?"

Appreciating the offer but ready for their time together to be over, Carolyn placed a hand on her stomach. There was only so much small talk she could manage. "I can't eat another thing, but you go ahead. It's been good to see you."

Part of her truly meant that, but it had also reminded her of how much freer she felt now. He seemed marginally more relaxed, too. Even if he hadn't been quite able to erase his frown since hearing Isla's news.

Isla and Sylvia had already leapt up to fetch their coats at the mention of dessert, and they were fussing with them in the hallway.

Marcus pushed out his chair. "It's been good to see you, too. And the new place. I have to confess I was a little worried about how all of this would go. The move, I mean, and the two of you being so far away on your own."

Carolyn offered him a warmer smile than she'd managed earlier. She knew he hadn't meant it with any condescension. They still cared about one another. "I know. I worried a little about you, too, but I think it's safe to say we're all fine." She gestured to where Isla was hastily buttoning Sylvia's coat, the two of them bantering back and forth. "Isla has appreciated this trip. I know she misses you."

Marcus took a step around the table and squeezed Carolyn's shoulder, finally managing to return her smile. "Thank you for saying that. Take care and I'll see you tomorrow."

"See you tomorrow."

Carolyn waited for them all to leave and then drummed her fingers on the table as she considered her options. Jax would most likely still be out. Was it fair to call her, even though she'd offered? In the end, Carolyn opted to send a message. Then she set her phone back on the table and picked up her mug, taking another sip of coffee. Less than thirty seconds later, a call flashed up.

"Is it over already?" Jax asked slightly breathlessly.

"Yes. Marcus has taken Isla for dessert in town."

"He might struggle, the town centre is without power. We ended up at Jenna's house because the pub had to close. Your estate seems to be one of the only ones not affected."

Carolyn smiled. Not at anything in particular, but just to hear Jax's voice. "Where are you going now? It sounds like you're walking."

"I said I was going to the shop for supplies whilst they argue over a board game."

"That wouldn't happen to be the shop around the corner from *my* house?"

"You know, I think it is. Why don't you join us for a while? You haven't caught up properly with Abi yet and she's asked after you a few times."

Carolyn looked around all of the dirty dishes. She really should tidy them away. Then again, it would be nice to get out for a while before another day with Marcus tomorrow, so she found herself agreeing to meet Jax outside the shop.

## 17

## JAX

"I have a confession to make," was the first thing Carolyn said after they'd kissed each other hello in the glare of the shop sign, and Jax wondered briefly whether she was about to hear an admission of murder. There was never a pen or tape recorder around when you needed one.

"Are you only here for an alibi? Marcus isn't really buying dessert, is he? I knew it."

Carolyn chuckled and took Jax's hand as they wandered across the car park. "Dinner actually went well, even if we did end up moving it because Sylvia lost power. I think it was a turning point. Mainly small talk and chit chat, besides a tense moment when Isla announced her latest plans, but everyone behaved. I'm glad we can still spend time together for her benefit."

"I'm glad, too, but what's the confession?"

"It came up that I'm seeing someone, so you've become John temporarily. Are you mad? It's only until we're ready to tell Isla. I didn't know how else to get around it."

Jax laughed. She'd take John over Jacqueline, although she'd have preferred something edgier. "No, of course I'm not mad."

"Thank you for being so understanding."

They slowed down as they reached the corner because Jenna's house was in sight, and Jax wanted a little more time alone with Carolyn. The beer and biscuits she'd bought for her own alibi jangled together in the bag by her side, the cheap plastic cutting into her fingers, and she adjusted her grip.

"I think I quite enjoy being your dirty little secret," she mused, deciding to see the positive. "Besides, I know it's complicated. Marcus's opinion doesn't matter but he'll likely still have one, which impacts Isla. Plus we were in a grey area five years ago and it makes more sense to me why you might be nervous about that, after you explained he had an affair, but you haven't told her."

"Precisely. I hate all of these lies and half-truths. It's not the way I usually operate, I'm straight down the line."

Jax stopped and wrapped Carolyn in a hug, her bag clinking again. "It's all going to be okay, whatever happens. We'll work it out when we're ready. For now, let's just try to have some fun and forget about it. Well, as much fun as you can have when you're being forced to play Monopoly with the most competitive woman on earth."

Carolyn's laughter was muffled by the shoulder of Jax's coat where they were still hugging, until they both submitted to holding hands again and continuing down the road. "Jenna's grown on me. The more I learn about her, the more I like her, and the more I see similarities with Isla. Sylvia's given her some money she wants to put into a business. That's what Marcus was unhappy over."

"Funnily enough, that's how Jenna started her first business." She was working as a hairdresser but noticed how many upscale barbershops were popping up, so she did a barbering course and borrowed enough from her grandparents to open her own shop.

"Yes, Isla's already given me a full biography. She's loving her job and so full of enthusiasm, although I am a little embarrassed that I thought she had a crush on Jenna when it was just professional admiration."

"Don't be. I got some enjoyment out of teasing her."

Carolyn gave Jax's hand a little tug. "You're always teasing her. It's like watching a pair of kids sometimes."

Jax laughed again because that was just how she saw Jenna. Kind of like a kid sister. "She's had a lot of stuff to contend with and she doesn't have much family, which is relatable in a way because mine are all thousands of miles away. I love that she can walk into my house and feel comfortable enough to steal my food, but please don't tell her that or she'll start doing it more regularly and I don't think I can afford her cookie habit."

They reached Jenna's house and Jax let herself in, always finding the assault of Jenna's loud motivational posters a bit much. She slipped off her trainers and waited for Carolyn to remove her shoes, then poked her head around the living room door to find Jenna knelt by the coffee table setting out the Monopoly board and Abi opposite trying to decide which piece would be her counter.

"Look who I found," Jax said, causing neither of them to look up.

"Yeah, who?" Jenna asked absently as she engaged in her favourite activity—counting money.

"Carolyn. I ran into her at the shop. Do you mind if she joins us for a while? She's just sat through dinner with her ex and she needs some excitement but failing that, you two will probably do."

"Of course!" Abi showed enthusiasm at last, getting up and giving Carolyn a hug.

They chatted between themselves for a minute or two whilst Jax added her beers to the stash already in Jenna's fridge. Dry

January had obviously resulted in a very wet February. She also opened the packet of chocolate chip cookies she'd bought, and ate one whilst taking the tops off a couple of bottles.

When Carolyn had been furnished with a drink and a biscuit, they all gathered around the coffee table to begin their game. Jax was handed the boot, Carolyn got the ship, and Jenna insisted on the dog for reasons unknown.

"Guess who came into the new shop whilst I was there this week?" she asked, taking the first roll of the dice.

"The Pope?" Jax replied.

"No, although he thinks he's God's gift, so you're not far off."

"Greg?"

"Bingo. He wanted a Turkish shave. We got chatting and I asked if any of the lads were coming to our fundraiser because I know Isla circulated the poster, but he didn't seem to think so. It's a bit rich given his whole stance on closer cooperation and merging. If he really meant it, you'd think they'd make a little effort to integrate."

"It's academic," Jax reminded her for at least the millionth time, sick to death of hearing about this non-merger. "He's only interested in money for the boys club. I don't think he even understands any purpose for our committee beyond that."

"And have you ever explained it?" Carolyn asked, organising her money into piles.

"I've told him we're not merging."

"Yes, but have you ever actually explained to him why having our own committee is important? Greg only thinks in money, I agree, but from what I can gather of him, that doesn't make him the devil. He seems to really believe that this is best for both clubs, in order to make sure there are always funds and the facilities are maintained."

Jax huffed, partly because Jenna had already landed on a street she wanted to buy and partly because Carolyn had a point. "I bet he's never felt the tiniest bit marginalised in his whole life."

"No, I don't expect he has. But this is why I say that reacting to him doesn't help. It isn't making him understand and he won't get it on his own, because it's outside of his frame of reference. So tell him and see how it lands."

Jenna mouthed, "Yeah, Jax."

"Don't you start," Jax replied, trying not to laugh when Jenna stuck out her tongue. "I know she's got me totally whipped."

"And I'm still enjoying it. You know she's right, though?"

"Yeah, I do. I'll think about it and try to play nicely next time I see Greg."

They were *all* playing nicely until Carolyn was absolutely rinsing them. She'd amassed four whole colours, plus three of the train stations, and had put hotels wherever she could. The rest of the board was divvied up between the remaining three players and two of them were taking it with good grace, but Jenna got into a sulk over landing on Carolyn's Mayfair hotel after thinking she'd successfully run the gauntlet.

"It's not fair."

"How so?" Carolyn asked, holding out her palm for Jenna to hand over her remaining cash. "I thought you were a capitalist?"

"Yeah, Jenna," Jax teased, getting her back for earlier. She was very happy to have Carolyn beat them all, if it knocked Jenna down a few pegs.

"I am, but I'm starting to see a different perspective."

Abi laughed. "Oh, so your girlfriend almost losing her entire livelihood to a pandemic doesn't teach you anything, but losing at Monopoly does?"

"Hey! That's not fair. I know how tough it is when you don't have money." Jenna slapped down her last note and then folded her arms. "I've been there. And I've been watching it recently, seeing you struggle to get together enough money to move out of your mum and dad's house."

"It hasn't been much of a struggle for *you*, though, enjoying my mum's fry ups every weekend."

"I'll admit there are perks. I'm going to miss her cooking when you do finally move out. Maybe you should just have this place and we'll trade. Then she can cook for me every night of the week."

"Or maybe," Jax suggested, tired of hearing them bicker and circle around the same topic. They'd been doing it all night, before Carolyn arrived, with Jenna dropping increasingly unsubtle hints that she wanted Abi to live with her rather than finding a place of her own. "Abi could move in here and cook you fry ups whenever you want. Problem solved."

"Yes, that would also be very nice." Jenna chewed her thumbnail, all bravado dissolving until she looked like a nervous child. It happened on the odd occasion when something really mattered to her and she didn't know how to ask. Jax had seen it many times over.

"Do you actually want me to live here or are you joking?" Abi asked, rubbing the dice in her hands. As usual, she was far more upfront, which was exactly what Jenna needed when she was feeling vulnerable and in need of reassurance. "Because you know the minute you ask me, I'll have my bags packed in about a minute flat."

"Really?"

Their eyes met and Jax felt a warming feeling in her chest. It might be rising bile at how sickening they were, but it could just as easily be real affection or satisfaction that she'd once again played a part in advancing their relationship.

"You're welcome," she said, resting back against the sofa next to Carolyn. Their hands met on the carpet and she rubbed their little fingers together.

"Watch out or we'll start on you next," Jenna replied, beginning to pack away the board. She'd clearly decided there was no point in continuing now. "I ran into a shared ex of ours the other day. We had lunch. She asked after you."

There *was* no shared ex, Jax had only slept with her a couple of times, and she shook her head. "You really have been busy with people I have no desire to spend time talking about, haven't you? For the record, she's *your* ex-girlfriend, not mine." She hooked her finger around Carolyn's, hoping to reassure her. "It was a fling. Mutually agreed. I hope she's okay, though."

"She is. She's also still single. Maybe you should've made more of a go of it."

"Absolutely not. Leave this alone."

"Why? She's your age, successful, attractive." Jenna missed out distant, cold, and ruthless. "I don't know why you're insistent on having these flings that don't go anywhere and telling me there's no one you'd have a relationship with, when you won't even try with people who could actually be good for you."

Carolyn withdrew her hand and tugged on her chain. Jenna really needed to leave this, now.

"Honestly, buddy. Drop it. We were never compatible like that." Jax reached into her pocket and pulled out her phone, looking for a distraction and finding one. "The game is off. Pitch is waterlogged."

"Does that mean you could help move in all of Abi's stuff tomorrow if we need you to?" Jenna asked, her fingers slipping around Abi's as they both looked at each other like someone was about to be eaten alive.

"Tomorrow? Sure. I guess I'm free now."

"Great. Nine AM?"

This was Jenna all over and Jax smiled at Carolyn, who'd dropped her chain and looked more relaxed. "Shall we leave them to it? I'll walk you home." They all said their goodbyes and when they reached the end of the drive, Jax had her hand back around Carolyn's. "Would you ever live with someone again?"

She considered for a second or two as they ambled again, trying to eke out their time together. "Yes, I think so. But I'm very accustomed to having my own space, and managing my own schedule. I would struggle to become so entwined with someone that my every spare minute was spent in their company. However much I loved them."

"Same. I can see why a complete merge works for those guys," Jax replied, thumbing over her shoulder. "Neither has properly lived with anyone yet, so it's new and exciting, and they both want a family someday."

"Jenna didn't live with this... *ex*?'"

The way Carolyn said 'ex' made Jax inwardly cringe. She might be the one committing murder tonight. "I'm sorry Jenna brought that up. It was just a silly fling. A couple of nights that we both agreed would be nothing more than a little fun."

Carolyn let out a small sigh. "I was under no illusion that you slept with other people, but I have to admit to being little jealous. You haven't done anything wrong, though, and you don't need to apologise. I'm sure Jenna wouldn't have been trying to set you up with people in front of me if you could say something, which is mainly my fault, so I can hardly be upset at having to listen to it."

"No, even Jenna isn't that insensitive. You know that the way I feel about you is entirely different, though, don't you?" Abi wasn't the only one more than happy to make their intentions crystal clear. "I don't see you as a fling or just a bit of casual fun and if I hadn't been serious about wanting to explore our feelings for each other, I wouldn't have said it. I'm straight down the line, too. Well, a little bent and wiggly all down the line, I've never been straight..."

"I do know that but thank you for saying it." Carolyn

laughed and pulled her coat a little tighter around herself. "And thank you for inviting me tonight. I really enjoyed being let into your normal day to day life and spending impromptu time with the people who matter to you."

"You see Jenna and Abi every week."

"I know but that's at the club where I'm Chairwoman Carolyn. Tonight, I was... Friend Carolyn. It was nice to get a casual invite."

It would be even nicer if she was there as Girlfriend Carolyn, and Jax smiled to herself for thinking that as she reluctantly walked Carolyn home.

## 18

## CAROLYN

Carolyn fiddled with at least the third pair of earrings, then checked her reflection in the gleaming door of the oven. "Do I look okay?"

"Relax, mother," Isla reassured her, placing a hand on Carolyn's shoulder and also staring into the oven. "They look fine."

Fine? That wasn't a good word. She wanted to look better than fine tonight. It was the first time she'd been so excited for Valentine's Day in more years than she could count, outwardly writing it off as a Hallmark holiday whilst internally wishing she had someone special to share it with. Now she did, and she'd allowed herself to descend further into a swirl of romantic expectation than even her teenage daughter. She'd bought an expensive box of Belgian chocolates to remind Jax of their trip and also indulged in new underwear. So far, the night had run to about a hundred pounds, so it needed to be better than 'fine'.

"You will be alright tonight?" she checked for the umpteenth time. "You'll make sure you're home by eleven and at school on time without me here to nag you?"

Isla rolled her eyes dramatically and then her face settled

back to an amused smile. "I've never seen you like this before. It's kind of adorable."

"What am I being like?" Carolyn asked, finally stepping away from the oven and deciding that the earrings would have to do. She was running out of time to change them, and she still hadn't grilled Isla about her own date.

"I don't know." Isla picked up a packet of cereal from the central island and flung a handful into her mouth. "Happy. Excited. And you've sort of jacked your boobs up too."

Stunned by the last comment and the casual nature of its delivery, Carolyn frowned down at her cleavage. Had she gone too far with the push up bra? It wasn't padded because she needed no help in that department, but there had been a definite lift and pushing together.

Seeming to sense her concern, Isla laughed and offered more reassurance. "You look fantastic. Honestly. John is a very lucky guy. When do I get to meet him?"

Carolyn winced. "It's too soon."

"Will you at least tell me where you met?"

After brief consideration, Carolyn had to say no. She could hardly tell Isla it was someone involved with the football club because it narrowed down the options considerably. "You're very nosy. Shouldn't I be the one asking you questions?"

Isla threw more cereal into her mouth and shrugged. "Fire away."

"Where is Curtis taking you tonight?"

"What makes you think *he's* taking me anywhere? I thought you were a feminist. Maybe I've made all of our V-Day plans."

Carolyn laughed. She shouldn't be at all surprised by her daughter's response. "Fine, where are you taking him?"

"I don't know. A bus shelter maybe. Or the park. Where do teenagers have unprotected sex these days?"

Grabbing the box of cereal so that it spilled onto the floor,

Carolyn tried her best to glare rather than laughing again. Not least because of where she'd been kissing Jax a few short weeks ago. "You're doing nothing to help my nerves, young lady."

Isla frowned. "Nerves? Why are you nervous?"

That was a good question and Carolyn desperately wished she had someone to hash it out with, but it couldn't be Isla. They shared a lot, but she didn't need to hear how her mum was worrying over falling for someone new so quickly. Or falling for someone *old* again.

Instead, Carolyn crouched to collect the cocoa pops littering her tiles and tried to remind herself that her feelings were good ones, and it was a welcome change from feeling nothing at all. "You aren't a little nervous about your date with Curtis?"

"No, not really. We always have a good time so what's there to be nervous about?"

Carolyn smiled. "That's true. And I always have a good time with my person, too, so I don't suppose I should be nervous either."

"Aw." Isla pouted and cocked her head. "Your person. That's so sweet."

As Carolyn straightened up and tossed the handful of cocoa pops onto a plate by the sink, she tried to work out what Isla had found to coo over. Then she clocked the implication of what she'd said in trying to dodge the John lie and disguise Jax's pronouns. "No, well, I didn't mean that they're *my* person. It's not... we haven't talked about even officially being a couple yet but..." She placed her hands on her hips so she couldn't keep using them to dig this hole. "I just mean, I like them very much but it's still very early."

"Sounds like you need to lock it down and make things exclusive."

Exclusive? She hadn't really considered that, and it made Carolyn's stomach churn. They'd agreed it wouldn't be a one-night stand but that didn't mean Jax wasn't still having those with other people. "Oh god."

"What?"

"You think they're seeing other people?"

Isla's eyes widened. "How should I know? But maybe. I mean, there's no reason they shouldn't if you haven't had that discussion."

"Oh *god*," Carolyn repeated.

Isla placed a reassuring hand on her shoulder. "Don't start panicking again. I think it's great if you've met someone you can see a future with. Like... I'm happy for you. I hope you do make it official and that it all works out and that John *is* your person. Just say how you feel."

Carolyn smiled again. "When did you start dishing out advice to me?"

"I love that I know more about something than you do. It's made my life to be honest." Isla snatched her box of cereal back. "I'm totally here for this. You deserve to find your knight in shining armour and live happily ever after."

That was sweet, but something new had just troubled Carolyn, and she couldn't help throwing out a bit of her own advice. She didn't want Isla to think that forever was the only goal. She didn't want her to stay in anything because she'd promised forever, even if it wasn't what she wanted anymore. And she certainly didn't want her to judge the quality of her relationships based on how long they lasted.

"I will say how I feel," Carolyn said, finally letting her hands drop by her sides. "But I really don't care if we're forever. I don't need forever, or a knight in shining armour, or a fairytale ending. What I need is someone who supports me and makes me happy for the time we are together. Someone who's an equal partner. Please don't ever think you need another person to complete you. You're whole on your own, not a half seeking someone else to fill a void. Relationships can be wonderful and life enhancing but the only person responsible for your happiness is you. Don't give it away to someone else."

Isla looked a little dumbstruck for a second, then her eyes darted around the kitchen. "Wow. That suddenly got deep."

"Yes, and it'll get deeper if you have unprotected sex with that boy in a bus shelter."

Isla laughed and accepted a peck on the cheek. "Have a great time tonight."

"You too."

Carolyn hurried towards the hallway to find her coat and bag, deciding that Isla was right and it probably was about time they had a proper discussion about what was happening between them beyond 'not a fling or casual fun'. She didn't quite know where to start, though, so opted for the truth.

"I love being with you," she said a little breathlessly when Jax opened her front door.

It seemed to take her aback, because Jax shook her head slightly. "I love being with you too. But have I missed something?"

"I just felt like telling you." Carolyn smiled as she kissed the worried look from Jax's face. Then she dropped her bag in the entrance hallway, next to the rack of Jax's various sports shoes, and slipped off her coat. Before she could say any more, she was halted by Jax's arms winding around her from behind.

"You look so incredibly sexy," Jax whispered against her ear, which was exposed because Carolyn had decided to sweep her hair up for tonight. "I just felt like telling you *that*."

Carolyn had thrown her coat over a peg and begun to laugh but was halted when kisses travelled down her neck, her breath hitching. Maybe there would be more advantages to an up-do than just showing off her earrings. "If you keep kissing me there, we're not going to make it to dinner."

"That's okay with me."

"It's not okay with me!" Becky shouted through from the living room, causing Carolyn to jump and clutch the arms still wrapped around her middle. She'd presumed they were alone.

"Don't worry," Jax called back. "I'll wait long enough for you to finally decide what you're wearing tonight." Then she lowered her voice. "Becky has her first date since the breakup and she's a little nervous."

Carolyn nodded her relief and crept forwards with Jax still attached to her, until they were both in the living room doorway. It was good to know she wasn't the only one. "You look great," she reassured Becky, who was sat on the sofa rapidly applying makeup whilst squinting into a handheld mirror. Her hair was bright pink all over today, which was possibly a nod to the occasion, and she had on a black dress not dissimilar to Carolyn's except far shorter and accompanied by a pair of hefty Doc Marten boots. "Do you want a hand?"

"Yes please," Becky replied, turning her head to reveal heavy and uneven eyeliner. "My hands are shaking so much that I'm going to end up repeating my goth phase if I keep trying to correct."

Carolyn tapped Jax's arm to get her to release her grip and sent her off to check on dinner, with only vague protests. Then she joined Becky on the sofa and cupped her cheeks gently, tilting each eye to the light and trying to assess the severity of the situation. "I think you might need to wipe it off and start again, sorry."

Becky huffed and slumped back into the sofa, closing her eyes. "Maybe I should just cancel. I don't know what I was thinking agreeing to a Tinder date on Valentine's Day. It's too much pressure and I've already made a fool of myself."

"How have you made a fool of yourself?"

Becky peeked through one eye. "Letting you see me like this. You must think I'm a complete idiot."

Carolyn chuckled, hoping it conveyed the warmth she felt and not any derision. "I don't think you're an idiot at all. It's difficult to put yourself out there again. Believe me. I'm learning it's a minefield."

"Yes, but you've got Jax, who's spent the whole day prepping the perfect evening for you and who would still think you were the best thing on the planet, even if you looked like... well," Becky paused, pointing both fingers at her own face and finally reopening her eyes. "Like this."

The thought both warmed and reassured Carolyn, but she had to stay focused on Becky for a little while longer. "Come on, now. You're a beautiful young woman and you deserve all of that too. Try to give tonight a chance and if it isn't fun, you'll just come home and chalk it up as another anecdote."

"Yeah, except I promised I *wouldn't* come home tonight and ruin Jax's plans. I don't want to cause her any hassle when I really need to live here right now."

"Jax isn't going to want you to stay out all night! Believe me, she'll only want you to be safe and have a good time. And please don't compare your night to ours. You must remember that Jax and I have known each other for a long time, even though there was a break in the middle. It's not the same as meeting someone for the first time from a dating profile, and even so I spent far too long earlier this evening worrying about who else she might be seeing and fussing over what I'm wearing. Give yourself a break."

Becky nodded and even managed a little smile. She blew out a deep breath and then shuffled forwards on the sofa before hoisting herself up. "Okay. Thanks, Carolyn. I really needed that."

"You're welcome. Any time."

After Becky had made her way out to the hallway and

ascended the stairs, Carolyn tidied the lids back onto her various make up pots and sticks, then brushed the excess foundation from the coffee table into her hand. She carried it to the kitchen and bashed her palms over the pedal bin, feeling a little more relaxed and trying to work out what was on the menu.

"Italian?" she asked, needing only one gentle sniff to recognise the scent of basil and tomato.

Jax was sat at the table, staring intently at the page of a recipe book and running her finger down a list of instructions. "Mhm," she mumbled, pausing to read to the end of the line and then pushing out her chair. "It seemed traditional and romantic, but don't tell Jenna. She thinks I'm devoid of all emotion just because I hate romcoms and can't stand over-sentimental mush."

Carolyn laughed and slipped onto her lap, hooking an arm around Jax's shoulder and tousling her hair. She'd worn it down, and had even applied a touch of makeup. Unlike Becky's, her blue eyes popped and Carolyn stroked the feint lines tracking to her temples. "I don't like either of those things either. I'm far too much of a realist." She dropped a gentle kiss on Jax's lips. "But I do think it's very sweet how much effort you've gone to. Becky said you'd spent all day planning our evening."

"Yeah, I heard your whole conversation. Thanks for giving her a pep talk. I know she's been missing her mum a lot lately so I expect she really did appreciate it. I'll make sure she knows I wasn't suggesting she had to go and pimp herself out for my benefit."

Was that how everyone saw her? The mum? The thought made Carolyn chuckle again. "Maybe I'll hire myself out as a surrogate parent. First Jenna and now Becky. I don't seem to be able to help myself. Not sure it fits the sexy image I was going for tonight, though."

Jax hooked her finger into the front of Carolyn's dress,

pulling it down ever so slightly to reveal the lace of her new bra. "I love how caring and nurturing you are. I also don't think you need to worry about anyone seeing you as mumsy when you look like this."

Gratified that Jax had noticed her new purchase, Carolyn couldn't resist a wicked smile. "Oh, that's right. I'd forgotten how keen you are on that part of my body."

"Like hell you had."

Jax dipped her head, brushing her lips ever so gently over the exposed skin of Carolyn's cleavage. It was an exquisite tease and Carolyn wanted her to continue but Jax stopped. "I heard the other thing you said, too. You know I'm not seeing anyone else, right?"

Carolyn nodded. She trailed her hand from Jax's chin, down her throat to the top button of the black shirt she was wearing. Then she flicked it open and stroked under the fabric, her fingertips delving under Jax's bra. "Yes, I know. We hadn't ever officially talked about it, though, and then Isla got in my head."

"It's very hard to have a serious conversation with you whilst you're doing that."

Laughing, Carolyn rubbed her nose along Jax's. "I'm sorry. I'm so intensely attracted to you and it's steamrolling my usually sensible brain. Things have been going so fast between us and I think I got a bit unbalanced tonight."

"I have to admit it's a bit scary being back where I was and knowing you could break my heart again. And this time it would be worse because I know what it's like to be with you and I don't want it to stop."

The thought of breaking Jax's heart again made Carolyn's hurt. "I'm safe to assume we're an item, then?"

Becky cleared her throat in the doorway. "I was going to say have a good night, but it looks like you already are. Also, I don't think you need to worry about that. The only person with genuine romantic problems is me."

Carolyn laughed and slipped off Jax's lap. "Sorry, I didn't realise you were there." She gave Becky's shoulder a quick rub. "Please try to have a good time and just in case, we'll save you a chocolate."

"Speak for yourself," Jax countered, getting up and wrapping her arms back around Carolyn's waist to hug her from behind again. "But no, you definitely don't need to worry about whether we're an item." She pressed a reassuring kiss to Carolyn's temple. "I only want you... and chocolate."

Becky laughed and made her way to the door. "Good luck with her hormones!"

## 19

## JAX

As soon as they'd finished their meal, Jax quickly decamped them to the sofa with a bottle of red and Carolyn's box of assorted truffles, sending some gentle acoustic music to the speaker and dimming the lights.

"For someone who doesn't do romance, this is very romantic," Carolyn pointed out as she hitched her feet into Jax's lap.

The log burner roared in the background, filling the room with warmth, and yet she shivered. Jax pulled the blanket from the back of the sofa and draped it over Carolyn's legs. She left her feet exposed, though, rubbing them through a pair of sheer tights.

"I said I don't do over-sentimental mush. Tacky cards. Bears with hearts sewn to them. Over-priced lingerie. It's just rubbish and it doesn't mean anything."

"I agree. Mostly. The way to my heart is definitely through this foot rub."

"Really? I thought it would be via those chocolates," Jax replied, nodding to the box they'd left on the coffee table. She'd been craving chocolate all day and was still desperate to get her hands on them. "Guess I'll just have to eat them all."

"Nice try." Carolyn leant over to pick up the box, then settled back into position and pulled off the lid. "I wonder how Becky's date is going."

Jax hadn't wondered about it once, she'd been too preoccupied with her own, which was going spectacularly. The ragu had been delicious. The conversation was stimulating. And the profiteroles she'd bought for dessert because there was no way in hell she was attempting to make them had been a triumph.

"Does it ever occur to you to think of yourself for a while?" she asked as she watched Carolyn shuffle again but this time to peek at her phone, no doubt to check Isla hadn't texted. "I meant it when I said I love how caring you are earlier, but maybe you could do with a little TLC too. In between healing the sick, smashing single parenting, dishing out advice, and all the other very important stuff you do."

Carolyn chuckled as she selected a chocolate and bit off the top, holding out the other half for Jax to eat. "How do you take care of yourself?"

"Well, if I had a hot tub, I'd definitely start there."

"Of course you would. And I expect that if I was going in, you'd come too, just to make sure I truly relaxed."

"It's a service I'm happy to provide." Just like the foot rub, because Carolyn was perpetually moaning about how much they hurt. "I also got you a gift that I think is going to help."

"You got me a gift?" Carolyn picked up another chocolate, this time slotting the entire thing in Jax's mouth. "But I thought you said Valentine's gifts were rubbish?"

They were, but this wasn't strictly Valentine's related. It was something Jax had ordered on the way back from Brussels and forgotten about until the box arrived earlier that day.

"Hang on," she replied, tapping Carolyn's feet and encouraging her to lift them. After wriggling off the sofa, Jax ran upstairs to collect the package, still in its plastic postal wrapping.

"I know you won't give up your heels, and I'm not asking you to, but this is just something to give your feet an occasional rest." Jax had begun tearing off the packaging as she re-entered the living room. She revealed an orange box, and from it she pulled a wad of tissue paper, followed by a pair of Nike Air Max. She threw the wrapping on the floor, then held up each shoe. "Comfy sneakers. I went for black because I figured that was classier than white."

Carolyn laughed and slid the chocolate box back onto the coffee table. "Sometimes I forget you're American and then you keep saying things like *sneakers*. That's very sweet, though. Thank you."

"You're welcome." Jax knelt by the sofa and slotted them onto Carolyn's feet.

"What do you think?" Carolyn asked, wiggling them alternately and tilting her head. "Do *sneakers* go with my dress?"

"I think it's a hot look, yes. Very sexy."

"Very sexy, huh?" Carolyn pulled the blanket off and discarded it back over the top of the sofa. Then she took a handful of Jax's shirt and drew her forward. "How sexy?"

"What's the highest number?"

Carolyn hummed as she considered. "Ninety-three."

"Then you're ninety-three sexy," Jax whispered close to Carolyn's mouth. Possibly even a ninety-four right now, because she was always perpetually aroused at this time of the month. Jax crawled over Carolyn's body, pushing her back into the sofa. When they kissed, she tasted of smooth chocolate and the sweetness burst on Jax's tongue. She had exactly what she craved right now, bar one thing. "Shall we take this upstairs? You know how I love our sofa time but I'm not sure how long Becky's date will last and I was thinking maybe we could revisit our Belgium trip in a few other ways."

"Yes?" Carolyn wore a lascivious smile, gripping around the

back of Jax's head and pulling her down for another kiss. It was hard, her touch a little rough, and it made Jax's nipples stand to attention. "I take it you're experiencing hormonal horn today."

"Is that a medical term?"

"No, it's a personal one."

"Sorry, I'll try to behave."

Jax went to climb off but Carolyn gripped her shirt to pull her back down. She sucked Jax's bottom lip and bit it gently, and Jax felt her hips buck involuntarily. Then Carolyn rubbed her nose along Jax's seductively before kissing her again.

"I showed you mine last weekend," she whispered, tousling the hair at the nape of Jax's neck. "So maybe it's time you shared some of your toys. What do you think?"

At the reminder of watching Carolyn pleasure herself on the bed in Brussels, instructing when she wanted Jax to join in—mostly to suck her nipples—Jax let out a low growl. She could do with Carolyn taking charge again tonight but this time, it was entirely selfish, because she was so turned on that she could think of little else but letting go and having Carolyn pin her to the bed. Given how open she seemed, Jax decided to just make her thoughts known.

"I am definitely up for showing you my toys. I want you to use them on me, though, tonight. Full audience participation. Are you up for that?"

Carolyn's lip curled at the side again and she raked her fingertips down Jax's back, sending a shiver right through her spine. "You really are hot, aren't you?"

"Uhuh. I love when we tease but right now..."

Raising her lips so close to Jax's ear that her tongue flicked over it and sent out another shiver, Carolyn whispered, "You can say it if you just want a rough fuck." It almost sent Jax's hips into convulsions of desire because she rarely used language like that, and Carolyn let out a deep, throaty chuckle, still close to Jax's ear. "Do you enjoy it when I talk to you like that?"

*Mmm* was all Jax could get out by way of reply because they were back to kissing, and Carolyn's fingertips were digging into her ass this time. The kiss was broken, though, when Carolyn reached between them and pushed Jax up with a palm on the middle of her chest.

"We're going upstairs," she said, kicking off her new trainers and pulling her hair out of it's up do. She shook her head so that it cascaded over her shoulders and then ran a hand through it, before standing and making her way for the stairs. "Are you coming?"

Seeing Carolyn all wild had brought her a little closer, yes, so Jax agreed. She followed up the stairs until they reached the landing and Carolyn didn't know which door to go through, pushing open the one on the far right. Jax had already changed the sheets, drawn the curtains across, and left a couple of candles on the night stands, so she went to light them rather than switching on the harsh overhead light.

They burned with cedarwood and jasmine, which was apparently sensual, but right now all Jax could smell was Carolyn's luxury perfume as she slipped out of her dress and the fabric wafted the scent throughout the entire room. Carolyn stood in black lace underwear, the bra lifting her breasts into an exquisite kiss, and Jax wanted her mouth around them. She was stopped, though, when Carolyn laid a palm in the middle of her chest again.

"Not so fast. Take your clothes off."

Jax unbuttoned her shirt while Carolyn watched. When she was also down to only her underwear, she gave Carolyn a searching look, wondering if she'd meant everything. Carolyn nodded and she unhooked her bra too, then wriggled out of her briefs.

Carolyn paused for a beat, then closed the gap between them. She wrapped her arms low around Jax's waist and started the kiss slowly, nibbling from one side of her mouth to the other. All the while, she made a light trail over Jax's lower back with her fingertips, leaving her buttocks rough with goosebumps. She gradually kissed with more intensity, her tongue slipping into Jax's mouth, the taste of chocolate lingering. Her touches became harder, too. She dug her fingers into Jax's ass to bring them closer, the rough lace of her bra slipping against Jax's sensitive breasts until they were punding and she was struggling to maintain the kiss because she was breathing so hard.

Carolyn dropped to Jax's neck so that she could catch her breath, but it didn't help. She sucked her way up to the base of Jax's jaw with greater pressure until she'd surely left her own mark this time, not that either of them cared. They were lost in each other now, stood beside the bed clawing each other closer and creating an urgency that was making the entire lower half of Jax's body throb with pleasure and anticipation. She could feel herself growing warmer and wetter, her internal walls pulsing as if Carolyn were inside her already.

The desire to touch Carolyn was becoming overwhelming, too, and Jax let out a breathy moan as she raked her hand between Carolyn's legs, finding her hair damp. Carolyn grasped Jax's wrist and wrestled it above their heads, then pushed her back onto the bed.

"Where are your toys?" she asked, her chest flushed so red that it was visible even in the low light of the candles. "Are you happy for me to use something other than my fingers?"

The answer to that was "very happy" but Jax didn't have time to reply because she was busy opening the larger bottom drawer of her nightstand. She pulled out two satin bags, holding a mixture of dildos and vibrators. "Take your pick. You're in charge."

Carolyn let out the dirty laugh Jax had heard in her hallway the first night they'd slept together, and it made her stomach do a series of somersaults. She rested back on her elbows whilst Carolyn inspected the stash.

She held up a long, thick black dildo. "This is ambitious. Really?"

"It's fine with a run up."

"Noted. I'll put that in the same category as fisting."

Jax was the one to laugh this time. "You're a dark horse."

"Am I? I'd always considered it fairly run of the mill but I suppose that's a very personal viewpoint. We all enjoy different things and have our own boundaries." She held up a double-ender Jax had bought to experiment with but soon discarded when she struggled to make it work. "I'm not so sure about this. I think I'm a one cock per play sort of girl."

"One cock per play?" Jax shook her head, once again wondering who the person was, standing before her giving opinions on sex toys. "I love this side of you."

"I still don't know why you're surprised that I enjoy sex and I'm happy to talk about it. Do I really come across as so buttoned up?"

A little, actually, but it seemed unkind to say. "It's more just that this *is* your first time having sex with a woman, and I have to admit that whilst I absolutely don't think it means you should be having some huge epiphany, I did expect you might want to take things a little slower. Not that I'm complaining at all."

Carolyn shrugged. "I've felt very comfortable with you. And you make me feel very desired. Very sexy. Very able to be open and try things. I'm having a lot of fun." She held up a ridged red dildo. Then she bit her lip for a second before asking, "Would you like me to show you one of my favourite positions?"

"Is that a trick question?"

"I'm just not sure how it'll work with me holding this, so you might have to go with the flow."

"Do you want to use it with the harness? Then you could wear it?" Jax swallowed hard and tried to stop the gymnasts in her stomach, who were having a great time at the thought of Carolyn wearing her favourite red dildo. She hoped desperately that the answer was yes.

Carolyn's lewd smile suggested Jax was about to get exactly what she wanted. She looked into the bag, though, and it faded. "You might have to help me out here."

Jax pushed herself up and wriggled forward, then reached into the drawer to pull it out. She loosened the straps and took the dildo from Carolyn, slotting it into the front. "Just step in, tighten, and you're good to go."

Carolyn did as instructed and then turned to admire herself in the full-length mirror in the corner of the room. "What does it say that I feel very powerful right now? Is it horribly anti-feminist of me?"

"I'm sure there are plenty who'd argue it is but so what? Just because you're queer, doesn't mean you don't necessarily like some of the same sexual acts. I find getting fucked, or fucking someone else, with a strap brings out this really primal urgency. I think it's the contact, and the hip movement, and..."

Jax trailed off and growled because now all she could think about was Carolyn's thighs against hers and their hips thrusting together. She stood and pressed against Carolyn from behind, hands raking over her stomach and the tops of her legs. Then she tightened the straps a little more because she could see they'd end up too loose, whilst Carolyn considered and decided, "I don't really care what it is, I just know this is a turn on."

"That makes two of us."

Jax cupped Carolyn's breasts but was quickly stopped, once again, when Carolyn turned and backed her onto the bed. Then she crawled on and rested back on her heels, the dildo flopping into her lap.

"Back into me," she instructed, I want us where we were a second ago but with you in front.

Jax could see where this was going and obliged. She mirrored Carolyn, wriggling into position until she was sat in Carolyn's lap. Carolyn's breasts pressed into Jax's back and the dildo was cool under her ass cheek, stopping her from putting down her full weight.

Carolyn raised them both up as she took hold of the dildo. When Jax sat again, it slipped inside and she let out a long, low moan as each of the ridges popped over her entrance.

"It might take me a second to get the hang of this," Carolyn whispered as she pulled Jax's legs a little wider. Then she ran her hands up to cup both of Jax's breasts as she tilted her hips, the ridges having a similar effect in the opposition direction.

"I don't know, you seem to be handling it pretty well."

Carolyn went slow at first, finding a rhythm, but Jax didn't mind. She enjoyed every sensation, including the feeling of Carolyn's soft breasts massaging into her back. As she found her confidence, Carolyn thrusted a little faster, grunting as she flicked her thumbs over Jax's swollen nipples. Then she dropped her hands to Jax's waist and pulled her down onto the shaft, her touches becoming firmer and more urgent.

Jax hooked a hand behind Carolyn's neck, twisting for a kiss. When she withdrew, it was to briefly run her fingers over her own clit, so inflamed that it ached.

Carolyn took a handful of the hair at the nape of Jax's neck, like she often did, but this time she gripped it at the roots and tugged back gently, sending prickles all the way over the top of Jax's head and down her back. She did it again, twisting slightly so that she could suck down hard on Jax's neck.

Jax was burning up, sweat running down the middle of her

chest and heat flickering across the tops of her thighs. It was tough to tell which of the erogenous zones Carolyn was attending to had most stoked the fire, but she could feel it ripping through her, and let out a low, rumbling moan when she was pushed forward onto all fours.

The dildo slipped out momentarily, giving Jax just enough time to grip the sheets in her fists as Carolyn slid fully inside her. She arched her back and let Carolyn well and truly fuck her, then buried her face into the soft duvet when fingertips stroked her vulva, Carolyn's palm then giving her something to rock into as she was engulfed, the orgasm exploding through her in all directions.

She let out another low groan as it radiated to every extremity, the ridges popping slowly one last time as they were withdrawn, allowing her hips to fall forward.

She lay completely motionless, until Carolyn cut through the sound of their heavy breathing. "How are the hormones doing? Has that helped any?"

Jax lifted her head and let out a slightly delirious laugh. "Much better. Thanks."

"It's hard to tell given they're both red, but I think there's a little blood."

"Shit, sorry."

When Jax rolled over quickly, Carolyn laughed. "You don't need to look so worried. I've seen far worse. May I remind you what I've done for a living for the past three decades?"

"I know but that's... work." Rubbing the pain in her abdomen, which was starting to take hold, Jax sat up.

"Are you okay?" Carolyn had begun to loosen the harness.

"Yeah, but I won't be in about twenty minutes." It always happened like this and Jax knew that she was in for a few hours of agony.

"If I wasn't here, what would you be doing to make yourself feel better tonight?"

"I'd be eating chocolates in my PJs whilst watching Match of the Day under the blanket. I still haven't seen Saturday night's episode because I was out most of the weekend."

"Then that's what we're doing for the rest of the evening. Chocolates and cuddling are both activities I'm more than happy to indulge in. You may just need to lend me something to wear, and I draw the line at supporting Chelsea."

The thought of Carolyn in flannel pyjamas caused Jax to let out a burst of laughter. "You're going to slob out on the sofa with me?"

"I'm not only in this relationship for sex, you know." When Jax smiled at her, Carolyn frowned. "What?"

"Nothing. I just loved you calling this a relationship."

## 20

# CAROLYN

Carolyn peered through the barbershop window, a hand shielding her eyes from the glare. She was interested to see where Isla worked and it was as she imagined from the detailed accounts. Isla was stood behind a rough wooden reception desk at the back of the room with a phone pressed to her ear, looking every bit the professional. Until she waved, that was, and held up her fingers to signal she'd be two minutes.

They were spending their evening doing a little shopping so that they could spend some proper time together and because Carolyn wanted to find a dress for the fundraiser. It might be nice to wear something that wasn't her black one for a change, and maybe add some colour. She had other options but they were mainly work clothes and she didn't have a lot for going out anymore.

"I thought I'd treat us to dinner," she said as Isla finally appeared on the high street, still wrestling with her coat. "What do you say? We've both been a little caught up with other things recently."

"If you're paying, I'm always in. Can we get Japanese?"

"Since when do you like Japanese?"

"I don't know that I do, but Curtis keeps going on about how much he loves Katsu and I want to try it."

Carolyn liked Katsu so she had no objection. She was also enjoying all of Isla's anecdotes about Curtis and happy to indulge her. He seemed, from all Isla had said, like a decent and level-headed kid. She didn't take after her mother at seventeen, that was for sure, and it was a relief to find that she was unlikely to be thrown from any motorbikes or get caught smoking pot behind the school bike sheds.

They made their way to the station and caught a train into London, connecting by Tube to Oxford Circus. When they reached the bustle of Oxford Street, it was still only five-thirty, and they had a good two hours of shopping time.

Even in the early evening, there were throngs of people milling around the shops, and an hour in, Carolyn was losing patience.

"I'm not sure this was the best way to relax," she said, rifling through a rack of dresses and seeing nothing she liked. All the while, the sound of a woman screaming at her toddler cut through her ears like a knife. "And I'm losing the will to live, as well as any hope that I'll find something."

"What about this?" Isla popped up over the top of the rail holding a royal blue jumpsuit. "It's even team colours. Am I a genius, or what?"

Carolyn had to admit that she liked it, even if Isla had gone off-piste and not technically delivered her a dress. "The jury's out," she said, rubbing the fabric between her fingers and finding it was good quality. "But I'll definitely try."

They scuttled past the screaming woman and into the changing rooms. This time the sensory assault came from the overhead lights and the piles of clothes dotted around. The store assistant looked equally frazzled and as if she might be found rocking in a corner later, and Carolyn smiled at her so she knew she wasn't alone.

Isla waited outside the door whilst Carolyn changed, then wolf whistled when she came out. "That's hot. You should totally get it."

"Do you think?" Carolyn made an adjustment so that her bra wasn't showing. The jumpsuit was cut into a low V, which was her usual style because it showed off her best asset, but that didn't mean she wanted to give too much away. Then she turned to get a view of her side profile in the full length mirror, pleasantly surprised. "I'm going to agree. This is a departure but a good one."

Isla did a little fist pump. "Amazing. I think you look *so* good in that. John's eyes are going to pop out of his head."

"Yes. John. I'm wearing it for me, though, not someone else."

Carolyn wanted to get them off that topic but it was tough because Isla had probed for information at various points since dinner with Marcus, and she wouldn't let it drop. They were going to have to tell her, before the lie got out of hand, and Carolyn planned to run the idea past Jax at the match tomorrow. Now they were official, it made sense. That didn't stop her from feeling a little nervous, though, and Carolyn was unsure which bit was the most terrifying.

"Yeah, totally for you," Isla agreed, fiddling with a loose thread. "But, you know, if he *happens* to also think you look smoking hot, that's a bonus."

"That's true." Carolyn slipped back into the cubicle and unzipped the jumpsuit, changing into her regular clothes. "Is there anywhere else you want to look or are you ready to eat now?"

"Eat. I didn't have time for lunch today so I'm starving."

"You didn't get a lunch break?"

"I did, but I used it to sort some fundraiser stuff and forgot to eat. Executive burnout is such a plague in our modern age."

Carolyn laughed. "Yes, it's tough at the top. Is there anything you need me to do before next weekend?"

"I don't think so. Curtis asked his older brother to DJ, so that's sorted now, and the only other thing I personally want to know is whether Dad is coming. I suggested he bring Nancy since it's her birthday, and because it would be nice to get to know her properly. Do you want to bring John, too, or is that weird?"

Carolyn draped the jumpsuit over her arm and opened the cubicle door. "Can I let you know about John? I appreciate the offer, though, and I'm sure your dad did, too."

"I hope so. He's tried to call a few times today but I couldn't answer at work so I'll phone him back tomorrow. See what he says."

"Are things feeling a little better between you after last weekend?"

They made their way out of the changing rooms, towards the cash registers at the back of the shop, dodging through racks of clothes.

"Yeah," Isla replied a little distractedly. She let out a huff and hung back whilst Carolyn paid. "I think we're trying to make it up to each other for what happened at dinner the other week."

Carolyn still had no idea what on earth had happened at that dinner, and she couldn't leave it anymore. "What is this all about?" she asked, thanking the assistant who'd served her and taking her bag. They began walking back along the store. "I can't work out why you won't just tell me."

Isla huffed again. "I suppose now I know you're seeing someone, it's probably fine. Dad brought Nancy to dinner and he didn't tell me in advance, so I showed up thinking it'd be the two of us, and it was really so I could meet her. I guess things were getting kind of serious between them and I was worried that might upset you."

It had clearly upset Isla, given she'd wanted to leave, and Carolyn could hardly blame her. "He didn't warn you?"

"No. It's fine, though. Honestly. He's apologised about a million times and we talked it through last Sunday when we spent the day together. You're not upset, though, are you? I mean, I know you have John, but this has still moved fast."

It hadn't moved *that* fast because Carolyn now presumed that Nancy was from the pre-divorce era. "I'm not upset your dad is with Nancy, no. I don't have any lingering feelings like that for him. I appreciate you worrying about me but I'm more worried about you. I'm sorry it happened and you didn't feel like you could tell me."

Isla shrugged and then pushed open the door, so that they spilled back out onto the busy street. It made more discussion impractical for five minutes or so, until they reached the restaurant, and it gave Carolyn a chance to process. Everything made a lot more sense now, and she could see why Isla had wanted to escape to football.

Once they were seated and looking over the menu, Carolyn returned them to their conversation. "Did you get on with her?"

Isla shrugged. "She's nice. If I'd met her under different circumstances, it would've been fine. It's kind of why I hope they come next weekend."

"That makes sense. You know I'm proud of you, don't you? Not just for the way you're approaching this but for how you're handling work and the fundraiser."

"Yeah, I do. Thanks, Mum." Isla set down her menu and picked up her phone instead. "I'm going to text him now. Make sure he knows why I want him to come. Can I also let him know that you're okay with it?" She paused with her thumbs poised over the screen. "Are you?"

"Yes, of course! I'm more than happy to meet her and I'll do anything you want to make this easier. Okay?"

Isla nodded and began to tap out her message. Then she returned to her menu, but before she could read it, her phone buzzed. She held it up and smiled, but it soon faded. "Oh."

"Is he not coming?" Carolyn reached over to rub the top of Isla's free hand where it lay on the table. "I know you're disappointed, but there will be plenty of other chances to meet her properly and put this behind you. Maybe they could both come to dinner instead. Or we could go up there and all share a meal out. Hmm?"

"Yeah, maybe," Isla replied, her face pale and her eyes downcast. She pulled her hand away and used it to nudge her menu around the table. "Mum?"

"Yes."

"Can we just go home?"

"I thought you were hungry and desperate to try Japanese?" Sensing they were back where they started and that Isla was keeping something from her, Carolyn pushed this time. "What's wrong, sweetheart?"

She shuffled and flicked at the menu again. There was an interminable pause, before she quietly said, "Dad and Nancy got engaged on Valentine's Day. That's why he was trying to call me. It wasn't about next weekend."

Engaged? And he'd delivered the news over text? Carolyn's hand curled into a tight fist, and she wished momentarily that it was around Marcus's throat. Had he learned nothing? This wasn't about her own feelings, though, and Carolyn flexed her fingers, trying to remain calm and focus on Isla. "Are you okay?"

"Yes. Totally. I'm just a little surprised. They can only have been together for what, six months? Tops. And I haven't had a chance to spend much time with her yet. What if she's not as nice as I thought? Or Dad stops wanting to see me?"

Isla swiped a tear from under her eye, and Carolyn felt her own welling to see it. She wanted to wrap her daughter in a tight hug and make it all better but she knew she couldn't. And it only made her own lie sit heavier on her conscience. They really did need to come clean soon, and she'd make sure Isla found out face to face, with a proper explanation.

"Your dad will always want to see you. I promise. He loves you, and marrying Nancy won't change that." Carolyn knew Marcus well enough that she whole heartedly believed her own words, even if she did still think he'd handled the situation badly.

"I hope so."

"Well, I'm sure. And I'm also sure that whatever happens in my relationship, I'll never let it change anything between us, okay? I'm sorry if it's seemed like I'm hiding John from you but it was just a little too soon. I think we're getting there, now, so give me a chance to check in and then you can know everything." At least, nearly everything, and Carolyn prayed there would be no tears on either side, because she really didn't want anything to change with Jax, either.

# 21

# JAX

Jax scanned the car park for Carolyn's Lexus. She'd been quiet the past twenty-four hours and it wasn't a problem, but it was unusual. There was always a good night text but last night it came alone, unaccompanied by anything about her day, even though she'd had a busy one meeting friends and taking Isla shopping.

That was probably the reason, and Jax shrugged off her slight worry, choosing to lay cones for the warm up and put it out of her mind. Whatever was happening, Carolyn would tell her later.

She was in a chill mood, and even the sight of Greg walking up the drive didn't fill her with so much dread today. She'd decided to take Carolyn's advice and try to explain her point of view, so for once, she was glad to see him.

"I've been meaning to speak with you," she said when he stopped at the edge of the grass. It was wet, and he probably didn't want to cover his shoes in mud, so she moved a little closer.

"That makes a nice change."

"I wouldn't necessarily get used to it. Carolyn suggested I try to reason with you but if it doesn't work, you should know that I plan to go back to my usual vitriolic comments and resume hating your guts."

Greg laughed. "Now you've got me intrigued."

As well he might be, because this could finally be advantageous for everyone. "The thing is," Jax began as she dropped her last cone and bashed the mud from her hand. "Carolyn's got it into her head that you actually think you're helping us by suggesting this merger."

"I do. A pitch and clubhouse require money to maintain. You've seen how many bills come in for maintenance, and we're trying to plug some of the gaps by hiring this bar manager to run the facility better, bring in hall bookings, and keep it open longer, but we could do more if we worked together. That would help everyone. It's why I can't understand why you're so against the idea."

"I don't object to us working together. There's a distinction to draw here. I don't want our committee swallowed by yours. But, to be clear, I am prepared to work more closely, perhaps by having an overarching committee to deal with matters affecting everyone who plays here, whilst retaining both existing committees and autonomy over our day to day running."

"Why, though? Why bother with three committees when we can have one?"

This was the crux, and the bit she wasn't sure Greg would get, but Carolyn was right that he needed a better explanation. She couldn't just assume he'd be a tool about it. "Because we don't want to end up outnumbered and overpowered. The women's game is still rising and it's taken a lot of work to get where we are. I've got players who can remember being pushed out of boys clubs and having nowhere to go, or told they were shit and not worth bothering with. Even now, we get girls turn up who are in disbelief that they're being coached by a woman, because they didn't know it was possible. We also have quite a few LGBTQ players who feel similarly that this is their safe space, and some of that sense of it being safe comes from knowing we've been there and have their backs. I get that you probably think I'm just a pain in the ass and I am, don't get me wrong, but it's because I'm protective of what we've built in the face of historical marginalisation in schools and pretty much every other arena you can imagine."

Greg considered for a second, rubbing a hand over his chin. "Okay. So if I can get everyone else on my committee to agree it, you're happy to work closer? I just need to explain all of that."

"Yes. Absolutely. I'll make sure Carolyn knows that a closer working relationship is fine by me, so long as we get to keep our committee."

"I have to say, she's had a big impact already. I never thought I'd see the day where we'd have a civil conversation." Greg finally stepped onto the grass, his foot squishing into wet mud. He nudged Jax with an elbow. "Speaking of which, I wouldn't mind a closer relationship with Carolyn. What do you reckon, can you put in a good word? You did say I should find a woman my own age."

He smirked as if they were sharing an inside joke, and if the subject were anyone else, he might have got away with it. After all, it was clearly his way of breaking the tension. He'd picked the wrong woman to chase, though, and Jax felt her shoulders scrunch as she resisted the urge to nudge him back far harder.

"Carolyn's seeing someone, so I think you're out of luck," she replied, reminding herself that he didn't know, or have any idea that he'd just put his size tens in it. "You and I should quit whilst we're marginally still ahead and I need to warm up the team, but she'll be here soon so I'll leave you to have a chat."

No sooner had Jax said that, but Carolyn's car pulled up in the car park. Greg didn't hang around to chat, though, instead heading into the clubhouse. Perhaps he was less interested now he knew she wasn't going to sleep with him. Not that Jax minded. She was pleased with how that had gone and planned to gloat a little, until Isla ran off without saying hello and Carolyn didn't have so much as a smile for her.

"Are you alright?" she asked, a little worry returning and gnawing gently on her insides. "You seem a little out of sorts."

Carolyn nodded. "Yes, I just had an intense evening with Isla. I'll tell you about it later."

"Okay." The team were in the changing rooms, and Jax glanced over her shoulder to make sure the door was closed before confessing, "I've really missed you this week."

"I've missed you too," Carolyn replied, before diverting her attention to the grass beneath her feet. She had her hands in the pockets of her coat as if she was also struggling with the same urgency for touch all of a sudden. It was a relief because the issue was clearly not between the two of them. "Can I help you with anything?"

"Yeah, you can kiss me."

A smile threatened on Carolyn's lips for the first time. She glanced up, then over Jax's shoulder, then pecked her on the lips. "Better?"

"Yes. I'm finding it harder than ever to pretend we're not a couple."

This time, the smile that had threatened spilled into a wide grin. "I'm finding it hard, too, and I actually wanted to check with you that you're happy for me to tell Isla about us. What do you reckon? Shall we go official?"

"Really?"

"Yes, really. I don't want to lie to her anymore, so if we both agree this relationship is going to continue…"

She left it hanging, as if there might be a question to answer, and Jax was quick to offer reassurance. There was no doubt in her mind that she wanted to be with Carolyn. "I am one hundred percent in."

"Good." Carolyn glanced over Jax's shoulder a second time and kissed her again. She stayed close, shuffling from one foot to the other. "Because I'm falling in love with you and this time, I want everyone to know."

Before Jax could reply, the door to the changing rooms burst open and from it spilled clacking boots and raucous players. She hoped the dopey smile on her face conveyed what she'd confirm with words later: that she had stayed by Carolyn's side on every moment of that free falling descent. For now, though, she had to focus on the game, and let Carolyn leave to the warmth of the clubhouse until kick off.

"Are you okay, champ?" she asked Isla, who jogged over and stopped to tie her laces. Whilst things seemed good with Carolyn now, Isla still hadn't said anything.

"Yeah. Sorry. I found out my dad is engaged last night and it was a bit of a surprise. He texted me, and it was... well..."

The penny dropped. Jax also started to understand why Carolyn suddenly wanted them to go public. She'd be worried about Isla finding out by another means. "I get the gist. And it'll have been a surprise for your mum, too."

"Yeah. She'd only just found out that he brought his girlfriend—well, fiancée now I guess—to dinner the other week when I bailed for football. So I think she's doubly mad. I'm over that, though. Now I just need to get my head around this..."

She straightened and Jax put a hand on her shoulder. "Are you sure you want to play today?"

The suggestion that she may not be up to it seemed to affront her more than anything else, and Jax saw her usual spark return. "Of course I can play."

The rest of the team were running a lap of the field already, and Jax pointed at Jenna, way out ahead of the pack. "Catch up and get your head in the game. Hopefully it'll help."

After the warm up and team talk, Jax went to stand by the dugouts as usual. What was unusual, though, was Carolyn's presence by her side.

"You're a sight for sore eyes," Carolyn said as she stood alongside Jax on the sideline, her hands wedged in her pockets. "I hope you don't mind me being over here but I wanted more of your company after stewing in the clubhouse on my own for the past hour."

"Yeah, Isla told me what happened. I'm glad the mere vision of me has improved the day for you."

"I knew there was something going on. I can't believe he foisted this on Isla without warning her first. She knew he was seeing someone, so that wasn't a surprise, but she turned up to dinner expecting to catch up with her dad, only to be ambushed. I'm furious with his lack of consideration, and also a little angry that he sat in my house last weekend acting like everything was fine. There was me telling you we'd turned a corner. What a fool."

"You're not a fool." Jax went to put her arm around Carolyn and had to stop herself. "I'm sorry."

"Thank you." Carolyn let out another sigh. It was longer this time, and full of resignation. "Isla says she's over it so that's the main thing."

It might be the main thing, but it wasn't the only thing, and Jax once again had to suppress the urge to hug Carolyn. Some of this must be affecting her, it couldn't all be about Isla. They could hardly get into deep and meaningful conversation on the side of a football pitch, though, and instead had to watch the rest of the game play out.

Isla was doing well, despite the problems in her personal life, this time alongside Becky in the centre of midfield rather than instead of her. Even so, it was a tight game and still nil-nil when the referee blew his final whistle.

"You don't see many scoreless draws at this level," Carolyn pointed out. It was inane but she at least seemed a little brighter, handing Isla her water bottle as she came off the pitch. "You all look shattered. Maybe we should go and sort the food today. To hell with whoever's on the rota."

Jax agreed, up for helping if it would give Carolyn a purpose. She seemed to cope best when she had something practical to do, and given Jax was also starving, she was happy to hurry things along. "If you're not careful, you might end up the most popular chair this club has ever had."

"That's my aim. Unlike you, who is quite happy to argue wherever possible."

"Actually," Jax countered, seeing another opportunity to distract Carolyn and improve her mood. "I think you'll be proud of me. I spoke to Greg earlier and floated the idea of having three committees so that we can work together as well as apart. *And*, I also explained my reservations about losing autonomy."

She held open the clubhouse door for Carolyn to pass, then followed her out to the kitchens behind the bar. When they were on the other side, she shut the door and was taken completely by surprise when Carolyn backed her up against it, planting a hard kiss on her mouth.

"What was that for?" she asked, not complaining but also finding Carolyn's mood a little erratic today.

"Nothing, I just wanted to kiss you. And why shouldn't I?"

"No reason at all. I love it when you kiss me. I'm still worried about you, though."

Carolyn wandered to the other side of the room and opened the fridge, with Jax following and peering over her shoulder to see what they had today. "Worried? Why?"

"Because I don't buy that you're only bothered on Isla's

account. It's fine to be pissed for yourself, too. You left your friends and your job behind to move with Marcus, and he's now marrying someone else whilst you pick up the pieces for Isla. I get he didn't mean to cause either of you hurt but I think he has, and it's okay to forgive him but I'm worried you're not even acknowledging your own pain. Aren't you pissed?"

Rummaging in the fridge, Carolyn replied, "No." She took out a large pack of sausages and set it on the counter. "Why should I be? I didn't love him anymore so what do I care if he's marrying someone else?"

"Because he cheated on you multiple times and I get that maybe you had feelings elsewhere, too, but you chose to put your family first rather than yourself and on the surface of things, he didn't. I don't think anyone would blame you if you're narked that he put himself first."

When Jax heard a timid "what?" she looked over her shoulder to find Isla in the doorway. She ran off and Jax raised her hands to her face, rubbing them down her cheeks.

"Oh, god," Carolyn whispered.

"Do you think she heard?"

"I'd say so," Carolyn replied, slamming the fridge shut and jamming her hands on her hips. "What was that? I tell you that I want to be with you openly and share this with Isla, I lay myself on the line by admitting that I'm falling in love with you, and you see a chance to even up the score?"

"What? There is no score! Not between us, anyway, although I think you still have one to settle with Marcus. I would never want to punish you or Isla."

"Really? Because it sounds like the only person who has unresolved anger is you."

"Hey! That's unfair and you're not talking to Isla now. I'm a goddamn adult. A forty-year-old woman with a career, a mortgage, and four decades of life experience who knows what they want and can manage their own emotions."

"I'm not talking to you like you're a teenager, I'm talking to you like someone who isn't being honest about their feelings. There's no such thing as an accident."

Jax laughed and clutched her own chest. She was so incredulous that it took her one or two seconds to compose words that would explain how ridiculous that was. "I have been nothing but honest about my feelings. Always. I took a huge chance telling you how I felt five years ago and yeah, being rejected hurt like hell. But being hurt doesn't mean I'm not able to take a step back to understand why you made the choice you did. And you know what? I've been honest with you about my feelings again since we reconnected, even though I know it could hurt me a second time. Because I think whatever we have is worth it."

"Where are you going?" Carolyn asked as Jax headed for the kitchen door, her hand already slipping into her pocket to find her keys.

"I need to cool down and *someone* needs to find your daughter."

## 22

# CAROLYN

Hanging around to argue had made the task of finding Isla ten times harder because she was nowhere to be seen. She wasn't in the bar, the changing rooms, or anywhere else in the clubhouse. Jax had also disappeared, and Carolyn stood in the car park with her hands on her hips trying to decide what to do next. The only thing for it was to drive home and hope Isla was on the route somewhere, so that's what Carolyn did.

She pulled up on her own drive, cut the engine, and ran into the house, calling up the stairs to see if Isla was inside. There was no reply, not that it was a surprise because she'd have to be Mo Farah to make it back that fast on foot.

The next try was a call to Sylvia, but she hadn't heard from Isla either. Curtis was a strong possibility, but Carolyn didn't have his number or address, and she was running out of options.

Deciding to drive back to the clubhouse, Carolyn made a reverse trip, scanning the streets again to make sure she hadn't missed Isla the first time. But when she crunched over the gravel again, there was still no sign of her.

Despair was setting in until her phone flashed up with a

message. She read it aloud, almost in disbelief. "I'm at Gran's. She's making us dinner."

Carolyn frowned. Was that it? All this worry and Isla had gone to Sylvia's?

"I called your gran and you weren't there," she replied before realising it was a pointless observation.

"Yeah? I'm there now. Are you coming or what?"

It took her less than ten minutes to make it to Sylvia's house, pulling up in the vacant space where her BMW had once sat. When Carolyn reached the front door, she let herself straight in, and peered through the living room doorway to find Isla with her feet up drinking a cup of tea in front of the television.

"Are you okay, sweetheart?" she asked, her voice quivering slightly when she could see that Isla was plainly fine and the memory of her argument with Jax came flooding back. She cleared her throat and tried to push down the desire to cry.

"I'm fine," Isla replied, frowning and setting her tea on the side table. "I was feeling a bit rubbish when I heard what dad did so I went for a walk, but Jax found me and we had a chat. Then she brought me here and gran made me tea, so the evolution is complete."

"Jax drove you here?" Now there was no hope of not crying, and Carolyn wiped a tear from her cheek. "That was kind of her." Which was completely at odds with how she'd just been treated.

"Yeah. I'm sorry I worried you both. Just needed a minute to myself, you know?"

"What did she say?" Carolyn slipped off her shoes and perched herself on the edge of the sofa, whilst Isla turned down the volume of whatever football match she'd found on the television. It looked to be Tottenham, which wasn't helping any.

"Just that relationships are complicated and I shouldn't judge my dad too harshly. She reminded me that you're both human, and you're making the best decisions you can with what you know at the time, and I'm lucky to have a mum who would do anything to make me happy. Which I totally am."

Carolyn nodded, unable to get any words out right now. Her mouth was glued together by saliva and guilt as she tried to keep from sobbing.

"I still don't feel good that he was with someone else, but if you're okay with it, I guess it's not my place to get involved," Isla continued with a little shrug. "I do want to tell him that I'm upset with the way he let me know about his engagement, though. Will you be on the call with me?"

"Of course I will. I think that's all very level-headed and I'm so proud of you. I know I keep saying, but only because it's true."

Isla nodded. "Are you okay?"

She wasn't, but wouldn't add to everything Isla already had going on. "I was very angry with your father earlier, and last night, but I'm going to speak with Gran about it. Will you be alright in here?"

Isla nodded again and returned her attention to the television, tucking the blanket around her legs. Carolyn watched her for a moment, wondering how she'd managed to raise such a considerate daughter. She may be a little sheltered but she'd proven all of her most wonderful qualities recently.

Carolyn hoisted herself from the sofa and wandered back into the hallway, clicking the living room door shut. She could hear the whoosh of steam and whir of the oven coming from the kitchen and moved towards it, smiling to see Sylvia in full flow in front of an array of pans.

"There you are my dear," Sylvia said without turning around. "I hope you don't mind me taking charge but it seemed everyone could do with a little TLC and I happened to have a leg of lamb in the fridge for just such an occasion."

"What did we ever do without you?"

"I've been asking myself that regularly."

Carolyn pulled out a chair. "Isla told me that Jax had a word with her and smoothed things over."

"Yes, she did. She was very worried about you."

Carolyn fell apart, her hand covering her eyes as the tears fell freely. She was worried about herself, too. She'd spent so long trying to do the right thing for everyone else that she'd become miserable. Now, she finally had the chance to make something for herself, and she'd ruined it. Worse still, she'd completely underestimated Jax. Whether it was Carolyn's disbelief that things could possibly be as good as they felt, or her disbelief that she deserved it, she'd thrown Jax right under the bus.

"I was so awful to her," she said through bursts of crying. "I took out all the anger I was feeling towards Marcus and myself, and punished her. Again."

"Yes, I know what happened. I dragged it out of her. For what it's worth, though, she was very understanding. I think her main worry was losing you."

"She's always understanding, that's the problem. The more love she shows me, the more I realise what I've missed out on, and the harder it becomes to pretend I don't question whether I made the right decision five years ago. Marcus took what he wanted and I didn't, she was right about that. Sometimes I really wish I'd followed my heart rather than my head."

"Many wouldn't thank me for saying this but I will anyway. It's always the woman who ends up holding things together. You can be with Jax now, though, so just be honest. If you tell her what happened, she'll forgive you any words spoken in the heat of the moment. I'm sure of it."

Carolyn nodded. She just needed to find the *right* words, because she wasn't entirely sure of it all herself yet. She would also need to work out how and when she could sneak out to see

Jax, because Isla still needed her. "Do you think Isla will be okay here for a while this evening so that I can speak to Jax?"

"No need, my dear. She's only gone to the shop to fetch me supplies. She'll be back any minute."

"What?" Carolyn's head snapped around, her eyes fixed on the kitchen door as if Jax might come bursting through it. "She's coming back here?"

"That's right. I was missing a few bits for dinner, given the last minute nature, and she kindly offered to help. I also thought it useful to keep her here. I hope I wasn't wrong."

"You weren't wrong." Once again full of gratitude, Carolyn pushed out her chair and dabbed the tears from under her eyes. Then she pecked Sylvia on the cheek. "Thank you. I'll go outside and wait for her."

She took a deep breath and tapped her foot on the pavement, stood on the street corner no doubt looking like she was up to no good. Jax would have to pass her and would hopefully stop. At least here they would have some privacy from Sylvia and Isla, even if the neighbours got an eyeful.

When Jax's car came into view, Carolyn held up a hand to flag her down. She felt like she was back in the clubhouse the first time they were reunited. Their exchange was stilted and cold at first, and she desperately hoped they weren't about to have a rerun. She wanted the alternate movie scene, this time, where they really did end up lost in their love for one another. So long as Jax could forgive her for being so hot-headed.

"Hi," she said, when Jax pulled up on the curb and walked towards her with a carrier bag in hand.

"Are you okay?" were the first words out of Jax's mouth and it gave Carolyn some hope that Sylvia might be right. She looked desperately worried, the lines near her eyes deep set from her frown. "I don't know how to convince you that it really was an accident. I was trying to help, I promise."

"I know you were." Carolyn took Jax's outstretched hand. "I'm so sorry for what I said to you."

"I was beginning to think I'd misjudged this. Misjudged us. Maybe we can't leave the past where it was."

"*You* have. I can see that now. You were right and I was the only one who hadn't. I kept telling myself that I was fine about how I've spent the last five years, but the truth is that I'm not sure I am. I think you were also right that seeing Marcus, then learning he was engaged, reminded me that he got what he wanted, and I didn't. I wanted you, so desperately, and I gave you up. The closer we've become, the more I've realised quite how much I've missed out on. I'm sorry I directed that at you today because you didn't deserve it, and I'm worried I don't deserve you."

"Of course you deserve me," Jax whispered, the bag rattling as she pulled Carolyn tight against herself. Then she peppered Carolyn's face with kisses, taking away the tears that had fallen over her cheeks. "I was also a little naïve, I think, in believing you when you kept telling me it's fine. How can it be? You've had so much to deal with, not even figuring in that you lost your dad as well, and you're not a superhero. Despite appearances." When Carolyn let out another burst of tears, Jax stroked her hair. "Do you believe me now that I'm on your side? Whatever you said earlier about me keeping a score or looking to get even, that's nowhere near true."

"Yes, I know. I'm so sorry I said that. The only true thing I've said to you is how much I want us to be together and tell Isla. If you still want to, that is?"

"Of course I do."

They stood and held each other for a few minutes, and Carolyn cried again. They were cathartic tears now, releasing some of her pent up feelings.

"I wish I could just hold you for the rest of the day," she mumbled.

Jax laughed. "You can. Not sure what the neighbours will think."

"I'm pretty sure that at some point, Isla or Sylvia would come looking. We might have to wait and do this another day."

"We can definitely hug lots next time we're alone. I have a conference Wednesday to Friday but how about Friday evening? Can we spend the night together?"

"Oh." Carolyn's stomach sunk with disappointment. After everything that had happened, she wished they could spend some time together sooner than Friday. "I feel like I've barely had a chance to see you this weekend. Maybe I can use the time you're away to have a chat with Isla, though." Trying to put a positive spin on things wasn't really working, and she held Jax a little tighter.

Jax dropped a kiss on Carolyn's head and stroked her hair again. "I'm sorry we won't get any alone time before then but I'm sort of looking forward to dinner with Sylvia tonight. I wasn't sure she liked me before."

Carolyn untucked her head from the comfy position she'd found, nestled in Jax's neck, and finally smiled. "You're staying for dinner?"

"Yes. I know she isn't your mum, she's Marcus's, but she's a really important person in your life so I'm glad she's decided to accept me."

"Sylvia always liked you. If she was ever cool, it was because she was enjoying teasing me. It wasn't personal."

Jax slipped her hand around Carolyn's and began leading her along the road. "Teasing you? Now *that* I can get behind."

## 23

# JAX

Jax pushed back her plate, wiped clean of any gravy traces. She could definitely get used to Sylvia's cooking and wondered how she felt about some sort of rent-a-granny service. "That's the best meal I've eaten in a long time. I couldn't fit in another bite."

"You won't want dessert then," Sylvia replied, already scraping out her chair to collect it. Jax had come back from the shop with a lemon cheesecake, in addition to the various items on Sylvia's list, as well as a box of after dinner mints encased in dark chocolate because she knew Carolyn loved them.

"I have a second stomach for that, don't worry. Let me clear these plates away first, though."

Sylvia wafted her hand to dismiss the offer. "Absolutely not. You're our guest. Isla will do it."

"Isla will *what*?" Isla's head shot up from her phone. She'd been tapping intermittent messages to Curtis all evening and Carolyn had grumbled initially but then decided to allow it, just this once.

"Isla will clear the plates and load the dishwasher. Then you can give me an update on this boy you're so fixated on. Are we sure he's good enough for my granddaughter?"

"Gran, he's like a star sports player and total nerd. We're just talking about our history essays and then he's going to help me go over my final playlist for the all-ages club night next Saturday."

Sylvia nodded slowly. "Is this the event you sold me a ticket for?"

When Isla didn't show any signs of moving to clear the plates, Jax got up and bussed them for her, with Carolyn's help. They listened to Isla try to explain her concept, sniggering as they heard the phrases 'target market' and 'profit margin'.

"I still say she's turning into a mini Jenna," Jax whispered as they both scraped leftovers into the bin. "I hope you're prepared for this. I might have to leave the country."

"There are worse people she could turn into than Jenna. I still don't think you should be so hard on her, given everything you've told me."

"Like I said, it's done with love and affection. When I stop winding someone up and cracking jokes, that's when they should worry."

Carolyn smiled. "I'll know if I'm in real danger, then?"

"Yes. I'm always honest with you."

They were snapped from lingering eye contact when Sylvia nudged between them to find bowls.

"Well," she surmised. "That all sounds very impressive. I shall be there. Although Lord knows what I'll wear." She looked from Jax to Carolyn and back again. "Do you have sporting hero outfits prepared?"

"I sure do," Jax replied, returning to her seat and readying herself for dessert. "I'm going as Abby Wambach, retired US women's national team player and hall of famer. We'll just skim over the DUI charge."

"And what will that involve?"

"Wearing my normal clothes. Conveniently."

Sylvia laughed. "And Carolyn?"

Carolyn had found the box of mints and was sneaking them whilst she started on hand washing the pots and pans. "I will be going as whoever will allow me to wear the new outfit I bought last night."

Isla folded her arms and let out a huff. "Is anyone taking the theme seriously?"

"Of course, sweetheart! I just don't know that many sports stars and I'm unprepared to wear a tracksuit. Have you and Curtis picked your costumes?"

"Yes. I'm going in England kit as Millie Bright and ignoring the fact she plays for Chelsea. I wanted a Tottenham player but there aren't many England players on their women's team right now. Curtis is going as some rugby player I've never heard of. I'm trying to show an interest but it's tough because rugby confuses me."

"Little shorts, big thighs." Sylvia set the cheesecake in the middle of the table. "That's all you need to know."

"Gran!" Isla shook her head. Then she spotted the cheesecake and finally put down her phone. "Can Jax come for dinner more often?"

"She's welcome any time."

Sylvia squeezed Jax's shoulder as she walked past to get them spoons from the drawer. It warmed her heart to be included. "I've really enjoyed myself. I usually only get a big family meal once a year when I visit my parents. Unless you count eating sausages with the team on a Sunday." At the mention of the team and sausages, Jax remembered that they'd completely abandoned the food prep. Hopefully, someone would have taken over, and she'd check with Becky later. "I guess they're like my proxy family."

"How long have you been coaching?"

Jax thanked Sylvia when she set down a spoon and cut off a

large wedge of cheesecake, dropping it into Jax's bowl and licking her fingers clean. "More years than I can count. I started playing for The Blues when I first moved to the area because my girlfriend at the time was the keeper. Then we split, but I stayed. I busted my ankle a while after and took a year out, by which time the coach had left, so I got back into it as the manager instead of a player. That must have been a decade ago."

"And you've never wanted to move on?"

"Never. I probably sound like I have no ambition. I do, in my career, but football is different. I became really tight with Abi, our left winger, and her folks have always been there for me, too. If I went somewhere else, I'd lose my whole social support network."

It wasn't Sylvia's hand that rubbed into Jax's shoulder this time, and when she craned to look over it, Carolyn smiled back at her. "We're lucky to have you."

Jax got the sense that she wasn't just talking about the team, and she longed for them to be alone. She wanted desperately to hold Carolyn and stroke her hair like she had in the bed in Belgium. Just the two of them, close and connected. They'd have to wait until Friday, though, and Jax should finish eating so she could leave and prepare for work and the conference. She hated those things and had been trying to forget about it for weeks but part of being ambitious in her career meant going to dumb events.

There was a quarter of cheesecake left by the time they'd all gone in for seconds, and Carolyn boxed it up for Jax to take home to Becky. Then she left Isla and Sylvia in the kitchen and shut the door behind them, following Jax down the hallway.

"Are we definitely okay?" Carolyn whispered, her hand on the open front door as Jax zipped her coat on the step outside. "I hate the thought of not seeing you for five days with anything hanging over us."

"I promise you we're good," Jax whispered back, before giving her a quick kiss. "I don't do grudges. Once it's dealt with, it's dealt with. Trust me."

"I do trust you."

"Will you please just do one thing?" When Carolyn agreed, Jax said, "Take care of yourself this week. Stop trying to push down anything you're feeling, and call me when you need to talk. Okay?"

"I'm sure I can manage that."

Carolyn stepped down for one more quick kiss and then waved as Jax walked along the road to where she'd left her car. It was dark and cold, and she shivered as she climbed inside, leaving the cheesecake on the passenger seat. She was also exhausted, all of a sudden. It had been a hell of a day.

When she arrived home, Becky was in the kitchen, kneading dough.

"Looks like you've had about as rough a day as me," Jax noted, because baking bread was Becky's stress reliever. She set the cheesecake down on the counter alongside. "Everything okay?"

"Yeah. I just got dumped again, that's all. I should be used to it."

"Oh, no. The Tinder date from Valentine's?"

"Yep," Becky replied, throwing a fist into the dough. "I thought it went pretty well in the end and we've been talking ever since. We were meant to meet up again tonight, just for a drink, but she's bailed. Doesn't feel a spark, apparently."

"I'm sorry, bud."

"It's fine. I wasn't that into it, anyway. Why was your day so rough? Is it anything to do with why you disappeared and left the sausages out?"

Jax pulled off her coat and hooked it over a chair. "Yeah. Sorry about that."

"Jenna and Abi dealt with it. No one stands in the way of their food. They both asked after you, though."

She'd text them later and check in because she also wanted to find out how they were getting on after the big move. They would usually have caught up after the match. "I had an argument with Carolyn but it's resolved now. A load of stuff came out that needed to so it was good. Oddly. And we've decided to tell Isla."

"Wow. That's big. How are you feeling about it?"

"Right now, I'm tired." It was the honest answer, but besides that she meant what she'd told Carolyn. Despite probing herself to see if there were any lingering doubts or resentments, she couldn't find any. "Do you think I'm odd?"

Becky laughed. "You'll have to explain, I think."

"It's just... Carolyn seems so surprised that I don't hold any resentment. I'm wondering if I've buried it but I just can't find any part of me that wants to hate her. It's all... love. I love her, more than I've ever loved anyone in my life, besides my family. I honestly think that she could go away for another five years and come back again, and I'd still love her. Not that I want her to go anywhere. She's flawed, and human, and wonderful, and I want her so passionately."

"That doesn't make you odd. I think it's lovely. I just hope someone feels like that about me some day."

"I hope they do, too, because you're awesome. Screw anyone who can't see it."

## 24

# CAROLYN

Deciding to tell Isla and actually doing it were two different matters, especially when they'd both been out of sorts all week. Carolyn was still working through her anger and resentment and Isla was, most likely, doing the same. The only person who had taken it in stride was Jax. They'd hashed it out on Sunday, left it there, and seemed to have become even closer because of it, which was a welcome surprise.

"How are you feeling today?" Jax asked, resting back on the hotel bed with one hand behind her head, the other holding her phone. They'd ended up video calling both nights whilst she was away.

"Tired," Carolyn replied, her body choosing that exact time to yawn as if it needed to make the point. "But I'm glad you're coming home tomorrow. Isla will be out with Curtis so you can come to my house for once."

"Do you know what's great for relaxing if you're tired and have had a difficult week? It's the hot tub in your back garden."

Carolyn laughed at Jax's obsession with that hot tub. "Is that a yes, you'd like to come over?"

"Of course it's a yes. I'm guessing you still haven't told Isla and I can't stay, though...?"

That was a no, and Carolyn knew she was stalling. The longer the week went on, the harder it seemed to become. Now it was Thursday, and she was no closer to telling Isla anything about her relationship with Jax. Or explaining exactly what had happened on Sunday, despite Isla having checked in on various occasions with what felt like genuine concern for her mum.

"I don't know where to begin. I'm just worried where the line is, given how upset she was about Marcus's affairs, and how she'll feel if she knows there was something between us whilst I was still married." Carolyn let out a short sigh. "It's hard knowing how much to tell her."

"I know, honey. Would you like me there when you tell her? We could do it tomorrow evening before she goes out?"

Carolyn bit back a smile. Jax had never called her that before. It seemed at odds with her usual brashness. "What did you just call me?"

Jax faltered, her forehead creasing. "Oh, honey? Sorry, I'm around a bunch of people who say it all the time. I think because they can never remember anyone's names."

"Oh, I see, so you were just calling me that through indifference. Good to know where I stand."

"You know that isn't true, I just didn't think we were pet name people. You'll always be my honey. My sugar. My—"

"Okay, you've gone too far." Carolyn laughed, enjoying this latest interlude of light relief. "I love how you can always cheer me up."

"Who always cheers you up?" Isla asked, launching a stealth attack from the hallway. She'd been upstairs studying and had somehow made it down the stairs without Carolyn hearing, probably because she was so engrossed in teasing Jax, who had just run her fingers over her lips to zip them.

"No one," Carolyn replied, pivoting so that Isla couldn't see the screen, however hard she tried to peer over her mum's shoulder.

"Hmm," Isla mumbled, taking her empty glass to the sink and filling it. "I don't believe you. I think that's John and you've been video calling *every* night this week. Ask him if he wants to come to the disco on Saturday so I can meet him."

Carolyn's eyes widened as they met Jax's, and hers did the same. Then Jax smiled and mouthed, "Here's your way in, good luck honey!"

She blew a kiss and disconnected, then sent an immediate follow up text to say, "Good luck!"

Jax was right. She had the perfect conversation starter, and Carolyn needed to take it. She set the phone down on the central island and scratched the back of her neck, then tucked a loose wave of hair behind her ear. "You've rumbled me, then."

"It was hardly a secret who's been making you so happy again this week, and I told you I'm cool with it. Especially if this John person is cheering you up after you were so upset on Sunday." Isla pulled up a stool and set her glass down next to Carolyn's phone, then stared at her fingers as she wiped the condensation along them. "I've been worried about you. That maybe you were lying and you *aren't* over dad or something."

"No, I promise it's not that." Carolyn also settled on a stool, picking up the mug of tea she'd poured before beginning her call with Jax. "Well, not exactly. I was angry with him because I hate when anyone lets you down, but there was a bit more to it than that. I've not really known how to explain this to you, though, because I don't want to hurt you."

Isla frowned. "The only thing that's hurt me so far is not being told the truth."

"I know that, but things go on in a marriage that aren't appropriate for a child to know. That's why I never wanted you to find out that your dad had been with other people before we split up. We didn't feel the same way about each other by that point and I knew all about it, so I didn't want you to view him too harshly."

"But you were still angry with him for seeing other people?"

"Yes, as it turns out I was carrying unacknowledged anger. It's what came out on Sunday. But it wasn't because he'd been with other people, exactly. I think it was more that I hadn't. That I'd had the chance to be with someone who meant a great deal to me, and I chose not to take it." There it was, the first of the secrets Carolyn knew had the power to hurt Isla, but she had to go with it now. "Back when your dad was offered the Manchester job, I had feelings for someone. I don't regret deciding to keep us all together and I want to make sure you know that I love you more than anyone else in the world, but that doesn't mean it didn't hurt to lose the bits of happiness that I might have had with them."

"So," Isla asked after considering it for a second or two. "Are you saying you only went to Manchester with Dad for me?"

That was also complicated but partly true, and Carolyn took a deep breath before delving into another difficult topic. "Sort of, but it wasn't all for your benefit. I wasn't ready to do that to any of us. Neither was your dad. We hoped we could be happy together again." Even if that hope had ultimately not lasted long. "We wanted to give our family a shot."

"You were unhappy pretty much that *whole* time, though?"

Carolyn drummed her fingers on the mug. The difficult questions were coming fast but she wouldn't lie. "We were friends at best and nothing more, but that doesn't mean we didn't enjoy all of the good times we each got to have with you. Or that we hated each other. Even now I'd consider your dad a friend." Regardless of the friction that seemed inevitable when navigating such a tricky transition. "We just weren't in love anymore and hadn't been for a long time."

Isla's forehead creased as she tried to process, and she pointed from side to side with her index finger as she connected the dots. "But you were in love with this other person you met? And Dad fell in love with Nancy?"

"I loved them, but it sort of snuck up on me because I thought we were just friends. When I realised, and made the decision to go to Manchester, I cut contact with them. And yes, I believe your dad loves Nancy. I'm happy for him if he's getting to experience that again."

"But also pissed because you didn't go there, and he did? I think I get it." Isla sipped her water as she took it all in. Once again, Carolyn was impressed by how maturely she was managing this. How considered her questions and responses were. Maybe she could handle the whole truth now, and she was about to provide another easy lead in. "This guy you're seeing now. Is it the same one from before Manchester or someone different?"

"It's the same person," Carolyn admitted, her heart fluttering at the thought of where this was heading. "We've reconnected since you and I moved back here, and our feelings are still there."

Isla smiled. "I'm happy for you, Mum. I guess it's a bit like me with Curtis."

"How so?"

"Well, just because I messed up and I thought he'd never be interested again, but he was. And you messed up by choosing Dad over this person who makes you happy, and you got a second chance too. So, if you think about it, we should both just support each other, you know?" Isla took another sip of water and shrugged. "If you want him to stay, I'm totally cool with it."

Seeing this wasn't going the way she'd expected, Carolyn

sighed with vague amusement. Perhaps there was also a little relief mixed in. "And let me guess, you'd also like it if Curtis can stay?"

"Wow, what a great idea. Or, if you're more comfortable with it, I could stay over at *his* house tomorrow night. Because his parents have already said it's cool and you can even ring them to check."

Carolyn folded her arms. She'd thought the worst thing she had to deal with was telling Isla about Jax, but that had gone to the back of the queue. "Since we're having a fully honest conversation tonight, I presume you're telling me you're sleeping with Curtis."

A little pink flushed Isla's cheeks and she fiddled with her water glass. "Not yet but... we've talked about it, and I think I'm ready. You said no bus shelters or unprotected sex and I can absolutely promise it's a check on both of those."

It was tough to argue with that, however hard Carolyn might like to try. Isla was seventeen now and at least she was being sensible about it. So why was the idea causing such a swell of anxiety? It beat out anything Carolyn had just felt at the prospect of revealing her relationship with Jax. "Tomorrow night is very soon. I feel like you've landed this on me with no time to think. Are you sure it's what you want?"

"Yes, but consent is a thing, right? If I decide I don't want anything to happen, I know Curtis won't push me. Sharing a bed tomorrow night doesn't change that. It doesn't give him any rights to my body."

Wow. Carolyn sat in awe, equal parts proud and terrified. "Will his parents be in? Tell me about them."

"They're lovely, I think you'd get on. His mum works as a teaching assistant and his dad is an engineer but I don't know what type. I did try really hard to find a bad boy but that's not how it worked out. Curtis is nice to me. He even keeps asking to come over for dinner so that he can get to know you better."

Carolyn laughed, echoing Jax's earlier sentiment. "Are we sure he's a seventeen-year-old boy?"

"I know, right? So, can I give you his parents number? And can he come over before the disco on Saturday night so you can meet him properly?"

"You mean the all-ages club night?"

"Whatever."

Letting out a whirring noise, Carolyn unfolded her arms and rubbed her temples. "Fine. Okay. You're growing up and I need to trust your judgement."

"Great." Isla jumped down and wrapped her arms around Carolyn's shoulder, kissing the side of her head. "Thanks, Mum. I'll go grab the number, unless there's something else you wanted to talk about?"

There was, but right now, Carolyn was struggling to think straight. She floundered before wafting a hand to dismiss it. They'd covered enough for one night. "Nothing that can't wait." Isla was halfway out the door when Carolyn remembered one other piece of information she should probably share. "Oh, but I do have my... John... over tomorrow night. Will you be coming home at all?"

"No, don't worry. You can keep him your secret a little bit longer since you're clearly desperate for me not to meet him, but I still say you should invite him on Saturday night." Isla swung off the door frame and turned back, leaning against its side. "Hey, Mum?"

"Yes?"

"I just want you to know that if things don't work out with *John* and you want to get with a woman, I'm cool. Okay? So long as you're happy and they treat you right."

She darted off up the stairs and Carolyn's scorching face fell

## 25

## JAX

The swell of anxiety Carolyn had phoned to tell Jax about after her conversation with Isla had grown to a tidal wave about to destroy everything in its path by the time they were reunited on Friday evening. She was right and the parents, or at least the mum, sounded lovely. But this was still a step that Carolyn wasn't quite ready for. When Jax arrived at six, straight from her work conference, she'd heard all of the reasons why it was fine, but wasn't convinced that Carolyn believed any of them.

"Hey, honey," she whispered against Carolyn's ear, hugging her from behind after entering via the back door and finding her at the sink scrubbing something to death. "I'm here to distract you with a hot tub, Champagne, and *spectacular* love making." Carolyn raised a soapy hand to Jax's cheek and twisted her head for a kiss. She was in sports clothes today for the first time in history and Jax couldn't help wondering if this was a sign of her descent into madness, or just that they were now more comfortable around each other. "Are you okay?"

"I'm better now you're here. I've even put on my swimming costume in anticipation."

That explained the tracksuit bottoms and running T-shirt at

least, although Jax was a little disappointed to hear they wouldn't be going in the hot tub naked. "I think you're going to love it." She slipped her thumbs into the waistband of Carolyn's trackies and pulled them down.

"I've taken the cover off, so all I'm waiting for is the glass of bubbly you promised me and for you to change."

Carolyn dried her hands on a tea towel hanging next to the sink, then finished undressing herself. All the while, Jax busied herself on the list of tasks, excited to finally get into the tub she'd been eying up for weeks. She'd been able to think of little else all day besides relaxing under the stars with the woman she adored. It was perfect, or at least it would be, if Carolyn could master the relaxation part.

Jax hung her coat in the hallway, popped the bottle she'd picked up on the way, poured their glasses, and then removed her jumper before revealing that there was a possible snag. "The thing is," she said, shimmying out of her jeans so that she stood in only her briefs and a tee. "I didn't bring a costume because I've come straight from the train station, so I think I'll have to go topless. Is that alright?"

Carolyn laughed. "Have I ever minded you being topless before?"

"Never."

"Then you have your answer."

Buoyed by one positive result, Jax then set to work on the relaxation part. She pulled off her tee and threw it over the back of a stool, then returned to her place behind Carolyn, this time rubbing her newly bare shoulders. "Try not to worry about Isla, okay? Or the fact that you didn't manage to tell her about us."

Carolyn had been melting into the touches but stiffened again. "I wasn't worrying about not telling her until you said that."

"Good. You shouldn't," Jax whispered, nipping Carolyn's

neck. She'd swept her hair up once she'd stripped down to a simple black one-piece. It had given Jax easy access to even more of her favourite erogenous zones and she was keen to resume exploring them, except Carolyn was still rigid under her touch. "There's no rush to tell her anything you're not ready for, okay?"

A little more reassurance seemed to work because Carolyn took hold of Jax's wrists to wrap them around herself in a hug. "Are you sure?" she asked, reaching to stroke Jax's face as it rested on her shoulder. "I said I'd tell her this week and I haven't done it."

"Yes, I'm sure. I promise there's no resentment, anger, tension, or anything bad from my side. Right now all I want to do is get into the hot tub and spend an evening with my honey."

When she said honey again, Carolyn chuckled. "I can definitely give you that." Her hand stilled on Jax's cheek. "I've missed you this week."

"I've missed you too." More so than she felt it was right to admit. It had been only two months since Carolyn had sashayed back into her life, and Jax had fallen for her again with alarming ease. Only this time, with the freedom to act on their attraction, her feelings ran far deeper than they had before. Their relationship was mostly theoretical five years ago. It was a good friendship with a spark that hinted at more. Now that 'more' was revealing itself to be better than anything she'd ever imagined or fantasised about when she'd asked Carolyn to leave Marcus.

They stood and held each other for a little longer, until Carolyn shivered and patted Jax's cheek. "I'm getting cold. Shall we go and boil ourselves in the garden?"

"Do I have to let you go?"

"Only temporarily."

She could cope with that, and so Jax unwound her arms. The cold didn't hit her, though, until Carolyn threw open the patio doors to let in a strong gust of wintery air. She shivered far more theatrically than Carolyn had, her arms pulled in close to her sides as she tiptoed across the kitchen to pick up their glasses of Champagne. Then she ran through the back doors, set them down on the side of the tub, and got in as quickly as possible.

The water was so warm that she let out a long *mmm* of appreciation. "This is heaven."

"If you say so," Carolyn replied with less enthusiasm as she slid in and tried not to get her hair wet. Once she'd settled and picked up her drink, though, she mellowed on the idea. "Perhaps I could get used to it." She closed her eyes and inclined her face to the string lights hanging around the pergola. "Anything to take my mind off the fact my daughter is in a stranger's house about to have sex for the first time."

Jax laughed. She knew Carolyn was still struggling with that. "Would you rather she was here at home, having sex in her bedroom?"

"No!"

Flicking water at Carolyn's scrunched face, Jax laughed again. "Why did you say yes if you weren't happy about this?"

"Because it isn't really my decision. I can't tell Isla when she is or isn't ready to have sex. And credit to her, she does seem to have thought it through."

They were only going over the same discussion they'd had three times already, but Jax didn't mind. She loved that Carolyn was sharing with her and wanted her advice. Especially when it came to the most precious thing in her life: Isla. "She's done a great job with this disco, too. Even I've noticed how much she's matured the past couple of months."

"Yes, I'm very proud of her for that." Carolyn opened her eyes and fixed them on the moon, glowing white above a line of houses. "She's going to be gone one day soon and I suppose this is just a reminder. Part of her becoming an adult. Selfishly, I'm struggling. I'm not sure I know who I'll be when I'm not being her mum."

"You'll never stop being her mum. I called mine just yesterday because I couldn't work out how to use the trouser press in the hotel room. I told her about you, too. It wasn't planned but she always asks about the state of my love life. And yes, state is the word she uses."

"Really? What did she say about me?"

"As soon as she found out you have a daughter, she mainly asked about Isla. She wants to know when she can meet her. And what she wants for Christmas next year. Sorry."

Carolyn laughed. "I've never visited any of the flyover states before."

"Flyover?! Ouch. I thought we were past these assaults on my roots. Besides, we're getting off topic. Isla is going to have all sorts of new and exciting experiences over the next couple of years and they're going to be tough, sure, but they'll also be great." Jax smiled at Carolyn, her eyes once again fixed on the night sky, and for the first time wondered what might be in store for the two of them over the next couple of years. She rarely felt so sure about someone that she wanted to consider even a month down the line, so it was new territory.

Carolyn returned the smile. "Why are you looking at me like that?" she asked, now the one to flick water in Jax's face.

"I was hoping we also have plenty of good stuff to look forward to. We haven't really talked about what will happen past telling Isla we're a couple, and it made me happy to imagine our lives for a second."

"What were we doing in your imagination?"

Jax swam-walked to close the short distance between them. "Travelling featured heavily. I'd love to explore more cities with you. Eating good food. Making love all over the world, including the *flyover* states. Then coming home and cuddling up in front of the log burner."

"Let me guess, watching Match of the Day?"

With a little laugh, Jax shrugged. "If you insist."

"Sounds mostly perfect," Carolyn whispered, her fingertips caressing Jax's cheek as their lips met, but they sprung apart again when a bang sounded from inside the house.

"What was that?" Jax asked, standing so that water cascaded off her shoulders. She leant forward with her hands planted on the side of the tub, trying to peer through the patio doors. "Stay there. I'll go and check."

Carolyn wrapped a hand around Jax's leg to stop her. "No, I'll go. It's probably Isla."

It took several seconds before Jax was prepared to sit down and let Carolyn go into the house alone. What if it wasn't Isla? She eventually sat back down but didn't relax, listening intently as Carolyn wrapped herself in a towel and crept through the patio doors.

"Isla, is that you?" she called from just inside the kitchen.

"Yes!" rang through the house and garden.

Jax let out a puff of air, relieved but only briefly. The next threat was to her anonymity, and she slunk down as far as she could whilst Carolyn ventured further inside the house and shut the patio doors behind her. Minutes passed before she appeared again, a hand clutched to her chest.

"She forgot something." Carolyn unwound the towel and shivered as she climbed back in.

"Has she gone back to Curtis's house?"

"Yes. She knows I've got someone here but she doesn't know it's you. She's just told me to *be safe*."

Jax laughed. "That *is* good advice. Can I still stay tonight so long as I promise not to murder you in your sleep?"

"That's the way I've chosen to take it. We just need to make sure you're gone before Isla comes home after work tomorrow. I really need to tell her, though. We can't keep sneaking around like this."

She would get no argument over that, but there was nothing they could do about it tonight. "Will you agree to let me help you tell her once the fundraiser and your big introduction to Curtis are out of the way?"

Carolyn nodded and slipped onto Jax's lap. She wound her arms over each shoulder, resuming their earlier kiss. "Yes," she whispered close to Jax's lips. "Let's do it together, but first I want to enjoy being clandestine for one last night because so far as I can tell, Sunday was our first ever fight and we forgot something very important."

"Throwing things?"

Carolyn laughed. "No." She nibbled on Jax's ear and then whispered, "The make-up sex."

"I think you're meant to have that in the heat of the moment."

"I'm bending the rules because I'm finding the idea of finally being able to have you in my own bedroom, in my own bed, oddly arousing. I've even put on fresh sheets, laid out candles, and bought massage oil, so will you indulge me?"

"Will I indulge you by making love in candlelight again and giving you a massage? Is that a trick question?"

"No, I want to give *you* a massage and take care of *you* for once. So it's a little like make up sex but really more *I appreciate you* sex. A twist. Starting with agreeing to the hot tub, and moving on to cooking you a meal. With dessert ready and waiting upstairs. What do you say?"

"It still sounds like a trick question. So long as this isn't about last weekend. You know you don't have anything to make up for over that, don't you? It's done."

"I know. But it still struck me that you planned us a

wonderful trip, and a perfect Valentine's Day dinner, and are generally just always there when I need you or there's some crisis with Isla, and I want you to know I see it."

"As I recall, you were also there for me on Valentine's Day, but fine. I accept."

## 26

# CAROLYN

*He's a nice boy* played on repeat in Carolyn's mind. Sometimes she even said it out loud to herself. It stopped her every time she wanted to ask Isla for more details about her evening, because she seemed in a good mood when she returned after work on Saturday. Whatever had happened, that was a positive and reassuring sign. If she wanted to say more, she could, but Carolyn was trying to respect her privacy.

"Can you check the food for me?" she yelled down from the top of the stairs. She'd usually go to more effort when entertaining but they had a fundraiser to get to, so would have to settle for pre-made pizzas. Jax was meeting them in the clubhouse at six-thirty to help set up, and there was no time to cook properly.

"Yeah," Isla shouted back from the living room.

She'd been ready for ages but Carolyn was still fussing over her outfit. It would help if Isla had chosen an easier theme, but sporting legends wasn't really within her comfort zone. The only sporting legend she could think of was Dame Kelly Holmes, whom she'd met at a charity fundraiser, but she wasn't about to try and pass herself off as a black woman. Instead, she'd taken inspiration from Jax. Carolyn had no idea who Abby Wambach was but she had heard of her partner, Glennon Doyle, because she'd read one of her books. She may not be a sporting star in her own right but nor was Carolyn.

The doorbell sounded and she took one last look in the full length mirror, admiring her new jumpsuit. It really did suit her. Then she slipped on the trainers Jax had bought her for Valentine's Day in an effort to look at least a little sporty and ran down the stairs because Isla would be dealing with the pizza and someone needed to greet Curtis.

She opened the door, startled when she found Sylvia on the doorstep.

"Aren't we meeting you there?" she asked, standing aside to let her pass. "You know we're going early?"

"Yes," Sylvia responded, already wriggling out of her coat and hooking it over a peg. "But Isla called earlier and asked me to join you for supper. She said something about meeting the boyfriend and I couldn't resist."

That rang true and actually, Carolyn was grateful for the ally. "Well, you know you're always welcome. The food is almost ready so head through." She followed Sylvia into the kitchen, where Isla was peering into the oven with a glove on her hand, poised to take out their pizzas at the optimal moment. "Your gran's here."

"Hi, Gran. Thanks for coming. Can I get you a drink?"

Carolyn shook her head, wondering when Isla has begun paying attention to her guests rather than simply assuming they would care for themselves. This was the same girl who hadn't managed to text Sylvia and let her know she wouldn't make dinner a few weeks ago. Before there was any time to point that out, though, the doorbell sounded again. Carolyn trotted back down the hallway, pulling open the door to find that it was the guest of honour: Curtis. What stopped her in her tracks, though, was who flanked him.

"Jax?" Carolyn asked, although she knew exactly who was stood on her doorstep.

"You look surprised to see me." Jax frowned, and then so did Curtis.

"Um, hi. I am supposed to be here, right?" He shuffled from foot to foot, trying to glance over Carolyn's shoulder.

"Yes, of course," Carolyn replied with another quick shake of her head, this time intended to snap herself back to reality. Whatever reality was right now, because it looked like Jax had turned up for dinner too and she had no idea why. "Isla's in the kitchen, go straight through. I just need to speak with my friend for a second." She stepped aside to let Curtis pass and when he'd gone, Jax moved closer, her eyes fixed on Carolyn's outfit. Usually they'd get into everything she loved about it but right now, Carolyn had bigger questions. "What are you doing here?"

Jax tugged on the lapels of a black velvet blazer. "Isla texted me about an hour ago and asked me to come over," she whispered. "I tried to call you a couple of times because I wondered if it meant you'd told her, but you didn't answer. I didn't know what else to do but... turn up."

"I haven't told her," Carolyn whispered back. "But Sylvia is also here unexpectedly so maybe she just thought she'd get together the people who are helping set up. I'm sure there's an explanation and I'm panicking over nothing." She placed a hand on her cantering heart and took a deep breath.

"You're panicking. Why?"

Before Carolyn could answer that, Isla was in the kitchen doorway. "Are you coming in or spending all night on the doorstep? Pizza's ready and I want to serve."

Carolyn finally let Jax pass and then closed the door behind them. When she returned to the kitchen, Isla was attending to

Curtis, offering him a plate and explaining the pizza options. Sylvia had taken a G&T to a stool and was more interested in drinking than eating. Then Jax found a spot on the periphery, drumming her fingers on the work surface and looking uncharacteristically uncomfortable.

"Do you want a drink?" Carolyn asked, trying to make her feel more at ease. She walked to the fridge and pulled out a bottle of lager, then held it over her shoulder. "It's Belgian."

"Then how can I say no?" Jax took it and twisted off the cap, then turned and surveyed the pizza options. "Can I help myself?"

Isla slid a plate across the central island. "Yes, but don't make a mess."

"I'll consider myself told. Is this your way of bribing yourself into the starting lineup for tomorrow's game?"

"Is that an option?"

Jax laughed. "No, but I'll take a slice all the same." She added a couple to her plate, then licked her fingers clean and nodded hello to Curtis. "Hi. You must be the boyfriend."

Whilst Jax had found her confidence, Curtis has just lost his, and his laugh gave away that he was nervous. "Yeah." He wiped his hand on the back of his trousers and stretched it out, then let out another burst of laughter when Jax fist bumped him.

"Maybe you should introduce people properly," Carolyn suggested when Isla didn't take Jax's hint. She was too busy stuffing her face with pizza.

"Oh yeah," she said through a mouthful of food, at least waiting until she'd finished chewing to continue. "Curtis, this is my gran."

He waved a shy hello, engulfed by Isla the extrovert. They were complete opposites in that regard but perhaps it was why the pairing worked. Carolyn loved her daughter to bits but couldn't imagine two of her in the same room for more than a few minutes, especially when she had an audience.

Isla moved on to Carolyn, who offered Curtis a warm smile. He seemed a nice kid, as she'd been told on numerous occasions. Polite and well turned out. It set her mind at ease somewhat. "This is my glamorous mum, who I just have to say looks a knock out in that jumpsuit."

Poor Curtis fidgeted, clearly unsure what to say to that. He could hardly agree or disagree without it coming out wrong, and so Carolyn let him off the hook. "It's nice to meet you again. Don't look so worried, we're all quite normal, despite appearances tonight."

He let out another little laugh and seemed to relax at that, and so did Carolyn, until Isla turned to an unsuspecting Jax. She'd already introduced herself so had hung back to eat her pizza in the corner of the kitchen. It almost lodged in her throat, though, when Isla announced, "And that's John. Mum's secret boyfriend."

Jax gripped her chest and spluttered a couple of times, her face turning bright red, and Carolyn freed herself from her own horror for long enough to stride across the kitchen and whack her on the back. "Are you okay?"

"Yes," Jax rasped, banging the centre of her chest with her fist one last time. "Sorry, I think your daughter's just trying to kill me."

"I think she's trying to kill both of us," Carolyn replied, still rubbing circles on Jax's back. She looked up and smiled at Curtis again. "Do you want to take that through to the living room? Sylvia will keep you company. I just need to speak with Isla for a second."

Curtis nodded and did as he was told, which only endeared Carolyn to him more. He looked a little embarrassed, which meant he probably knew what she'd been cooking up, and had been dragged into the farce.

When Sylvia had the good sense to click shut the door behind them, Carolyn finally asked the question she'd been dying to. "What on earth was that?"

"What do you mean?" Isla shrugged and took another bite of her pizza. "I thought you'd be happy I let you off the hook. You were clearly struggling to tell me that you and Jax are a couple and John is a fake out, so I thought I'd just pretend it's as open and obvious as it is."

"Open and obvious?"

"Yeah, open and obvious. I've suspected for weeks and then last night I noticed her coat in the hallway and her perfume was all over you. Again. I don't see what the big deal is."

Carolyn only stood open mouthed, her hand coming to rest still snaked around Jax's waist. "The big deal is that I've been tying myself in knots trying to work out how to tell you this without upsetting you."

"Upsetting me? Why would I be upset? I told you, I just want you to be happy, and I've literally never seen you so happy. Plus, if it happens to mean I get more pitch time, so be it."

Jax laughed at this point, rubbing her thumb and forefinger into her eyes. "This kid. I love her almost as much as I love you."

They'd come close to saying it to each other last night but hearing those words still sent a shock of warmth through Carolyn's body. She felt it flush her chest, her fingertips curling into Jax's hip with a desperation to pull her closer and say it back. She was just struggling to be quite so open about her feelings with Isla still watching their every move. "You're not using this as a way to bribe Jax, if that's what you think."

"As if I was serious about that." Isla began stacking more slices of pizza on her plate. "There is one more thing I really have thought about, though. You and Dad are enough, okay? So we can be friends or whatever, but I only need one mum."

"Thank you for clarifying that," Carolyn deadpanned, her head still spinning. She rubbed her temple, wondering what on earth had just happened. "Am I in the twilight zone?" Pulled into Jax's embrace made her world feel a little more steady, and Carolyn let out a gentle huff into her shoulder. "I love you too."

"You don't sound very happy about it."

"I am, this just isn't the way I wanted to tell you. I suppose things rarely go the way you expect, though."

Jax pressed a kiss to Carolyn's temple. "You might have been kidding yourself to think she wouldn't see through the John lie."

"I sensed she'd seen through the John lie, I just didn't think she'd realised it was a cover for seeing you."

"Well, she did," Isla interjected, casually watching them as she munched through her pizza. "But I get why you didn't tell me. It's all started to make a lot of sense over the past week." She pointed at them with a slice. "For the record, I'm very happy about this. You two make such a great power couple. I do have some questions, though."

"Fire away."

"For clarity, Jax is the person you fell in love with before Manchester. Yeah?"

"Yes."

Isla nodded. "Okay. Understanding why you didn't realise it was more than friendship, then. And had you been with women before?"

"A few drunken kisses with women at university but everyone does that."

"Not everyone." Isla moved on apace, firing off questions as if she'd been storing up a list. Carolyn didn't mind, though. She was happy to have it all out in the open, at last, and relieved that it was interest rather than anger or upset. Isla didn't seem to feel either of those. "Do you think you'll get married or live together like Dad and Nancy?"

"We haven't talked about it but if and when either come up, we'll let you know."

"Appreciated. Does anyone else know about you guys?"

"Only your gran and Becky. They both caught us out. We didn't want to tell anyone until you knew, though, so we've been careful whilst we've figured out our feelings."

Isla tilted her head. "Aw." Something occurred to her and she raised the pizza slice to her mouth, nibbling on the crust with a little glint in her eye. "Can I tell Dad?"

"Absolutely not! I'll fill him in tonight, presuming he's coming?"

"Yeah. Nancy was apparently super keen even though it's her birthday so she suggested they head to London for a matinee so they could make the fundraiser afterwards. That's sweet, right? I feel like she's making an effort so I will as well. Jax is still my favourite, though."

Jax had been stood providing reassuring lower back rubs through that but Isla's last comment stopped her and she laughed. "Thanks, champ. I'm wondering if you'd feel the same if I wasn't in control of your pitch time, but I appreciate it all the same."

Isla laughed and headed towards the door but then turned back to add, "Oh, one last thing." She pointed to Carolyn's trainers. "I *love* the new look. If you're responsible for this, you can definitely stay."

## 27

## JAX

An hour later, after they'd finally circled back to the original purpose of dinner and spent some time getting to know Curtis, everyone bundled into Jax's car so she could drive them up to the clubhouse. Curtis's brother was meeting them all there with his DJ equipment and everyone else was tasked with setting up. The boot was full of items to sell, and Isla had them set up a stall next to the entry desk, where Jax was tasked with checking everyone had a ticket.

"How are we doing, champ?" she asked as Isla counted the money that was coming in from those who were choosing to pay on the door. Their number included Greg, who'd surprised Jax by turning up with a few of his committee.

"Still seventy pounds short of Mum's target. Any ideas?"

"Leave it with me. I don't think anyone else will come in now so put the money somewhere safe and let's have some fun."

For Jax, fun meant joining Jenna and Abi, who were sat on top of each other by a table in the bar area where it was quieter. By the looks of things, the move had only brought them closer together.

"Wow, Carolyn looks a knock out," Jenna said distractedly as she watched Carolyn walk past the door to the hall. "I hope I can still pull off an outfit like that when I'm in my fifties." Her eyes were still on stalks and Abi placed a hand on either of her cheeks to swing her attention back to Jax.

"Easy tiger."

"Why, you jealous?"

"No, you're just being a bit creepy. She does look great, though."

Jax laughed and sat down on the chair opposite. "Both of you need to put your tongues away. You wouldn't stand a chance."

"Yeah, well neither would you," Jenna shot back, folding her arms in a challenge.

It was one Jax would happily take, especially since she'd just thought of a way to get her own back for that rude assumption, and solve Isla's problem into the bargain. Isla had just sat down with them, and Jax gave her a quick nudge to signal there was a plan afoot. "You reckon, huh? What do you bet I can't get Carolyn to dance with me tonight? Better still, lets up the stakes. A kiss by eleven o'clock."

Isla tried to hide a smile. She had astutely picked up where this was going. "You won't get my mum to kiss you. No way. She loves to dance but she doesn't do PDA's."

Right on cue, Jenna reached into her pocket and pulled out a twenty pound note, slapping it down on the table. "Do you know what I'm looking forward to most? It's watching you make a fool of yourself."

Abi produced a similar note and laid it on top of Jenna's. It still only added up to forty pounds of the deficit but Jax would put in the rest herself, just for the fun of taking revenge on Jenna. "Okay, bet taken. If I can get Carolyn to kiss me in front of you before eleven, this is mine. If I can't, I'll give you each twenty pounds."

"It has to be a proper kiss, though. On the lips. I'm not letting you weasel out of this on a technicality just because she's given you a peck on the cheek as she's leaving."

It was a nice touch that Isla blew out a long jet of air through the side of her mouth, shaking her head to make Jenna think she was in with any sort of a shot. They made a good team and Jax smiled at her. "Do you know where your mum's gone?"

"Nope," Isla replied, glancing over her shoulder. "Think she was chatting to Greg and looking out for my dad."

Jenna smirked across the table. "I wouldn't take this bet with him. They actually make a cute couple." Her smile softened as she turned to Isla. "Sorry, we probably shouldn't be talking like this in front of you. It's just fun to wind up Jax."

"That's okay. You should cut her some slack, though. She's been pretty helpful with trying to hit my fundraising target."

At that moment, Carolyn's hand landed on Isla's shoulder. "Who's been helping you?"

"Jax. She's come up with a way to make up the rest of the money."

"That's great! How?"

Jax stood, then turned and leant forward with one knee on the chair, so she and Carolyn were facing. "I'll explain later but for now, I still haven't had a chance to tell you how incredible you look in that outfit."

A little colour rose on Carolyn's cheeks and she gave Jax a questioning look. When Jax gave her a nod back of unspoken confirmation that it was okay for them to be open with each other, she smiled. "Thank you. I hoped you'd appreciate it."

"I do, very much." Leaning further forward, Jax whispered low enough that Isla definitely couldn't hear over the sound of the disco in the hall behind, "I'm really looking forward to taking it off later, too. Do you both want to stay at my house? Isla can have the spare room."

Carolyn's hand came to rest on Jax's shoulder as she whispered back, "We'll have to be quiet if Isla's next door. Are you going to dance with me in a minute?"

"Yes. I just need to sort out the missing money with Isla and then I'll come to find you."

"Okay." The hand that had been on Jax's shoulder stroked her cheek as Carolyn kissed her goodbye. It was chaste by their usual standards but she still lingered long enough to leave no equivocation that there would be more.

After watching her walk away, Jax turned to take the money from the table, satisfied to find that Jenna's jaw was where it belonged: on the floor. Then she handed the two notes to Isla. "Add this to the rest. Your mum says it's okay for you both to stay at my place tonight, by the way. I'll drop you home with all the stuff tomorrow."

"Awesome, thanks."

Isla tucked the money into her pocket, smiling at Jenna as she left, and Jax hooked her arm over the back of the chair as she sat down. "Hard luck, buddy."

"What the *hell*?" Jenna got out, her eyes widening. "Are you and Carolyn an item?"

"Yeah, which is so funny given I'm clearly beneath her. I'm sure she'll come to her senses eventually but for now, I'm glad we worked things out this time and she hasn't ditched me for her husband again."

"Wait." Jenna shook her head, her eyes screwing now. "Carolyn's *her*? The married woman you were crazy over?"

"The woman I'm still crazy over only this time, she's no longer married so we can actually be together."

"What?!" Abi exclaimed. "We've been friends for a decade and I know Carolyn, too. How on earth didn't I find out about this?"

"Because it was a secret until today. All those times you guys said I should settle down and fall in love. Turns out I was doing it right under your nose and you never suspected. Not that it surprises me because you couldn't even work out you were in love with each other until I pointed it out."

"Wow. I mean, congratulations, obviously. But wow. She's like..." Abi's eyes were the ones to widen this time, but with a slow nod of her head that told Jax what she really wanted to say: "Carolyn's hot".

Jenna seemed to pick up on the real meaning, too, because she folded her arms and pouted. "You moved in less than a week ago and already you've been drooling over two other women."

"I wasn't drooling over anyone! But Carolyn's a very attractive woman and I'm happy for Jax."

"And the new barmaid?"

Abi laughed. "Yeah, okay. You looked too, though."

"I haven't seen her yet," Jax said, sitting a little straighter and trying to pick her out of the crowd. She knew that Greg would've picked someone pretty. "What's she like?"

"Early-thirties, blue hair, *very* curvy figure."

The last comment earned Abi a whack from Jenna. "You shouldn't be looking at her curvy figure."

"Why in the world not? You openly notice other women all the time but I understand it's just a bit of fun. Why is it any different for me? You know I love you and would never actually do anything."

It softened Jenna, and her pout dissolved. "I suppose."

"You suppose I love you?"

"No, I know you love me."

"Good, you should," Jax confirmed, starting to understand how disgustingly loved up they were. "I'm almost coming to find you two quite adorable. I can see the appeal with being in love. Carolyn's even managed to heal the rift with Greg and I spoke to him voluntarily the other day."

Jenna laughed. "Then she's not just an attractive woman,

she's a miracle worker. I have very much enjoyed watching her cut you down to size."

"I've enjoyed it too. I might have to keep pretending to hate Greg a bit, just so she can tell me off from time to time. Either that or find a new nemesis." She was tempted to put Marcus at the top of that list, although she'd behave for Carolyn's sake. She'd just spotted Carolyn at the bar with a guy who looked a little like Greg, and a grey haired woman in a coat like Carolyn's, and for a second she thought she'd slipped into the twilight zone again. "I think that's the ex and his fiancée."

Both Abi and Jenna craned their necks to get a not-so-subtle look.

"Isn't it a bit weird for her to be hanging around with her ex and his new wife?" Jenna asked, still gawping at them.

"You're a fine one to talk," Jax countered, given Jenna was very much still friends with her most recent girlfriend. "Weren't you the one trying to set me up with your ex the other night? Carolyn and Marcus have a kid together, though. They have to play nicely." And so did she, however she came to feel about Marcus when she met him.

"I guess. I hope that never happens to us." Jenna pulled Abi's arms tight around her middle. "I don't want to have to be nice to your next wife."

"I haven't had a first wife yet," Abi pointed out.

Jax laughed because she had a feeling it wouldn't be long. "I guess also when you've known someone almost your entire adult life, there's a connection that never goes away."

"And it doesn't bother you?"

"Not at all, buddy. They're done romantically and I know Carolyn loves me. It's why I'm going to charm the pants off him later."

Jenna smirked. "Yeah, well. Try not to also charm the pants off his new missus as well as his old one or he might be pissed."

## 28

## CAROLYN

Carolyn pulled her fingers across Jax's cheek, smearing them with luminous orange body paint. It was the first time they'd managed a moment alone all night and she wanted to dance, but there was one last matter to resolve first.

"What was Nancy like?" Jax asked, turning her head so Carolyn could do the other side.

"She seems lovely, as Isla said. Not that you can really tell from a ten-minute conversation in a bar."

"Hey, you can have a whole night of passion based on a ten-minute conversation in a bar."

Carolyn laughed. "I'll take your word for it. Do you want to go and find out?"

"She's not my type, sorry. I prefer smoking hot blondes with big—"

Before Jax could finish that sentence, Isla came bounding over. "We've smashed the fundraising target now that people are buying glow sticks and paint."

"That's awesome. Well done, champ."

"Thanks. There aren't many people dancing, though, so can you guys like... help?"

"Oh, so *now* you want us to dance?" Carolyn asked, wiping her fingers on a napkin.

"Yes, please."

"Fine. I need to have a conversation with your father before he sees Jax and I together, though, so wish me luck."

Carolyn set down the pot of paint and tried to remind herself that it didn't matter what Marcus thought. She was only telling him at all out of courtesy, but even so, her hands prickled with nerves.

She found him in the bar area ordering a drink, alone.

"Where's Nancy?" Carolyn asked, moving a stool so that she could stand next to him without hitting her leg.

"She's just taking a call from her son. She'll be back in a moment."

She had a son? That was interesting, but not the point, and Carolyn tried not to let herself become distracted. "While it's just the two of us, there's something I wanted to confess. It's about John."

Marcus's smile was annoyingly condescending and making it hard to break this gently. "He's not real, is he?"

"No. I made up a name because I was on the spot."

"I did wonder. I'm sorry if my talking about Nancy made you uncomfortable enough that you felt the need to make up a relationship. It will happen for you. I've no doubt."

"Oh, no. I *am* in a relationship. It's just not with someone called John and I needed to buy some time because I hadn't told Isla yet. It's been a little delicate to navigate because I'm actually dating her football coach."

Marcus frowned. "But I thought her football coach was a woman? Or is there another?"

"No, just the one." Carolyn turned and pointed to where Jax was chatting with Isla and helping her put on body paint. "That's Jax. Isla knows now so I wanted to make you aware, too.

After all, we should both know who's in our daughter's life. Perhaps the four of us could sit down and have a drink later. I'd like to get to know Nancy properly, now she's going to be Isla's stepmother."

"Of course I'd like you to get to know Nancy properly. I hope you won't take this the wrong way, though, but are we really suggesting that introducing the person you're having a fling with is on the same level? Come on, Carolyn. I'll meet her but it's hardly the same thing."

There weren't many ways to take that, and Carolyn had to remember a bit of the advice she'd dished out to Jax about Greg. Otherwise, she feared she might lose her shit, and that wasn't going to be good for anyone. He was clearly surprised, but that didn't give him the right to be nasty. "It's not a fling. I love Jax and we're committed to each other. Maybe we won't get married like you and Nancy, because I for one am not sure I want to do that again, but please don't ever suggest our relationship is any less legitimate."

Marcus held up his hands. "Fine. I'm sorry. If you want me to meet her, I will."

"I want *you* to want to, for Isla's sake if nothing else. She adores Jax."

"I don't doubt it, with them being so similar in age."

"Oh, for goodness' sake, Marcus. You know very well they're not. Jax is forty, not a child. Stop being churlish and insecure. We said we were going to be friends but you're making it very difficult right now."

He huffed and picked up his pint from the bar next to them. "You have to allow me a little time to adjust. I've just found out the woman I was with for twenty-seven years isn't quite who I thought."

"We've all had some adjusting to do. Let me know when you're ready and I'll buy us a drink."

Carolyn left it there and rejoined Jax and Isla. "It's all sorted. Marcus knows about us."

"Are you okay?" Jax asked, holding out her paint smeared hand.

Carolyn took it, despite knowing it would cover her in sticky mess again. "Absolutely. I've offered to buy us all a drink and I can do no more. Shall we dance and kick off this party properly?"

"You bet."

They danced for over an hour and succeeded in getting the floor packed with people, including Sylvia, who in turn managed to finally get her hands on Greg for a slower number. Carolyn was about to comment that it was the most fun she'd had in ages, except that she'd had plenty of fun lately, and it pushed any lingering thoughts about Marcus and his reaction from her mind. She'd done all she could to maintain relations, and it was up to him now.

When Jax was beginning to tire and cast longing looks at the bar, Carolyn pulled her towards it so they could take a break, surprised to find she still felt entirely fresh. It made a change that her feet weren't on fire.

"You're right about these trainers," she conceded, giving Jax's hand a squeeze. "I think I could go all night."

"All night, huh? Keep talking."

Before she could, Marcus was beckoning Carolyn over. She really hoped it was to make peace and not war.

Excusing herself and leaving Jax to join Abi and Jenna at the pool table, Carolyn took a deep breath and went once more unto the breach. At some point, this procession of difficult conversation had to end.

"Is everything okay?" she asked, smiling for Nancy's benefit more than Marcus's.

"Yes," Nancy replied, tugging on his hand. "Isla's done a great job. She's such a lovely girl. We just wondered if the two of you —you and Jax—wanted to join us for a casual meal tomorrow evening before we head home. It's hard to speak properly in here and Marcus is feeling a little unwell."

Whether or not he was genuinely unwell, Carolyn didn't like to guess, but she'd accept the olive branch. "Of course. Let me know where you'd like to go, and we'll be there. I hope you feel better."

"See, that wasn't so hard," she heard Nancy whisper as she walked away, and it made her chuckle.

"Who's winning?" Carolyn asked when she reached the snug.

"I am," Jax replied, potting a yellow ball into the corner pocket. "For the second time tonight."

"You tricked me!" Jenna shot back at her, looking for comfort in Abi's arms.

"I didn't trick you! It was pay back for the horrible thing you said, and you deserved it. Besides, the money goes to the club, so stop complaining."

Carolyn was still curious about that but had been preoccupied by other matters. "Is this something to do with how you helped Isla hit her fundraising target?"

"Yes," Jenna replied, one hand on her cue and the other around Abi's waist. "She made a bet that you would kiss her before the end of the night, but she didn't tell me that you're already a couple. It was unfair."

"You made a bet on me, huh?"

"I'm sorry about that." Jax rubbed circles in Carolyn's back. "But she said there was no way I ever had a chance with someone like you and it was a low blow."

Carolyn laughed it off for what felt like the hundredth time that night. It was the least of her problems and she really didn't care. "I'll choose to be flattered, but I'm sorry she hurt your feelings. Would you like me to kiss it better some more?" She raised her hand to Jax's cheek and guided their lips together, lingering over a kiss.

"I'm not paying you extra," Jenna grumbled as she let go of Abi and took her next shot. "It wasn't per kiss." She potted a ball and then rounded the table to line up another, so that she was now the one winning. "For the record, though, I *am* happy for you guys. You actually make a really great couple, and I was only joking earlier. Carolyn, you couldn't do any better than Jax. She's an asshole but she's also the best."

"Thanks, buddy," Jax replied with a little chuckle. "Same sentiment goes. You're also an asshole."

Carolyn banged her head against Jax's shoulder. "You two."

"I told you. It's love."

"Was that your ex?" Becky asked, joining the group and thumbing over her shoulder. It was a merciful distraction.

"Yes, and his fiancée."

"He downgraded," Jenna said as she stooped to take her next shot. When everyone turned to stare at her, she straightened and shrugged. "What? I'm only saying what everyone else is thinking as usual. For what it's worth, I reckon you're better off. He doesn't look like much fun."

Carolyn frowned. "In fairness to him, I think he's just had a bit of a shock. I said we'd have dinner with them both, though. I hope that's okay." She leant in to Jax's ear to whisper, "Do you want to get out of here?" They'd supported Isla with her fundraiser and had a good time, despite everything, but she was ready to call it quits.

"Definitely." Jax held out her cue. "Becky can take my place."

Becky had zoned out and was distractedly peering towards the bar. She bit her thumb and craned her neck to get a better look, then snapped back to face the group when the barmaid walked into view. "Hmm? What's that?"

"I was saying you'd play pool but now I'm wondering what's got you so interested. Or who."

"No one," she shot back, the colour of her face showing that to be a lie. She glanced over her shoulder again, then turned back and finally took the pool cue. "But just out of interest, who's *that*?"

Jax and Carolyn both looked at the bar, then at each other with matching smiles.

"That's the new bar manager," Carolyn replied, following Becky's line of sight again. "I take it you approve of Greg's choice?"

"First time for everything," Jax muttered, earning her a playful whack in the stomach. "You should go and talk to her."

Becky shook her head furiously. "No, I couldn't. She's so confident and... gorgeous."

Carolyn chuckled. "I'm sure she'd be flattered to hear that. Maybe you should tell her."

"Mmm," Becky mumbled, her thumbnail back in her mouth and her gaze once again fixed on the bar. "Not so sure about that, but I *will* play pool. You know, just for you."

"Of course. Nothing to do with having a great view. We'll see you later and the rest of you tomorrow."

"Congratulations on your win!" Jenna called out with a salute from the far side of the pool table.

Carolyn stopped and peered back over her shoulder. "My win?"

"Over the ex. I love that you flipped the stereotype and were the one to find yourself a younger woman."

Carolyn laughed again. She hadn't seen it that way, but the thought amused her. "To use football parlance, does that make it one-nil to me?" She continued to smile at the familiar rub of Jax's thumb into her palm, reassuring and exciting in equal measure. "I'm joking, of course. Enjoy your game."

They grabbed their coats, made sure Isla was okay to walk back with Becky, said goodbye to Marcus and Nancy, then left. It had been a hell of a night, and Carolyn let out a long, relieved sigh as they wandered down the drive. The cold air was a refreshing slap, reminding her that she had no one else to worry about. Isla was happy, Marcus would come around and if he didn't, too bad, Nancy seemed nice, and Sylvia was having a fabulous night. Even her feet were still feeling fresh by the time they made it back to Jax's cottage five minutes later.

They crossed the threshold, greeted by the smell of the wood burner and freshly baked bread. Carolyn hooked her coat on a peg, kicked off her trainers, and turned to help Jax with her jacket before pushing her back against the front door and kissing her.

"Are you okay?" Jax looked a little startled, her eyes searching Carolyn's. "This didn't end well last time."

"Don't panic, I promise we're not going to fall out tonight." She kissed Jax more gently, trying to remove the worried look. "I'm actually very happy."

"Really?"

"Yes. How would you feel about us getting into those comfy pyjamas again?"

The worried look returned. "Are you sure that you're okay?" Jax raised her palm to Carolyn's forehead. "I'm not qualified but I think you might be unwell."

Carolyn took hold of the hand still checking her temperature and curled Jax's fingers around the pulse on her wrist. "Aren't you going to check here, too? You should know the drill by now."

"It feels fast to me. I think that's just because you kissed me, though. I'm prepared to go with the pyjamas for now but I'll revisit this later to make sure it's come down."

"You be sure to do that." Carolyn smiled, once again amused

by their play. She hated Marcus's assumption that they were just having a little fun, but that didn't mean she wasn't enjoying herself. Who said that relationships had to be constant slog? It was refreshing to feel so at ease and happy.

Jax led them upstairs and pulled two pairs of fresh tartan pyjama bottoms from her drawer. She threw a pair at Carolyn and they began to change.

"Am I going to really worry you if I say I'd be up for watching Match of the Day with you, too?" Carolyn asked.

"No, you're going to make me very happy. You do realise, the only thing I was missing from my life was a beautiful woman to snuggle and watch the football with, don't you? You're basically giving me everything I've ever dreamed about."

"Imagine how happy you'd be if I finally got a television at my house so you could watch football when you stay over, too." Carolyn threaded her jumpsuit on a hanger from Jax's wardrobe, and hung it inside.

"Okay, *now* I'm worried again."

Jax instructed Carolyn to raise her arms so she could dress her in a T-shirt. It was odd to have her putting clothes on, rather than taking them off.

Once they were both in their matching outfits, they made their way back downstairs and cuddled in close alongside each other on the sofa. Jax pulled the blanket down but when Carolyn handed her the remote so she could turn on the television, she set it back on the coffee table.

"Hang on," Jax said, turning and hitching up her leg. She took Carolyn's wrist. "I promised I'd check this again. I don't want to give you anything too stimulating to watch, like the Chelsea game, until I know you're okay."

"Good thinking. What's the verdict?"

Jax bobbed her head. "Still feels fast to me."

"Oh dear. Well, you know what the cure is. Hurry, though,

because we might not have much time." Carolyn laid back and wriggled out of her pyjama bottoms.

It didn't take much encouragement at all for Jax to do the same. After briefly attempting to look shocked despite her eyes twinkling and giving her away, she was soon between Carolyn's legs, pinning her to the sofa. With a hand resting either side of Carolyn's head, she dipped her mouth to cover Carolyn's face in kisses.

It took her by surprise and she laughed, cupping Jax's face and trying to guide their mouths together. Once she had, she found a different set of cheeks and pulled Jax against her, the giggling replaced by an appreciative grunt when they ground together and Jax rubbed her palm firmly over Carolyn's breast. The soft cotton against her nipples was delicious and she willed Jax on with mumbles of pleasure, knowing it wouldn't take much enticement.

She often came close to orgasm from breast play alone and Jax was incredibly adept at exploiting her biggest weakness, cupping, rubbing, caressing, and then wrapping her mouth around a nipple. She created warmth and then a shiver when she moved on and the damp T-shirt cooled. Carolyn knew that by the time Jax touched her anywhere else, she'd be so close that it would only require a gentle push. Usually, she loved being brought back from the precipice and sometimes repeatedly, but not tonight. Tonight, she just wanted to enjoy the fall with the woman she loved.

When Jax began to work her way down Carolyn's body, she urged her back up. "Come here, I want to face you."

They kissed for a few moments until Carolyn tilted her hips, moaning as Jax slipped her fingers inside. She was always so purposeful as she stroked and caressed, coaxing Carolyn closer to the edge without rushing, her thumb splaying to give something to rock against.

Carolyn stroked Jax's face, kissing her gently and luxuriating in the weight of her, the warmth, the softness of her skin as they slipped together. They'd enjoyed each other every which way over the past few weeks, the highest highs and a few lows. Dressed up, unclothed, teasing, flirting, and finding out all the exciting ways they fit. Tonight, Carolyn was beginning to realise all the unexciting ways they fit. The way they always found their way back, their hands searching for one another at every opportunity, and the simple intimacy of lying unguarded on a sofa without any toys or games. Well, almost no games.

They rolled onto their sides, their legs slipping together as Jax ran her fingers over Carolyn's lips, up to her clit, stroking circles and groaning when Carolyn shuffled to free the hand from underneath herself and mirrored the movements, her other hand hooking under Jax's shoulder blade to hold them together as they kissed.

"I love you," she whispered, before slipping her tongue into Jax's mouth again. She focused on the slow rhythm, almost unaware of the one played out by their fingers, until she couldn't keep her hips from bucking into the touch. Every movement Jax made, she followed, until Jax was whimpering and unable to maintain their lip contact. She closed her eyes, her hand barely moving now, and then gripped Carolyn's wrist as she let out an uncharacteristically high grunt.

Carolyn laughed softly and kissed Jax's warm, pink face, her hips bucking again and the laughter stopping when Jax rolled her back over and sucked her swollen clit into her mouth, flicking her tongue over it. The move took Carolyn by surprise but it was a good one and she arched her back as her orgasm hit her all at once, gripping Jax's hair and pressing her hips forward one last time. The laughter came back just as quickly as she sunk into the sofa and Jax lowered herself on top.

"I love you too by the way," she said, kissing all over

Carolyn's face again. But then they both heard voices outside and they sprung apart, grappling for their pyjamas.

Jax stuck both legs through the same hole and toppled backwards, finally righting herself in time for the front door to clatter open. Carolyn reached to take the remote from the coffee table and then pulled the blanket over them, nuzzling into Jax's shoulder. Besides the fact that her hair was in disarray, no one would ever know. Or so she hoped.

"Hello, sweetheart," she said casually as Isla came in and sprawled herself across the armchair. "Did your gran get home okay?"

"Greg put her in a taxi," Isla replied, glancing around the room. "This place is really nice. I hope we're staying more often." Her gaze settled on the two of them, still cuddled up together with the blanket half covering them. "Mum, are you wearing flannel pyjamas? First those fierce trainers and now this. Are you totally sure this is a relationship and not a hostage situation of some sort?"

Carolyn laughed. "It may be, yes. I think I just found myself offering to get a television at home so you can both watch the football in 4K."

"Oh my god, really? Can we watch Match of the Day now?"

Jax took the remote from Carolyn's hand. "Sure can. We were just sat here patiently waiting for you to get home, so we could all watch it together."

"Great. Becky's making us tea and bringing me some of her homemade bread."

"You've got Becky waiting on you now, too?" Carolyn shook her head. She didn't know why she was surprised that Isla had adapted so quickly and was taking full advantage of the situation.

"She's not waiting on me, she offered. She also said I could borrow something to sleep in. When Jax stays with us, maybe *I'll* bake."

"*You'll* bake? You who couldn't successfully melt chocolate two months ago?"

"Yeah, well. You wouldn't have worn those trainers or those PJ's two months ago. We're all allowed to grow." Isla folded her arms, as if to say that was check mate, and then changed the subject. "I don't think Dad was very happy when he saw you two kissing earlier, by the way."

"No?" That was a shame, but it was none of his business.

"I told him queer love was beautiful and that it didn't invalidate the time you spent together."

Carolyn and Jax both spluttered with laughter. "You didn't…"

"I did. Nancy laughed. Then I got Becky to explain bisexuality. She seemed to find that quite funny, too."

"I like her more and more. You know you don't have to stand up for me, though? I'm a big girl. Although I appreciate the support."

"I know. I wanted to support you, though. I told Jenna and she said something about it being two-nil to you, but I didn't get that."

"It was a joke about keeping a score between your father and I. It was childish and silly. There's no competition and I don't want either of us to be bitter about the past. It's time to move on."

"Yeah," Isla replied absently as Jax turned on the television and entered the catch up service. "But I still agree with her that if it was a competition, you'd be winning."

Carolyn didn't reply but she would have to agree. Her daughter was happy and thriving, she had a wonderful and supportive partner, and her feet felt like they'd been dancing on clouds all night. She was definitely winning at life right now.

Printed in Great Britain
by Amazon